SPEAKING IN TONGUES

LINDA ASHOUR

SIMON AND SCHUSTER
New York · London · Toronto · Sydney · Tokyo

Simon and Schuster
Simon & Schuster Building
Rockefeller Center
1230 Avenue of the Americas
New York, New York 10020

Designed by Helen L. Granger/Levavi & Levavi
Manufactured in the United States of America

1 3 5 7 9 10 8 6 4 2

Library of Congress Cataloging in Publication Data

Ashour, Linda.
Speaking in tongues.

I. Title.
PS3551.S416S6 1988 813'.54 88-6648
ISBN 0-671-64090-9

To my family

"Oh! There's a big flag waving
and all the children are singing."
—My mother, watching a Dr. Schuller broadcast

Acknowledgments

I would like to thank Mona Simpson and the staff of *The Paris Review.* The publication of "Stories I'd Rather Not Tell" led to the writing of this novel. I would especially like to thank my editor, Robert Asahina, for his excellent guidance. His patience and faith in this project often exceeded my own.

I

The village train route is an odd voyage. Despite the enthusiasm of the driver and his obvious love of good narrative, there just isn't a lot to include in the tour. Forty-five minutes is printed on the ticket. For this reason and our proximity to the polar bears, our home, La Belle Eléna, is often included on the train ride. My son Sam and I were out gardening the day I recognized our presence on the tour. I had read somewhere that snails liked the taste of beer. They would drink their fill of it and drown. We trimmed down paper cups and planted them in the earth around the oleander trees. Sam poured the measures of beer in each cup, licking his fingers occasionally and twisting his face into fresh expressions of disgust. There must have been a couple of unwitting Americans somewhere on the train, for the driver switched to an impromptu English.

"We in the village believe La Belle Eléna was once an ill-reputed house. Others say no, it was only a place to dance and eat and have a bit of fun. Eléna is gone now, so we could never know the truth. What remains is fact or legend. It doesn't matter which, because the house is privately owned now and no one comes here."

The microphone is acting up and the driver taps it twice with his middle finger. I bend lower to keep out of the range of vision. The train has come to a full stop, as it usually does to maneuver a sharp curve.

"Now as I say before, La Belle Eléna is privately owned by a young couple, the woman of which is American."

The train moans softly, straining on the upgrade.

"If you will turn please to page four in the *Nice-Matin* I see some of you have with you, you can see a photograph of our local soccer team. The picture is taken by the man who lives here with the American wife. The pool, which you cannot see, is green. It is the only green pool in the village. The other three are blue. We going now to an original thirteen-century well. It was blocked up by the mayor in 1957 due to cats thrown in by village boys."

"Sam?"

He has changed projects and is making small wormlike objects out of dirt and beer.

"Put that down and come stand by me. That's right. Come stand by Mommy."

When he turned five years old, Sam dropped his round belly and some of the very small boy in him disappeared as well. Shadows appear sometimes on his face now. His expression can drop into a kind of darkness that seems quite literally a cloud or covering of a previous brightness. He's come despite himself and is standing so close I can feel his breath on my cheek.

"Would you let Mommy hold you for two minutes?"

He shakes his head violently.

"Je ne suis pas un bébé, moi."

"Then just one minute. A minute isn't long, Sam. I promise I won't kiss."

"Qu'est-ce que j'ai dit?"

This is what I have to do lately to get a whiff of my son. It's a begging, bargaining game. Sometimes I feel physically starved for him.

"Mommy's feeling sad and blue."

He edges in slowly. It is very difficult for both of us to keep from smiling.

"S'il te plaît, Sam."

I win a rigid hug. Perhaps because of the strain, the outlandish responsibilities of love, he sprints to the middle of the terrace. Our few chairs are pushed to the perimeter or lean folded against the house. In the emptiness and space, Sam's smallness is almost comic. He certainly doesn't think so. He gives out a series of staccato shouts, staring in disbelief at the house curved around him. For the house is still standing. His intention seems to be to bring the whole thing tumbling down.

An article appeared several months ago announcing that France and Disney were at a delicate point in their negotiation. France would be marketed using foolproof Disney methods. One ticket to France would include, instead of a trip to Magic Mountain or Small World, a visit to Versailles or a château in the Loire Valley. The article was meticulously written. There were long, ruminative passages on the advantages of group sales and the administrative problems the Disney deal would involve. Only midway through the article did I realize it to be a complete bluff. Long after this article appeared Paris was selected as the site for the next Disneyland. Many people assumed the choice was made on the basis of charm, rusticity. American officials challenged the capacity at Rungis, the marketplace that feeds the metropolis. Could it supply enough or would it be overtaxed? There was a slight edge to these discussions. Rungis administrators were miffed by the lack of faith and at times adopted the courteous, distant attitude a defeated nation displays toward its invaders. In what seemed almost an involuntary reflex, Jean Médecin, the mayor of Nice, announced his plans to construct a huge leisure park for his city. And an underwater causeway that would eventually link Nice and Antibes, freeing up the entire Promenade des Anglais to pedestrian traffic. The mayor's project logically will end at a corner dominated by the American Express bank.

The little white train that has come to the village is seen as a step toward prosperity. The first little train installation took place in Nice years ago. It was a very select concept back then, and many families drove in from the country after Sunday lunch and took a ride on the train. It wound first through the marketplace and the old city in Nice. The train made a brief stop for picture-taking in front of the olive stand. The olive merchant was a pretty young woman who spoke a proud, impenetrable Niçois dialect. She sold fifteen varieties of olives at her stand. Then the train scaled the hill to the château at the lower end of the city. When asked about the origins of the château the conductor shrugged and pointed to the sign indicating a dungeon somewhere on the premises. The waterfalls on the ascent, the extraordinary views at the top of the hill compensated for this lack of information. But now the white train with glittery gold trim is omnipresent. A second train was installed in Antibes, followed by another, until now there is even a little train bustling through the uneven streets in our village. Half empty, it stops in front of one of our young vegetable sellers. He has strung up a garland of plastic flowers in front of his stall. He has taken a new commercial direction because of the train and now sells only the most unlikely fruits and vegetables. He advertises eight varieties of winter lettuce.

I begin to think of how to frame my complaint in the mayor's office. I resent, Monsieur le Maire, being a tourist attraction. Or I could broadside the project from a hygiene standpoint, citing the trail of orange peels and half-eaten candy bars the little train leaves in her wake. Some families have been forced to put out rat poison. There is a sulphurous line of yellow powder outlining certain houses. As it turns out, none of this is necessary. The tour is not a success and the train becomes a sort of public servant. Ticket sales are abandoned and the driver makes a few desultory rounds each week, transporting the ill or the disabled to the market or the post office. On Wednesdays he makes a shuttle from the high school to the soccer field on the outskirts of town. The train is otherwise stationed at the foot of the mayor's garden and has become an extravagant toy for his grandchildren and the grandchildren of his best friend, Jean Lapelier, famous locally for his brave partisan efforts in the Second World War.

• • •

If I had been firm from the day we took ownership of this place it would never have happened. If I had said no to the Germans from Stuttgart, La Belle Eléna would not have undergone this halfhearted revival. But the red-faced Germans looked so disconsolate, so displaced when I said no. There was a baby squalling in the backseat, and I believed them when they said they had been driving all night. The man said there had been some mistake. They had been coming to La Belle Eléna for years. They came the day Chagall was buried. My husband was taking photographs of the small procession as they headed up the stone path to the cemetery. He was the first to reach Chagall's widow as she slipped and nearly fell. So I was alone with Sam that day. I was standing barefoot with Sam's grimy hand in mine and I didn't look like the proprietress of anything. I let them in. The woman immediately opened her dress for the baby and put her round white legs in the pool while the baby suckled. Her husband eyed the barbecue and his watch with increasing alarm. It was noon, Sunday, and with La Belle Eléna in such disrepair, what would they eat? I calmed them with some charcuterie, a good bottle of red wine. They were in luck—I had baked a faultless tart that morning. The baby slept in a wicker laundry basket under the palm tree while they swam and sunbathed. I didn't take any money from them and they never returned. Still, that was the beginning.

Before moving in we had borrowed a small truck from a friend and combed the area for defunct signs. They were everywhere. Handmade, secured with a row of thumbtacks or a bit of stray wire. La Belle Eléna. Snack. Piscine. A deux cent metres! A pile of these signs still lies stacked in a corner of the garage. The problem has something to do with inertia and habit. Maybe memory. A picture has emerged of Eléna.

She ran around because her husband drank. He drank because she ran around. To hang on to the house when it became clear that her husband would never keep a job, she turned it into a summer affair that would keep them alive through the winter. She could feed fifty people without batting an eye. An afternoon by the pool, lunch and the right to watch beautiful Eléna weave through the patio with platters of grilled steaks and merguez. All that for one hundred francs. The sangria was on the house. The hostelleries in the village referred their overflow to Eléna.

"Mais alors, ses enfants, les pauvres!"

My neighbor Madame Leconte washed Eléna's floors. She also scraped down the grill after the guests were gone and hung up fifty or so linen napkins on the clothesline each day because Eléna wouldn't have paper. Was it true that the children were so unhappy, I ask, watching Sam, who pulls on her skirts for a cookie.

"Non seulement malheureux, ils étaient malades."

To get his mother's attention, the little one once mounted a table, overturning a pitcher of wine in his haste. He must have been ten years old. He clapped his hands twice over his head and, bent in a sumo squat, swallowed a live lizard. The father walloped his son. Eléna, humming, began to string up a net for a game of volleyball. In the summer, my neighbor tells me, she always had a jasmine blossom wound through her hair. So that whenever she passed . . . Madame Leconte sighs.

And then she suffered a nervous depression. She took a sleep cure in a hospital in Nice that lasted seven days. Madame Leconte doesn't believe the work drove her over the edge. She doesn't think it was her husband's drinking or even Eléna's sex crimes. It had to do with a change here. The change on the Côte d'Azur. A camping site went up on the other side of the village years ago. Her husband was too weak, and when the clientele changed he never tried to stop those people from coming here. They would spend the afternoon here, Madame Leconte says, their children screaming and fighting, then get up to leave without paying. They always promised to come back the next day but they never did. They complained about the food. Des gens vulgaires. And then one day someone defiled Eléna's pool. Madame Leconte swears this was the end. When she returned from the sleep cure, she was so beautiful and lucid. Then she packed up and left. Leaving the husband and the boys to fend for themselves. Madame Leconte continued to wash the floors with oily black soap. She increased her efforts in Eléna's absence, feeding the children at noon when they returned fighting and crying from school. When Eléna's husband declared bankruptcy, she polished the wood trim on the stairs until it gleamed. She transferred all her best porcelain dessert plates and found clever ways of displaying them on a window ledge or an otherwise barren wall. She routed her own husband from the garden and implored him to replace the broken windowpane, for who would buy such a house! When we came round to look, Marc and I both assumed Madame Leconte was the fierce owner. The agent, a simple man who had just come to the region, quoted the wrong asking price. This house may have been his first sale. Years later I am still banging on our neighbor's door for answers to some house mystery or other. But this is a house that reveals its story niggardly, in bits and pieces and in its own time.

The insistent ones, the ones who knock and introduce themselves as former guests, must come from that first period when things were going well for Eléna and her husband. If Marc is home, I apologize and explain the changed circumstances. Yes, we own the house now. It's privately owned now. I direct them to the municipal pool and, if they get quarrelsome, draw myself up and say something like Look here! The Mediterranean is ten minutes away. Other times, I look over my shoulder and see a grill that can take care of fifty people. A pool tiled in seven thousand sea green squares and think why not. They tell me stories about Eléna and how pleasant things were until the area changed. If I have food enough for them I take one hundred francs. If not, they have their swim and go away. In the winter we are mostly left alone.

2

Well, mostly alone. For who can turn away the English? Marc corners me in the kitchen where I've come to get some extra place settings.

"They didn't come in with a battering ram, Marc. I *asked* them in."

"Worse. This is not a kibbutz, Lucy. It's no longer even a whorehouse. It's just our house, and there are two perfect strangers sitting outside with my son."

"Speaking English to him, by the way."

"Ah, yes. That's it. The mother tongue at any cost."

"I'm only saying we need to keep reminding Sam that English isn't something his parents invented just to annoy him."

"I'm taking this upstairs. I want them gone in an hour."

"I think you are mean-spirited."

"Stop dragging strangers through my house."

"Our house, damn it."

His back is turned; he's already carrying his tray upstairs. How chaste it looks. A plowman's supper of Swiss chard pie, a bit of cheese and bread, and the bottle of beer. Just who is a stranger to a Frenchman? Anyone not mother, father, immediately and irrevocably blood-tied, that's who is strange. I've made it under the wire by a nose. The Old Testament sometimes has an uncomfortable echo. Ezra 10:44, for starters, with its eerie emphasis. "All these had married foreign wives, and some of them had wives *by whom* they had children." I return to the English, who wait sweetly for their food. I ask them for still another profile of infamous Eléna.

"When Eléna was here there was dancing."

"Dancing, yes. Oh, and the colored lights! Yes, she strung up blinking colored lights. But of course, that was a festive time for us. We were gay then, weren't we, Harry?"

"Gay? I don't know about that."

"Perhaps I mean young. We had just enough money to make the passage. Then we worked a bit in Brittany until we were too discouraged by the rain. We were crew members on a private barge after that. We scrimped and saved, didn't we, Harry? So that when we came here, well, I don't know. It was rather like le grand luxe. And of course, Eléna was so creative."

"This is really rather good, Mrs. Laugier. Mind if I have just one more slice? What's it called again?"

"They call it a tourte de blette. Swiss chard. Simple, really. She was beautiful, wasn't she?"

"It was beauty but something else, too. Generosity had something to do with it. And bearing up despite it all. We rather liked that. You could see the husband was worthless."

"Have you got any more wine on board?"

"Oh, Harry! You won't be fit to drive. Toulon's so far away. Mrs. Laugier, I want to tell you how kind this is. Of course, we should have known, for all the signs are down now. Imagine taking us in like this for a meal. Perfect strangers. Would you mind if I used the ladies' before we leave?"

She tucks her blouse back into her skirt.

"They danced here? Under this palm tree?"

"Sometimes. Over there. There. Where you haven't any grass growing. She strung the lights up on a dead tree. Sometimes it was just the women who danced. The men liked to play boule down in the gravel by the garage. I'll go to the ladies' then and we'll be off."

When she has gone, Harry leans forward and motions for me to do the same. His wife's napkin is in her plate. She had blotted her lips and the red imprint took perfectly. Tiny, bow-like. A mouth that could slide easily into a sweet pout.

"Eléna was a perfect tart. Generous, alright. What my wife doesn't know won't hurt her. Let her dream's what I say. She hit it with all the young men who came here. In the pantry. Upstairs in her son's bedroom. Never gave a damn who knew. You couldn't get away with this sort of thing in England. La Belle Eléna, my behind."

I wave them off from the edge of the terrace. They drive a funny little English car that Harry said had the same motor as a sewing machine. He pulls down hard and moves it into reverse.

I stumbled on that string of colored lights last year and plugged them in to see if they still worked. The lights were lying in a dusty strand beside a stained mattress that was perforated in many places. There was also an empty wine bottle in the little grenier. A red wine that claimed to have been a family business for seven generations. The names of the growers were listed on the label, with the corresponding dates of their births and deaths. The last, José, was born in 1938. Madame Leconte's husband dragged the mattress into his own garden and burned it. I threw the lights away when they began to explode, one by one.

Now that the signs are down, directions to La Belle Eléna are ambiguous. We are in a covey of old buildings crouched near a village known primarily for its superior mechanic. Car knowledge runs in the mechanic's veins like blood. He is a man who has once held public office. He considers engines and human nature equally fragile and trouble-prone. Villas here have names or don't. There are no numbers anywhere. Though the newer buildings reflect the Provençal building code, they are fiercely individual, marked inside and out by the owners' preoccupations and unashamed notions of splendor. The unknowing wanderer would do well to read a passage in E.I. Robson's chapbook. Robson wrote in 1926, "You cannot be a mere hustling tourist in Provence. Something of the mystic must be about you, if you are not to go away cold and empty." He may refer to a Provence more deep and insulated than this stretch of hazy coastline. Still, Robson's theory holds in this maze of buildings that becomes, with time, something more than a charming pile of stone. Peering through a rickety fence, I can see an Icelandic menagerie—a stone polar bear and five penguins are distributed under a grape arbor. Farther down, a tropical trompe l 'oeil mural with turquoise skies. In the wall of the same building is an iron-barred niche harboring the statue of a saint whose deeds no one remembers anymore.

Tourist buses have stopped coming to our village. Travelers complain that there is nothing to buy for their relatives and friends. Only the dizzy quincaillerie named Mille Choses. You can buy thread and plastic plates, assorted camping equipment and false nails. No one in the village claims to be an artist. The tourists don't want their car repaired. They don't want to buy a patch of rocky soil in the Alps-Maritimes or a hunting rifle. An occasional carful of Danes or Swedes pulls up to the one dry monument to the Fourteenth of July and moves quickly away. Once the gitaines came to the village, fifty or sixty strong. They filled the parking lots with campers and roulottes, metallic Mercedes and Citroëns slung low as cats. They took over the two bars in town and everyone walked up to have a look at their bright jewelry and beautiful, foul-mouthed children. When they pulled out of town two or three days later there was not an ashtray to be found. There was no ill feeling. Everyone had had their fortune told and better, happier times were ahead.

Another Arab family is moving to our street. They work late at night and this is the third trip. Just now there is an overstuffed armchair bound to the top of their rusty car. There mustn't be any electricity in their apartment, for they work by the headlights of the car. They are soundless and polite, starting the old car with a puff of exhaust whenever someone drives up behind them, honking furiously for them to be up and out of the way. A suitcase or package tumbles to the ground each time this happens. The only thing that is really secure is the huge armchair strapped to the top of the car. One of the men strokes it appreciatively after each trip in and out of the apartment. Clearly the royal red chair is the finest thing they own.

The mother stands in front of the headlights of the car with a baby. Her young son has caught hold of her skirts and the two of them sway together, soothing the colicky baby. The woman gasps as one of the men stumbles with a piece of crockery. A pair of headlights wobble down the road toward the narrow alley they're blocking with their car. The driver gathers speed on the descent. There is a screech of brakes and a long horn blast. It's Marc and Sam, back already from my mother-in-law's house. I can't see Marc, but I hear his boots crunch on the gravel. I hear Mal Garé! and Passage! shouted out as the baby's cries increase. Sam echoes him, and then there's a duet of insults coming from my husband and son. Gravel spits out from the tires of the car and he gains the top of the hill. He is still fuming when he hits the garage. Sam runs past me without a word, straight to his room. His cheeks are puffed out like a toad's and his hands are in his pockets.

"Marc?"

"Bonsoir, ma chérie."

"Is that how the French welcome newcomers to the neighborhood?"

When he is angry or tired, Marc seems to contract. His shoulders look sharp enough to pierce his thin sweater.

"You frightened their baby. Did you hear him howling?"

"Ne commence pas, Lucy."

"I've already started. In front of Sam! Did you hear how he spoke to those people? Like a little Nazi. I won't have him talk like that, Marc. He's five years old and he repeats everything we say."

"They shouldn't have blocked the road like that. En pleine nuît. Ça peut faire un bel accident."

"You sound like a policeman. Good God, I married an aspiring cop."

My mother-in-law has fried something tonight. The smell of cooking oil still clings to his clothes.

"What kind of disagreement is this? I honk the horn and get a little angry with some foreigners, and you act as if I've committed a criminal act. Lucy? Tu m'écoutes plus. Très bien. Elle va bouder maintenant."

"I am not pouting. I'm thinking about Jean Marie Le Pen and Le Front National."

"You accuse me of being like that racist? You really compare me to that fat madman who wants to run all foreigners out of France? You exaggerate, Lucy. Tiens. De la part de Maman."

"My son wagged his finger at those people. I saw him do it from our window."

"Our son!"

He hands me a crystal bowl and stalks off to the darkroom. In his mother's crystal bowl several white meringue balls bob up and down in a caramel syrup. A ghastly Floating Island is perfect for this mean night. I draw off some syrup and throw the rest out. For these and other occasions there are spare bedrooms at La Belle Eléna. So spare, in fact, I spend the night wrapped in a bedroll on a convertible sofa bed. Cold white rods of moonlight enter the room through cracks in the wooden shutters. I make a mental note to purchase extra bedding and a length of heavy fabric for a simple curtain.

I'm awakened by the sound of Sam on the prowl. When he finds me he does not wish me good morning. He sits on the sofa bed with his back toward me until I suggest breakfast. His hair rises in stiff blond shocks. He gulps down his cereal and pockets the toast to offer to the roosting pigeons outside. They refuse his food and shoot straight up like rockets.

Marc has risen early. He's drinking coffee and warming his hands on the sides of the cup. To get us talking, I offer a fresh bit of data.

"If we were in America today, we might catch an afternoon movie."

"Would we?"

"We might. Or maybe someone would call us to watch a

football game on television. Take my sister-in-law's annual open house, for instance. She and Cody invite all their friends over for the Super Bowl. Becky carries on about him in funny ways, complaining like all her friends do about their husbands. But she never gets to the real heart of the matter. It's okay to make allusions to trouble, but people are careful to keep things nice and light."

"Ah, je vois."

"Marc? Have I made an orphan out of you?"

"At thirty-six years of age? Tu es folle."

"You should have chosen someone who could get along with your mother. Someone who knew how to choose the right Camembert. Or who understood De Gaulle, maybe. I screw up all the time, don't I?"

"Marc?"

Sam has brought his bike inside and is circling the table where we sit. He goes faster and faster. I'm afraid he'll hit his head on one of the sharp corners.

"Did you mean what you said to those people?"

"I didn't tell them to go back to Algeria. I told them to move their car. Qu'est-ce que tu me cherches ce matin? Bon Dieu."

In my favorite bar there is a wooden plaque mounted on the wall above a steady line of pastis and whiskey bottles. A proverb is burned into the wood. Female customers scoff at it. Some modern town-women even boycott this bar. It says, *La femme et la truite se prennent par la bouche*. I think it's funny and honest. I wish Marc would hook me right now. This water is icy and cold, full of surprising currents. Sam stops cycling. Watching us and sucking his thumb, he's waiting for the outcome. I wriggle around for awhile in the lap of a disapproving stranger, then give that up for dead.

"Regarde les amoureuses. Berk!"

"Ce n'est pas si facile, Lucy."

"Was it the Le Pen comment?"

"Entre autres. Dégage, Lucy. Laisse tomber."

"My grandmother used to say political talk between married people never amounted to a hill of beans."

"Un quoi?"

"A hill of beans. She thought that when a couple fought about who ought to be elected they really meant 'I don't like the way you lick your lips when you eat.' Or 'Suck in your stomach, why don't you?' She never held any stock in that."

I wipe Sam's nose and stroke his cheek.

"Go play outside, Sam. Dehors, mon lapin. Va regarder les oiseaux."

The whole day is full of blemished projects. Collapsing roofs of plywood birdhouses. Infinite Band-Aids for Sam, and a suspiciously brown, unleavened loaf of gingerbread. Funny smells collect in corners of the house. Eliot is by with a new almanac. His glasses fog up as he speaks. He removes them matter-of-factly and wipes them off. He is one of the few men I know who carry a white handkerchief.

"Have I walked into a squabble of some sort?"

"You might say. A pretty silly one. Here, eat some of this just to please me."

"Well, I certainly didn't have anything to do with it. Why was he so churlish with me? Would you like us to take Sam for a few days?"

"This was a minor skirmish, Eliot. Calm down and eat your gingerbread like a good boy. Tell me something. Do you and Marie-France ever come apart over political things?"

This picks him up considerably. A vulgar little something about who did or didn't do the dishes the last time is one thing. But a political disagreement! Eliot settles deeper into the chair and lights a cigarette, his eyes bright.

"Don't let this go farther than your kitchen. Once we were talking about the Occupation, and I don't know, maybe I'd been drinking. I started going on about the wormy French conduct. Yes, I think that must have been it. And my wife suddenly threw me into the wall. She really hurt me. I fractured a rib. Now, tell Eliot all."

I back up and recreate the night, the menacing crunch of Marc's boots on the gravel. The sight of grown men and women scurrying around in the dim light like rodents.

"And Sam—where did he get all that authority? Bellowing and gesticulating. Eliot, you're not listening."

His face is smoother than a crock of butter. He has not taken my dilemma to heart. Or perhaps he's dreaming of his wife's contorted face as she hurled him into a wall.

"Is that all?"

"Isn't that enough?"

"This has nothing to do with ideology. This has to do with conduct. You are describing a mediocre comedy of manners. A well-bred girl from Oklahoma doesn't shout. Why, I drove down the Turner Turnpike in 1965. You people don't even honk. Listen, well-bred cowgirl. This is years after the fact. You married an in-the-flesh Frenchman. He was taught to push and shove. Those people blocking the road could have been members of the Royal Family. They were blocking His Path."

"You really think so?"

"Of course. I have seen my beloved wife in too many street battles to think otherwise. My advice? Get out of the way. Step into an alcove, study a window treatment until it passes. Because it does pass."

"You sound sure of yourself."

"I am. Cut me a piece of this sludge to take to Marie-France. You've outdone yourself."

We have a tight fistful of close friends in southern France. I take the greatest solace, perhaps, in Eliot, the English-book merchant, and Chan, a long, tall displaced Texan. Together we form a kind of dispersed, wandering tribe. In each couple either the husband or wife is American, the spouse French. We are self-confessed oddities. Sometimes a child is present, by virtue of a babysitter who has fallen ill. These children are interchangeable, the women might think to themselves or aloud. The younger children all speak an incomprehensible English. As they grow, this becomes a kind of stilted, touching adultspeak that has no relation to American-kid English. The women wonder over the ease of linguistic hybridization. Humans cross-pollinate like wildflowers, a woman from Idaho I met at a party once said to me. Look at it! Her son, Sam's age, was fighting to the death over the pronunciation of Mickey Mouse. "C'est Mickay. Papa, je te dis que c'est Mickay." Invariably our bilingual evenings slide into a twangy French, ripe to bursting with appropriate argot. We no longer parrot the spouse, that was ages ago. We're linguistically who we are. Still, what sort of concession has been made? I will turn to an all-American girlfriend on that occasional late, wine-sodden night and plunge along witlessly in a language not my own, later thinking, Oh My God.

The culmination came before Sam was born. We were at a concert in Nice. Simon and Garfunkel were together again. Marc and I could just barely make them out, two sober figures far below us, just noticeable before a throbbing starlit backdrop of Manhattan. We had trouble getting tickets and were perched on the back row of an amphitheater. There was discomfort and displeasure all around.

"Merde. Je vois mal d'ici."

"Mais ils sont vieux, ces deux types."

Art was out of voice, but it wasn't for that I had come. They were together again! Down below the most ferocious activity was at a food concession. An enterprising young woman in a football jersey was selling slices of tarte aux pommes. They were singing a song I didn't like about cars, and I could barely hear above the din.

"Ils chantaient mieux avant. C'est sûr. Passe-moi une bière."

I turned to Marc, who was pretending to be enraptured for my sake. I held up one finger.

"C'est-à-dire?"

"I want you to send me home once a year."

Marc was by then a staff photographer. *Paris Match* had bought some pictures he had shot on an improbable day in Monte Carlo. He had caught a shy Saudi prince in the unlikely company of a burly blonde. She towered over him as he lost thousands in a casino. We were finally earning more than we spent. I've often thought he must imagine I'm composed of helium. That one day I'll simply float up and away from him. There's leverage in that constant possibility of loss. He answered as he always does when he's up against a wall.

"Comme tu voudras. It's not a problem."

And since that concert I've been going back, first alone, then with Sam like a soldier on leave. It is puzzling that these visits to Oklahoma remain so fundamental. I often wonder if without them my fractured life would rattle straight off the rails. I've fanned alive an ardent patriotism for all these years. It leaps up annually in deep blues and golds, then sinks back down into something warm, not dismissible, hot enough to warm the back of your legs if you stand close enough. My ideas are tipsy and vague, constructed largely on the disarming prejudices of my home state. When I get back to France, Marc wants headlines. A succinct little something from the State Department. What he receives is a Southwestern fait divers, a satisfying crime of passion full of frontier undertones. And the real news. My rotten brother Cody. Mom improbably spewing Schullerisms and my father, worn thinner than a strand of fine wire, mourning the vanishing scrub oak and dreaming of local politics. I never let them know when I'm coming in, but they must know from the particular low drone of the engine that it's Lucy. So they scurry around and order up hysterical events as soon as the wheels touch the earth. Life shouldn't be this episodic, but it is. For as long as I can remember I have arrived just in time, or too damned late. Collapse is imminent. Events, even given years, come continuously to a head. Lucy, thank the Lord you're home. Eliot rows the Schuylkill with middle-aged members of his old yacht club team and eats clear beef broth as a first course on the eve of his homecoming. Meanwhile Marie-France makes still another crossing to Corsica. As her husband swallows soup in a staid Philadelphia dining room, she keeps watch on a moonlit deck somewhere in the Mediterranean. I'm convinced it's all the same.

Eliot is gone, and I'm watching the results of the day's wind from a kitchen window. The sky has been swept clean and is a single shade of blue. What clouds remain are bullied over to one corner in the west. They're stacked high in a tower formation.

"Maman?"

Sam makes a wide detour, dodging the stove and the toaster

oven, then pushes and thrusts his way between my legs. He hides his face.

"Pourquoi ils ont voulu manger le petit garçon?"

"Who wanted to eat the little boy, honey? Qui?"

"Les gens à la télé. Viens voir, Maman. Il n'a rien fait."

He leads me to the television. A little boy stands before an outsized kitchen range. The oven door looms before him and appears ready to swallow him. Around him are other kitchen hazards—a huge stockpot, a wooden chopping block and a handsome set of gigantesque carving knives. All within easy reach of the sandy-haired boy. This is not a children's program. It is a cautionary tale for parents of young children. I turn off the television and Sam's tight shoulders relax. He slumps slightly and sighs. I carefully explain that no one is making a meal of the boy. He seems satisfied the child will survive the program.

"Maman. Raconte-moi une histoire."

"Alright. A story. Quel genre?"

"Une histoire de tendresse et de beauté."

"Of tenderness and beauty."

"Sans aucun monstre."

"No monsters."

"Pas de sorcières."

"Or witches."

"Par exemple. 'Il était une fois . . .' "

"Once upon a time. There was a boy. Or a fish. No one quite knew which."

"Oui, oui, oui. C'est celle-ci que je voulais."

"And so they called him Fishboy."

"Feeshboi!"

Sam has never let me finish the saga of Fishboy. I would like Fishboy to eventually swim to America, leaving a silvery trail on the dark water. His mother and father, long-suffering, persevere. They track that silver trail in a wooden boat until at last they are reunited with Fishboy in New York Harbor, where he is nonchalantly lounging at the base of the Statue of Liberty. Sam doesn't care for the ambiguity in the story. He picks up the thread of the story once the going gets rough and transforms him into either a whole fish or a whole boy. Today Fishboy isn't even getting his feet wet.

"Il a vu que la mer était pleine de crabes qui pincent et de serpents qui mordent. Alors, Feeshboi est sorti de l'eau froide et s'est transformé en petit garçon. Il a vecu deux cent ans après ça."

"Terminée, notre histoire de tendresse et de beauté?"

"Oui. Terminée."

When I finally get back to the kitchen window there's nothing left in the sky at all.

3

The summer I was fourteen, I took a bus out of town to visit Cody. He was spending the summer in the Panhandle working for our cousin who had a fried chicken establishment. Actually, my brother was doing time. He and some friends had taken a spin in a stolen car. Stolen? he repeated. We didn't steal it, Dad. We borrowed it. He was blowing up mailboxes right and left and had taken up membership in a tough boys' club called the Black Knights. Dad sent him out to the Panhandle to work it off.

It was a big Greyhound, but it didn't run like the sleek racing dog on the side of the bus. The air conditioner worked only intermittently, and we had to stop several times, every hour or so. The driver would make an announcement into the microphone, but he held it too close to his mouth and we couldn't understand anything he said. He would pull over and make some adjustment that got us moving again. It was a hot ride and the landscape was flat and dry under the August sun. Staring through the smeared windows, I waited for the scene to change. For the miles of barren landscape to suddenly give way to a carefully hidden secret. Cattle and working ponies stood about in shrinking water holes. I saw a cowbird or two. Every little town claimed to have the world's best barbecue. Nothing moved under the sun. The bus driver, seizing an opportunity, made an announcement we could all understand.

"Ladies and gentlemen. If you all look quickly to the left you will see an Oklahoma groundhog."

He was standing on two legs by the side of the road and looked like a potential passenger, his forelegs held up to his chest. He scuttled off into a ditch as we passed. The man next to me had brought a sack of popcorn with him and a can of cherry pop. He worked the residue out of his teeth with the nail of his finger, belching quietly as he sucked on the can of pop. He wore one of those hats with a slight bill on the front, poked through with airholes. When he finished his popcorn he looked at me, then out the window. I didn't know if he were actually addressing me, so I thought it better not to reply.

"I guess if you're gonna see God, you're more likely to see Him in Oklahoma than anywheres else. Sweet Jesus, it's hot on this bus."

I repeated that sentence to myself again and again. By the time we reached the Panhandle it wasn't cryptic anymore, it was as homey and comfortable as an old shoe. The number of evangelists that have risen since from that cracked, sun-baked soil have proved him right. The fact of God's presence has lost all its strangeness in Oklahoma. Some might argue much of His majesty has been leeched away with all the exposure. That He appears to man, that He speaks and, in fact, issues directives has become commonplace. Looking quickly to the left we might spot a groundhog. Or God.

My mother once mailed me a trade magazine in which a new brand of local evangelist was the subject of the feature story. City booster, born-again Christian. Keen businessman. It was a three-dimensional portrait of Kyle Lark.

July 4, 1979

Dear Lucy,

Please see page 38. Just look at what that old beau of yours is up to now!

Will write at length later. Must run.

In the photograph stood a man perhaps forty years old, with his hands spread out as if in welcome. He was standing in a pasture behind which lay the city skyline. The text explained Kyle's wish to construct a trolley car linking the north and south ends of the city. Actually, it went on to say, this was not really Kyle's wish, but God's. To quote Kyle himself:

"I had slipped outside to take a nap in the hammock. It must have been, oh, golly, four-thirty or so. Somebody was trying to mow his lawn but durned if he could get his mower started up. So there was this sound of the mower starting and stopping and the sounds of my girls, Kitty and Kelly, who happened to be playing blindman's bluff. Well, they tired of this game and my neighbor gave up on his mower and must have went inside. I began to nod off in my hammock."

"Then, when I was nearly asleep, everything turned golden on me. I mean the light in the yard. I became afraid. Until He spoke. And when He spoke, His voice was so gentle I knew I had nothing to fear. I knew then I had to get a trolley car built for this town. That's how the project came to me and that's why I need the support of this city."

I studied the picture closely. Maybe in the wide stretch of those welcoming arms Kyle meant to imply the breadth of his vision. I didn't know. I couldn't help looking at his feet to see if he was still wearing white shoes. The field was overgrown and I couldn't make his feet out. He was standing in a patch of thistle and dry grass.

That I would one day be Lucy Lark with little Larks tugging on my skirts was at one time quite plausible. But things happen to make young love die on the vine. Minor revelations that can make this love turn sour as rancid milk. One detail may be all it takes. I remember Kyle's deep commitment to white shoes. Often there was a white belt or handkerchief to set off his enormous gleaming feet. We were sitting in his convertible, parked in a lover's lane, and I was once more staring at those shoes, glossed and ready to roll. Between kisses he told me about the tent, the tent his family rented for their reunion every seven years. Wait until you see it, Lucy. Young and old, from points across Texas and Oklahoma. I want you to come with me. You'll never witness anything like it again. I sweetly returned a kiss by way of an answer and began applying red, red lipstick. He took a great interest in my future. Perhaps because of the difference in our ages he took on the role of counselor. Lucy, in the years that lie ahead, he would start—then he would take up my future, mine, and mold it with the concentration of a potter at work on a stubborn lump of clay. Those books of yours, for instance, and he would dismiss contemporary American poetry with a smirk. Foreign titles drew dark scowls. I jumped ship just as Kyle and his clan were heading full sail into another seventh year. Presumably the Larks were still gathering under a rented canvas tent in the far western reaches of my home state. I thought of this as a heroic concept, but one that had nothing whatsoever to do with me. I imagine the Lerners and the Laugiers, extended or even nuclear, herded together with a cattle prod, feigning solidarity under penalty of a sharp electric shock. For my own family to gather willingly, to lay down arms for one single afternoon under the big top, it would require nothing less than an act of God.

Cody had been at large for two months before I heard about it. My parents, reading the headlines about the paralyzing snowfall on the Côte, telephoned several times before they could get through. Worried friends and relatives were phoning nonstop and the lines hummed. It was the winter of 1984.

"Lucy! Oh, honey. We've just seen a UPI photo of somebody snowskiing down the Promenade des Anglais. I bet your husband is having a wonderful time shooting pictures. Everything alright?"

"Never better. They say it's the first time it's snowed like this in nearly forty years."

We had become an overnight community. A neighbor, not Madame Leconte but another, at last bent her head toward me in the snow-filled alley and sang out, Bonjour! as if we had known each other for years. I had been anxious to speak with her. She was a handsome widow who had moved here from Paris when her husband died. Her disciplined good looks attracted me. She worked late into the night at a drafting table. I could watch her from one of the back bedroom windows. I couldn't find a way to approach her until the snow fell.

"We have some bad news, honey."

My mother passed the phone to my father. I thought someone was dead and I started ticking off names to myself. The snow was melting, dropping off my boots to form a gray puddle where I stood.

"Lucy, it's your brother. Cody—"

"What happened?"

"—has disappeared. He's been gone for two months. We waited this long to tell you because we didn't want to upset you. We were sure he'd be back. Either that or Catch—we thought Catch would track him down with that private eye of his. We simply don't know where he is."

I heard my mother banging pots and pans beside him. It sounded like he was phoning from a cafeteria.

"Becky had a real time. Anita and Catch moved in with her for a few days until she asked them to leave. I guess some things you just have to get through alone. She seems to be back on her feet now. Has to with those girls. Your mother wants a word with you."

She cleared her throat and I could tell by the way she spoke she was sitting up very, very straight.

"I am tired. You can't imagine how tired I feel. We seem to go from one saga to another around here. To think that little bastard is my son."

"Maybe Cody was kidnapped. After all, Catch—"

"My eye. He abandoned his family. Period. Don't try to elevate this, Lucy. It stinks worse than a rotten egg."

I made coffee and planned my phone call to Becky. Nothing immoderate. Best to steer clear of too much feminine empathy. As the criminal's sibling, I might be, in Becky's eyes, as much a miscreant as my brother. I let the phone ring nine times. On the tenth ring, someone picked up the phone and placed the receiver down without answering. This was followed by the sound of breaking glass. I heard Becky cursing offstage.

"Yes?"

"It's Lucy. Have I picked a bad time?"

"These days any time is a bad time. Honestly, these girls! They sweep through the house in their big shoes with no regard for my things. They just throw their gym sacks anywhere. My favorite piece of Steuben. The absolute sweetest piece you've ever seen, too."

The volume of the music increased in the background and Becky placed something over the receiver. There were muffled shouts and an abrupt halt to the noise.

"Now, how can I help you, Lucy?"

"That's the question I wanted to ask you. I feel so—"

"Oh, that. Listen, I've got about a hundred people feeling just awful for me, so one more mourner isn't going to make any difference. Your mom bring you up to date?"

"Not really. All I know is he's been gone for two months."

"Right. Anything else?"

My left shoulder felt sore and tight. Maybe it was Becky's crisp tone. If she was affected, it certainly didn't show.

"Nothing."

"Two months ago, nearly to the day, I woke up at five o'clock in the morning. No Samsonite, no Cody. He left thirteen hundred dollars in cash on the dressing table."

"A note of explanation?"

"Zip. High and dry if you don't count the money on the table. Mind you, I'm not surprised. That's your brother through and through."

"You don't sound too—"

"Torn up? I'm not. I'm two months down the road, that's why, and already living my life. If Cody wants to walk out on the best thing that ever happened to him, I say let him go. Libby Lerner!"

The phone was slammed down again and a door banged. Becky returned, breathless and out of time.

"I've got to run, Lucy. Listen, I appreciate your calling and all. You might let your mother know in a subtle way that her pies are really not what the doctor ordered just now. Mincemeat, lemon chiffon. Rhubarb, ugh. They make me nauseous and, of course, Eleanor doesn't eat sweets."

"I'll see what I can do. What else?"

"Nothing else unless you can do a little long-distance counseling. Short of giving me a hand with these *girls* I don't need anything from anybody. Daddy's helping out with the money end. Say, though. I saw the prettiest gift suggestion in House Beautiful. Says these come from a shop in Antibes. Isn't that near you-all?"

"Not far. Why don't you describe it?"

"They are just precious. Straw hats with great huge brims. All decorated with ribbons and dried flowers. Wait a sec. It says here the hat part is full of potpourri. Don't go out of your way, but if you do happen to see one of these . . ."

"I know where to find them. Look Becky, I just wanted to say how crummy this whole thing is."

"We're going to find your brother, Lucy. You don't know Daddy. When he sets his mind to something, there's no stopping him. Cody's going to have hell to pay for what he's done."

"Let's keep in touch."

"Let's."

I hung up the phone, light-headed, and went to look at Cody's picture. To see if that, too, had disappeared into thin air.

At La Belle Eléna there are only three photographs on display. Marc's work is out of sight, locked away in his darkroom. But I have erected what amounts to a shrine near the corner where guests hang their hats and coats. In a dimly lit cubbyhole I have placed three photographs, aging and unframed, the edges of each curling up now under the heat of the small lamp.

One photograph shows my mother poised on a stepladder, dressed in painter's overalls, a fashionable gag shot at the Tulsa State Fair the year of my birth. I am nowhere in evidence. My mother's thin frame belies the fact that somewhere, out of camera's range, a three-week-old baby is squalling in a father's arms. "You gave me a hell of a time," she once told me. "Not that things were any easier for you. Your head was pointy for weeks." The second photo is again of my mother, standing on the deck of a small boat at the lake. My mother does not swim, a sober fact she has managed to hide behind a wide grin. That day was quite windy. Her hair in the photo blows across her face. She looks wonderfully sporty, a woman perfectly at home sitting around a campfire pan-frying a fat trout. I prefer these two photographs to any taken of my mother since. Their charm lies in what they manage to conceal. The third picture is of Cody. Friends reel back from it and do not believe this is my brother. Cody, shirt unbuttoned to the waist on a blistering hot day, sits astride a borrowed Yamaha. At first glance one supposes another young imitator of James Dean, a standard tough guy pose. But the look on my brother's face the moment the shutter snapped is intensely private and the only real proof I have of him. Below the photos I have casually lain a pair of brass knuckles. Friends slip them on and wriggle their fingers as I explain their function—jaw-bashing circa 1900. Their true value I hoard for myself. My father put them in my hands as I was making still another return to France. The man who sprayed our trees every summer found them out back in the woods when we were young, and handed them solemnly to my mother, who promised never to split them up, for they were a pair.

Did Cody criss-cross state lines or did he foresee a second professional life in some other place? Catch, Cody's father-in-law, was on his trail. Had Cody adequately covered his tracks? Only then, not knowing whether the sun was rising or setting in the place where my brother was, did I realize he was gone.

"You could stand a creed. A political doctrine of some kind. It's not enough to be just a little bastard who deserts his wife and kids. But you never entertained a political thought in your life. Or did you, Cody?"

"Ah!"

A fugitive can turn up just about anywhere. I thought at first it was him. The steady pressure on my shoulder kept me from jumping right out of my skin. I hadn't heard the knock on the door, if there had been one. I recognized the bony grip—it was Roselli, the senile old she-witch no one called Madame anymore. She had dropped her gender ages ago, existing now as a dry, whiskery little gnome. In the summer I sometimes found her in a corner of the garden, ripping out weeds. She always wore an apron and the pocket was filled with chewing gum wrappers and twigs. When I run her out of the garden she hands me a sticky candy paper or the label from a can of motor oil. Her own children advise caution. Lucy, if you're kind to her she'll come again and again, like a stray cat. She was excited by the snowfall and spoke in patois. I asked her what she was doing in my house.

"Le mari a froid. Mon mari a froid."

She claimed to hear her dead husband shivering and crying from the cold. I led her to the kitchen. Ordinarily after a cup of tea she forgets why she has come and wanders back to her apartment. The gate to her property is the side of an old packing crate. *Fragile* is still marked on the outside in fading letters. Each time the gate falls off she comes to Marc. She summons him with an extraordinary mixture of gratitude and impatience, as if he is responsible for the decrepitude of the gate and its repair. Other neighbors are called upon to unplug the sink or mop up the bucket of water that has somehow been overturned again. On days she is close to death she hangs a red beach towel over the side of her small balcony and someone phones the children. The daughters knit and laugh by the side of her bed.

I couldn't sidetrack her today with tea. She insisted we stand outside so I could hear the cries, which were actually the elated shouts of neighborhood kids.

"Ce sont les enfants, Roselli. Les enfants s'amusent. Ce n'est pas votre mari."

She was wearing a few thin sweaters but didn't seem to mind the cold. She studied the tracks left in the snow, pigeon-toed and shallow. She set her feet carefully in each fresh track and set off up the hill to where the children were sledding on plastic sacks. Her dead husband's agony was forgotten. She picked up a child's mitten and stuffed it furtively in her apron. Neighborhood kids say she once made a soup from bad boys. That the stones lined up on Roselli's windowsill were used to knock them cold before they were thrown into her pot.

Because of the snow, we fell into a state of heady emergency. Cars and trucks were not getting through and there wasn't a pair of snow tires or chains to be found. The village market was picked clean and for the next two days the baker was the local hero. He blushed with pleasure at the line that formed outside as early as seven o'clock.

We ate strange, wonderful grub with the widow from Paris. She managed to find canned peas and produced a potato gratin with the last of her milk and butter. Her butane was gone and we huddled around the fire after dinner, dressed in ski clothes. The inconvenience was festive, for the snow was melting off. We stood to lose some palm trees, the citrus growers would be hurt. The widow was an artist, steadfast about not selling her work. She seemed unused to speech and her questions were like shotgun blasts. I stared at the big-bottomed beauties that figured in her paintings. Sam curled up in front of her, punching out a space for his head in a soft cushion. She stroked him with her foot as she talked.

I mentioned as we left that I had a brother living in Mexico. It was a final flourish, a distinguishing signature on the evening. Marc took Sam from my shoulder, a sign that he considered me completely irresponsible. Unfit to engineer the slick street, the low passage where I might bump the head of a sleeping child.

When the snow melted and we slid into the traditionally rainy Mediterranean winter, that evening spent in the widow's apartment was annulled. We may have spoken too soon, violated some code of propriety. My waves and salutations were barely noticed and I went back to watching her work at night from my bedroom window. She sometimes fell asleep at her drafting table.

That spring when I would catch sight of her, poising a glass on a table or watering the potted plants on her terrace, I saw she had acquired a new outer layer of flesh around her middle. I thought of my uncle's line of unshod quarter horses and how they shed their winter coats in scruffy patches. If you pulled hard at the coat with your hand, it came loose effortlessly, like a piece of carpet. The strangeness of intimacy—I thought it might take another snowfall for the widow and I to exchange greetings again.

The palm trees were much worse for that snowfall. We were advised by radio and television bulletins not to cut the limp, brown fronds until the end of May. Retired people were hardest hit. They paced the length and width of their small plots with the increasingly warm weather. They studied the disorder, slapping the sides of their legs with sunhats and gardening gloves, resisting the urge to trim and uproot. Detritus was deceptive after that harsh winter and no one dared touch what might still contain life. They picked up books and newspapers instead, settling into armchairs. Or merely sat blinking in the warm sun. There was plenty of time to think.

4

In many ways my youth was misspent. Maybe Cody was right.

"There's no ball like an oddball. Why do you hang around with jerks, Lucy? You oughta see 'em, Dad. That delightful little number Jeanine, for example. She shakes her head and it's snowing. There's even dandruff on her eyelashes, for God's sake."

"Watch your language, Cody."

"Why doesn't she wash her hair? Cripes. You invite her here and we'll have to disinfect the whole house."

Cody was up to his elbows in flour when he made this assessment of my high school social life. He was making a pie crust. A lighter-than-air pie crust that no one could equal, not even my mother. It was a question of fingertips and speed. The minute the flat of your hand touched it, he said, finito.

"Both her parents are teachers in the junior college. Jeanine is an intellectual. Stop criticizing my friends."

"You can be smart and clean at the same time. Also that fat guy with the horn-rims. Forget it."

As usual my brother had made a bull's-eye.

"It's your fault for not telling me."

"Oh, this is good. For not telling you how to choose decent friends?"

"Of course not. For not telling me how it is at lunch."

The lunch pass was the key to the world. With it you won the right to one hour of windy freedom right in the middle of the day. With it you fell into a car, any car, and roared out of the parking lot toward the snack shop at the golf course. Or you went winging down Bishop Avenue, all the windows down. Without it you were caught in a sticky web of Jeanines and Lawfords. The Jeanines and Lawfords of the world didn't apply for lunch passes. They inhaled their food and rushed to the library with the twenty minutes gained. It didn't end there. They waited for me after class, sealing my fate. I wouldn't be a cheerleader or Girl of the Month. Teachers called on me first and wrote Very Promising in the margins of my papers. Not for those who dined out. They flew into class late, accepting proctor slips with equanimity, stifling laughter in the back row. They combed their hair furtively, peering into tiny hidden mirrors. Or designed faster cars still, in margins of their own. They had tasted freedom and just didn't care.

"Cody?"

Dad had left the kitchen and there were only the two of us. He was crimping the edges and I could taste it already. It broke into buttery particles on the tip of my tongue.

"Take me with you. Sneak me out at lunchtime."

He turned to me and rolled an unwanted bit of dough between his fingers.

"Little Sis. Do you really think I eat on my lunch hour?"

I blushed, caught out in the horrible act of not knowing.

"What do you do then? I mean if you don't actually eat."

"I do Sue Ellen Beardsley."

The Tractor Queen! I knew her from the picture in the paper. She stood astride a John Deer tractor in a halter top and short shorts. Riding that machine around in the hot sun, waving to sweaty bands of onlookers from under the brim of a wide straw hat had won Sue Ellen a one-thousand-dollar cash prize and a college scholarship. The agricultural college of her choice. Sue Ellen's goal in life? It was printed under the picture. To study veterinary science and to look after those less fortunate than herself. And to become the kind of woman Oklahomans could be proud of.

He raised his eyebrows and blew a shimmering series of smoke rings toward me though he wasn't smoking a thing.

"Shocked?"

"Of course not. You are a louse. A true scum. You know what, Cody? I wasn't sure until this minute, but I am now so I'll share it with you. There was an awful mix-up at the hospital and my real brother is somewhere else. I'll tell you what. When he reads, his lips don't move, because after all he's a junior in high school. And he doesn't act up and talk bad, because he *has brains.* Badness throws people off the track. You act the way you do to divert everybody. They're so disconcerted, they don't have time to think of your lack of intelligence. You're touching that with your hand. It'll taste like cement."

We once had a yardman my father nicknamed Demosthenes. We would watch him fly over the backyard on the wings of a new power mower. His arms flew out in wide circles as his ongoing, drowned-out oratory was piffled away on the likes of crickets and hissing squirrels in the tops of trees. That day, my outburst hung suspended in the hot kitchen, begging to be refuted. Cody didn't react. He offered no self-defense and turned back to the pie until I finally wandered off, as robbed of audience as poor Demosthenes.

I became rather popular in high school. My parents were secretly alarmed, for there had been no prior indicators. They thought I would stick it out at the library, dragging home occasional shy, lint-covered friends. My status was a fraud, a richness entirely unearned. The coins slipped into the palm of my open hand as I glided through the halls of Howard High School. I was Cody's sister. I carried a note around in my purse that proved it.

Dear Lucy,

I've just got to talk to you. Do you think we could meet after school? I've got my Dad's car. See you then!

Love,
Sherry

I knew what lay behind every flirtation, every invitation to see what was on at the Cinema West. I pressed these notes into the yellowing pages of old collie books by Albert Payson Terhune, every Caldecott winner issued since I was seven. They weren't notes to me, they were tributes to my brother. I tried not to play favorites, invited them all home one at a time and let them prowl through the house, The Cody Museum.

"Oh, gosh. This is your brother's baseball cap? Why didn't he go out for the team this year?"

"He does chin-ups on that thing? How many does he do a night?"

Walking solemnly down the hall to my bedroom, they gave into temptation and pushed a door already ajar. They fingered his bedspread, paused for a minute before the picture of a California surfer. They charted his comings and goings, studied his tracks with ardor. The lucky ones got a glimpse of him disappearing out a back door. They heard the swish of a nylon windbreaker that must have been Cody.

"Your brother's no stay-at-home. That much is for sure."

"Where's he gone off to now?"

He glanced off all those girls like refracted light, raised a hand in greeting and was gone. My heart flinched for them. Most went home satisfied, having seen him. Certain of them found ticket stubs in their pockets when they arrived home. A loose page of Jack London folded carefully in quarters.

So Cody's conduct in his senior year surprised us all. The only all-nighters my brother pulled were at Safeway. He didn't bask in the glory of his reputation as a ladies' man. He did not, as my father glumly predicted, become a hood. He bagged groceries. He bagged without malice. He bagged tenderly, paying attention to fragile eggs and tomatoes. He distributed weighty items so the long trek from car to kitchen wouldn't wear his clients down. He even bagged on prom night, waving to his drunken classmates who honked wildly for him in the parking lot. He volunteered nights and weekends when, on the strength of a generous allowance, he could have been courting Sue Ellen and others like her.

"Cody, where's the fire? Stop wolfing your food, for heaven's sake."

"I'm going to be late, Mom. I'm working the late shift."

The store manager had never seen anything like it. He smiled, tweeked rosy little cheeks and remembered the names of frequent customers. When business was slow he offered to stock shelves. He was free any night, and the only drawback, if it could be called that, was the women. They lined up at the register where Cody was working, leaving other baggers twiddling their thumbs. Women in their late thirties and forties, with tired, heavy legs and kids pulling on them for chewing gum. They endured the inconvenience for Cody, leaning into their carts and reading movie magazines. My brother greeted them politely by their names. He asked them how their soufflés had turned out the week before and drew their attention to an interesting punch recipe in *Good Housekeeping*. They responded with sweet smiles and stuffed new bills into his shirt pocket. The capper came the day Mrs. McHenry pressed a twenty into Cody's warm palm. She had on a playful white tennis dress and canvas shoes that had *FUN!* printed all over them in pink letters.

"Mrs. McHenry, I think there's a mistake here."

Cody winked at her daughter Megan, who stuck out her tongue.

"There's no mistake, Cody. I said to my husband the other day, 'Dickey, I've heard enough about taciturn teenagers. You ought to see the boy at Safeway. You'd eat your words.' Do something fun with that twenty, Cody. Megan, quit! Stop that this minute."

I volunteered a lot for errands that year. I enjoyed watching him work the parking lot. Cody could recover a tip for anything—racing after a grapefruit or hailing a woman who left her car headlights on. He was not ingratiating. He was smooth. His supremacy was clear. The other boys stood back a bit from my brother, giving him room to work the crowd.

I honked at him as he handed a baby back to a sunburned woman in plaid bermuda shorts. He pocketed his tip and came over to the car. I was parked under the only shade tree in the lot.

"You're terrific, Cody."

"Thank you, Ma'am."

"When you grow up are you going to be a politician? Kissing babies. That's too much."

He reached inside the car and bent the mirror forward. He flicked something off his cheek.

"Stop for gas on the way home. You're riding on empty."

"Cody?"

He has bluish circles under his eyes.

"What?"

"What's going on? Being a model bag boy is surely not an end in itself."

A smile started up on one corner of my brother's mouth and went away.

"You're clever with words. I like how you talk sometimes."

"You can trust me. What's cooking?"

"Mexico. The point is Mexico."

Cody took a wayward strand of my hair between his fingers and laid it correctly in place. We were not touchers and I flinched as he reached for me. The inadvertent gesture surprised me.

"Face it. You have a brother who can't read for shit. I'm not the kind of brother who is going off to college in the fall. You won't be able to visit me on the weekends and I'll never introduce you to my frat brothers. Sometimes I feel like I'm about to blast out of here. Like if I don't hook my ankles around the legs of the chair I'll just fly off into space. Only I somehow never do. I'm going to Mexico as soon as I get the money saved."

"Does Mom know?"

"You know. And me."

After that my eyes began to take on the same bruised bluish shadows Cody's had. My mother complained of the extremism that ran in our family. When she lay down to sleep she thought she heard page-turning coming from my room even when the lights were out.

"Isn't it time we all settled down around here?"

Cody's intention summoned up a whole empire. I read a novel about a young mestizo named Juan, biographies of Pancho Villa and Emiliano Zapata, while my brother hustled the parking lot of Safeway with all the élan of a pimp working his district.

5

When was it exactly that Cody's behavior seemed less and less predictable? I would have been saddened and ashamed if Cody had made it big as a loan shark or bank robber. But not the least bit surprised. When did my brother stop dreaming?

Cody didn't blast off into space or even into Mexico. His fist closed around a dozen jumping beans, Cody blinked hard, for Mexico was receding fast. He opened his fist and they hopped from his hand to the floor.

"Maybe the three of us can still go one day."

"You and me and Becky? Oh, let's!"

"Me and Becky and Garrett. Ass. I'm going to be a father."

Becky called and wanted to know if he could lay wallpaper straight. Yellow wallpaper with ducks splashing around in a big, big pond.

Luck, Cody's kind, ran downhill. The Mexico money evaporated. It disappeared before his eyes. It went for baby booties and terry cloth bibs. A hefty deposit on a two-bedroom apartment. We hung a solemn black robe and cap on the stunned father-to-be and he moved through graduation exercises in a daze. Later he rolled his diploma into a tight wand and held a burning end to a contraband Havana cigar. To celebrate this most joyous occasion, he said.

Becky Eckle twirled almost to the end. She was captain of the squad and wouldn't let them down for the world. Without a good captain, she exclaimed, they are helpless! Not one of my girls can hold a routine in her mind for long. It takes a special kind of memory to be a good captain, she said. Pregnancy added to her triumph. Round-bellied and increasingly glorious she worked through the summer with her squad.

"Now, of course, come fall, you all will follow Wanda instead of me. But I'll get you there. Let's back up and do the last number again. Get those batons up! I want you to keep smiling. I know it's hot out here, but if I can smile you can."

Right after practice she drove over so Cody could feel her stomach. He felt nothing, though she swore he was about to kick right through her. Let's call him Garrett, okay? How about if we call him Garrett?

My mother took Dad's advice and got hold of herself. There are times in your life when you need to be cool as a cucumber, she said to me, and this is one of them. Why, there are definite steps to be taken. This is not a defeat. Cody, are you listening?

She was always reaching for his hands, which he kept jammed in coat pockets. When he hung his jacket up you could see how it was going for him. The jacket slumped forward, as if still inhabited by someone standing in a slouch, the pockets all misshapen. This is not personal, Mom would say. This is not against Becky. That is one darling and beautiful girl. I am simply saying that it is never too late to rectify a mistake.

"I don't understand why you don't let yourself be helped, Cody. You are too young to be a father. I have volunteered at St. John's Home for Girls. I ought to mention that these girls were from every walk of life, but they were not unhappy. I worked with them on napkin folding, knitting and that sort of thing. We put on our own production of *Midsummer Night's Dream*. And the girls had their babies and went home. The rest was in the hands of the adoption agency. No lives ruined. I could present the idea of the school to Becky in a subtle fashion—"

"Agnes, I really believe enough has been said."

"But that's just it, Wade. Enough has not been said. My son has not been heard from. Just this nonsense of 'Becky wants the baby.' Well and good, but what about my son? And one more thing. Don't think me vicious, she is a darling, darling girl, but Becky doesn't want a baby. She wants a doll or cuddly animal. A baby! Cody, *your life.*"

She would change colors too fast and someone would run to the kitchen for a glass of cold water. My mother began to nap. Like a child or an aged person, she went to bed most every afternoon. She wheeled down the aisle of our local supermarket with the floral imprint of the bedspread still embossed on one cheek.

Cody had by then begun to take his place in a tiny, tiny world. Becky's father, Catch Eckle, was the undisputed miniature golf king of Oklahoma. A great business, he told Cody.

"You work spring and fall in this business. Seems like people here got nothing better to do than play putt-putt golf in spring and fall. I run a full crew for about six months. Cotton candy, iced drinks and miniature golf. It's crazy. Summer? Hell, I'm at the lake skiing. Winter place up in Snowmass. It's yours, Cody. I show you all I know and it's yours. It'll be a great thing for Garrett one day."

Cody wandered through the miniature golf parks with the king. They squatted before a little windmill that had stopped turning and Catch radioed maintenance from his car.

"You can't believe how much she wants this baby, Cody. I never saw Becky want something so much in her whole life. Me and her mother hardly recognize her. Ordinarily a father'd be upset. I mean, I'd hear about so-and-so's kid getting knocked up and I'd think, 'Jesus, why doesn't he kill the guy? How does he keep from killing the little son of a bitch?' And here we are today, Cody. Sitting. Talking. And the upshot of this is you've made my little girl happy. And I don't want to kill you at all, Cody. Fact."

Cody lay at the foot of my bed with one of the dogs after a long day with the king. Trade secrets had spilled out after lunch. Cody learned about trust, a thing Catch Eckle had teased out of people for years. Catch Eckle said trust was provoked. He said he provoked trust in his employees, his wife, his daughter.

" 'Take my wife, for example. I send her to Miami every year on vacation. I see to it she's looking good. Hair cut just right. I'm after her to take off a few pounds at the gym before she goes. Then I buy her a fancy dress and put her on a plane for Miami. I kiss her one on the lips at the airport and say, "Sweetheart, have yourself the time of your life." And that's how I provoke trust in my wife, Cody. And I've never had reason to doubt her.'

"So then he tells me in the same breath my job, my training at the moment, is to close down each of the big three locations. And the man's a lunatic. He says, 'Cody, don't make the deposit until tomorrow morning. My bank opens at nine.' I fought with him. 'Catch,' I said, 'I'm a walking murder victim.' He said in fifteen years he's only been hit once and all he had on him was ten dollars in cash. Lucy, he's a psycho and the man's going to be my father-in-law."

"He's just provoking trust. A sicko. Why don't you get a job on a rig? Go to Galveston with Becky. Uncle Rob knows people down there. Go to Texas and get away from him. You'll make a fortune and you won't have Catch Eckle breathing down your back."

"I can stand it. This could be a very good thing for me. Shep, you've got halitosis, buddy."

He pushed the dog off the bed and grabbed my foot.

"Swear you'll babysit or I'll tear it off."

"No way. What are you going to do with a baby anyway? Do you know what to do when they cry? They don't walk to the toilet, you know. What about all that?"

"It's under control. I've been going to this thing called Crib Counseling at the Y. It talks all about that stuff. For Christ's sake, you too? Everybody's bawling around here. If it's not you, it's Mom."

"The whole idea stinks. You shouldn't be burping babies. You should be in Mexico, fighting your way out of a sleazy bar or running illegals over the border at night. I don't know. But not hanging wallpaper. You won't last, Cody. And when you bolt it's going to be a big mess for everyone to clean up. Except you, of course, because you'll be gone. Cody."

His nose was running furiously.

"You're always waiting for the big disclosure, Lucy. So here goes. I made it up. Mexico City, can you picture that? Broken-down buses, spic kids begging for pesos and me with the trots. Mexico was a lie from the start because you're the one who's dying to bolt. I'd like a kid. And don't try to measure how much I love Becky or whether I love her at all. I'm sticking in place, and Becky and this baby of mine are going to help me. It's you who's flying out of here, not me."

They were married in a civil ceremony. Catch and Anita were resplendent. Before them, the Lerners looked like drab game. Trapped inside the courthouse we seemed less than we were, too literally earth-toned. There was only our cousin Ella, that perpetual exception, whose flamboyance rivaled our new in-laws. Heads turned as she rustled through the door in a cloud of uncontrolled taffeta. My mother fingered her strand of pearls and moved in to embrace Becky.

"I feel richer today by one. Oh, two I should say. . . . I am so happy for you both."

Catch and my father exchanged rough hugs. Catch swiped at the corner of his brow with a handkerchief and admitted to a case of the nerves.

"I nearly didn't make it here. Weddings! Anita and I ran off to Vegas ourselves. I just couldn't face it."

Guests lined the steps of the courthouse. They joined hands and formed a tensile human chain. When Cody and Becky appeared at the door they broke into applause. Pink paper dots piled up at their feet.

Becky turned and waved slowly, leaning on the door of a black limousine.

"Way to go, Cody!"

"Alright, alright!"

A brief reception was held at the airport, where Cody and Becky waited for a plane to Tahoe. Catch treated all the Flight 902 passengers to a glass of Dom Perignon and free passes to any of the big three locations. He knelt before an older woman carefully dressed in a wrinkle-free polyester suit. She nodded to him, smiling, as he filled her glass a second time. He told her the story of his happpiness.

"Now in my case happiness was a thing that just snuck up on me over time. Some men will look me in the eye when they're explaining a low, common thing they've done. 'Catch, I'm just trying to be happy,' they might say to me. I always figured happiness knew my address alright. I thought, 'Catch Eckle, you do right by your family and obey the Lord and you won't have to worry about happiness.' Then I happened to be sitting out on the patio one evening and Becky and Anita (that's Anita in the peacock blue) were putting steaks on the grill. We were drinking iced tea and watching the heat lightning. It occurred to me then that I'd been happy so long, the word just didn't exist anymore. Happiness had just up and moved in permanently. Do you enjoy miniature golf, Minah? Never played? We'll have to fix that."

Their flight was called and Becky moved toward my mother. She had been drinking Orange Crush and there was a slight mustache above her upper lip. She held my mother by the elbow as if she were lecturing someone younger and more inexperienced.

"Mrs. Lerner, I know you think I'm a bubblehead and that's okay. I mean, I do smile a lot and optimistic people are often misunderstood. I just want you to know that this is going to work out. Some boys can do all kinds of things for themselves, you see. They can become presidents of things and sales managers and college grads just to walk farther down their own road. But not Cody. Cody needs an obligation. A thing to look out for besides himself. Babies are cute and all. I really do love them. But I want this baby for what it can do for me and Cody. You just wait and see. Oh, I hope we'll be real close. I hope we'll often go out to lunch. I'm quite close with many women your age. I have recently begun keeping a notebook on all the important things women your age tell me."

She released her and started on Dad. I made my way over to Cody. He was standing by the window watching the final preparations for Flight 902, drinking off the last of the champagne. I thought about saying what was on my mind. Ditch her, Cody. She won't stay sweet long. When you hit Tahoe, make a run for it.

"Beware of air pockets over Albuquerque. It's notorious for

that. But I guess at your altitude you won't feel a thing."

We both turned to watch Catch. He wanted to take over the microphone in the waiting area for just one minute. The father of the bride wanted to congratulate the newlyweds before they climbed onto the plane. Catch reddened and pulled on his collar. He was up against airline regulations that wouldn't give way before his happiness.

"Cody, remember when we were in California that time and you got carried out on a riptide? Tell me what it was like out there."

Cody stroked the rim of his glass with one finger until it hummed, setting my teeth on edge.

"I was scared shitless. Once I passed the final point, that is. Remember the point out past the red flag? There were almost always divers out there, only not that day. They'd all crawled out of the water and were watching from the rocks. When I got past those guys I stopped trying. I was getting tired and had swallowed a lot of water.

"Then I started praying. I figured numbers were important. So I promised if He'd let go, stop pulling on me, I'd get back to shore and toss Him three others. My mother and father. My pretty little sister. And then the pulling let up and I swam in as far as I could. You know the rest. The patrol boat picked me up and I got the royal treatment for a week. My allowance went up. I became a hero."

After the plane took off, we drove to the Ramada Inn. Dad and I shared a dark beer. Every table in the cocktail lounge had a candle burning in a red glass bowl. The bowls were weighted so if you accidentally knocked one over it would right itself. The waitress brought us black olives served in a white saucer. She took my mother's order first.

"I would like something thirst-quenching, please. I am terribly thirsty."

"It's dusty alright. I was just listening to the radio and they were giving the dust count. There is a historic number of dust particles in the air today. Can I get you a martini, hon?"

"Please. And a tall glass of water."

Dad stroked his hair back several times. Said "well" like it was a complete sentence. We all held on to something. The table edge. A solid glass handle or the thin stem of a goblet. As if these objects would rise up into the air were it not for our fullest attention. Mom finally spoke and the heat was on.

"This evening I want nothing to go wrong. I don't want to hear a door slammed or a voice raised. The first dog that barks is going to the pound."

We drove home carefully. My father swerved, neatly missing potholes in the roads rutted and buckling from the extreme heat. He braked so gradually we hardly noticed coming to a stop. My mother kept her hands cupped over her eyes. The sunlight, she said, is just blinding.

Garrett was renamed Eleanor because of courage. There was no other woman in American history as courageous as Eleanor Roosevelt. The way she fought for what she believed in! If there was any disappointment in Eleanor's gender it didn't show.

"I've got all the *boy* I need."

They became public smoochers. My brother bought a pair of margarine-colored canaries that Becky named Lovey and Dovey. She called all the time with Eleanor updates.

"Lucy? Becky here. Guess what? I just moved into Eleanor's range of vision. She was lying in her tubby in the kitchen sink and all of a sudden her eyes just locked into place when she saw me. This is part of what is known as the bonding process between a mother and newborn."

"Mrs. Lerner, it's Becky. I had to call! Eleanor just rolled over and it's quite early according to Brazelton. Another thing I have discovered is that she prefers the milk from my right breast. There is a very clear appetite difference depending on whether she's taking from the right or left."

My mother was a model of restraint. She admired Eleanor, rediscovered Cody in eyes that tipped up slightly. She didn't beg to keep the baby so Cody and Becky could enjoy a night to themselves. She didn't coo. She held the baby only when it was suggested she do so. I am all thumbs, she repeated. Suppose I drop her? My dexterous mother was lying through her teeth.

Becky insisted, laying Eleanor across Mom's knees in the sun. She clowned behind her back, drawing chirps and whistles from the baby, smiles so spasmodic that my mother was ordered not to blink.

"You really have to watch her, Mrs. Lerner. Otherwise you'll miss it."

Becky drew me aside.

"She's really a tough customer. She's just not reacting like most grandparents. Look at your father, how he is. Beside himself."

"Give her time. It all happened so fast. She'll warm up to the baby. She's got a lot on her mind now."

I consistently underestimate my sister-in-law. In the months following Eleanor's birth she stalked my mother with the cunning of a trapper in a cold, snowy woods. She drew my mother in slow with blood-red bait, too tempting to turn down. Just when the view from every window seemed unbearably arid, Becky phoned with a wonderful idea.

"It was a lovely luncheon, Lucy. Just lovely. She invited a few women my age. Nice women, too. Unaffected. Becky wrote down several of our remarks. Imagine. She served us chicken salad from individual flower pots. I think I'll skip my nap. I've got a list of things to do a mile long."

My mother was the founder of a local book club. Many club members were grandmothers and one month they devoted their reading to toddler behavior. Excitedly, she phoned Becky with bulletins on Dr. Dobson. There's a whole new feeling about discipline with love, she would shout into the phone. They began collaborating gaily on textiles and recipes. That's how I left the two of them, my mother unequivocally nutty about her daughter-in-law, an energetic young wife and mother. And a first-class bitch.

6

In a children's book I've hung on to for Sam, the man in the moon falls from his handy lunar cradle. Because of space static, trouble in the heavens, the moon begins to rock and roll. The pale, limpid moonman is cast out of his home. His journey through space is meticulously recounted, full of information for budding astronauts and astrologists. The galactic details fascinate Sam. What strikes me about the moonman is his tearless conduct. When the moonman at last lands on the earth, he picks himself up matter-of-factly. Rubbing a sore bottom, he takes up a rock and puts it to his tongue for his first solemn mouthful of the new world. I have been in France for seventeen years. I was not cast out of my homeland as was the moonman. But I like to think that my conduct on foreign shores was as relentless as his own, full of touching and tasting, sensual knowing of the new land. Certainly I suffered my share of space static and trouble in the heavens. That followed my arrival in France. A certain chronology may be all that separates me from the ghostly man in the moon.

• • •

"Are you in some kind of trouble over there?"

This question, in one form or another, has tailed me for years. Contrary to what my mother thought in 1969, I was not in trouble. Sharon Tate and others had been killed by the Charles Manson "family" in what seemed to be a completely motiveless crime. That horror seemed to suggest that other horrors were out there ready to be unleashed on the unwitting.

"Your father and I just feel it would be best if you were to come home now. What with this Charles Manson crime and all."

I was watching television in the study of a doctor's house. At the Sorbonne, in the Academy of Letters, students were heaving chairs from an upstairs window. A nervous panel discussion was under way. Sociologists were discussing the student revolt of May 1968 and the future of the Republic of France. But there was no revolution in the doctor's house. Only a golden-haired baby girl who gurgled and laughed when I tickled her. The doctor and his wife spoke impeccable English and earnestly hoped that my first taste of France would be heady. I was introduced as the fille de la maison. I dressed the tiny girl in handsome embroidered clothing, covered her head with a blue velvet hood lined with soft fur and rolled her through the streets of the sixteenth arrondissement. Sometimes I was so happy tears stood in my eyes for no other reason than pure joy. Oklahoma?

"I'm not coming home. Not yet."

"Lucy. Are you in some kind of trouble over there?"

We were mercifully cut off in the middle of the phone conversation. I watched television closely. Smoke poured from the Sorbonne and the police were lining up with gas masks. Two bare-breasted women could be seen leaning out of the top-floor window. A magazine arrived for me ten days later. My mother's letter was crisp, the tone was one of wounded pride. In a postscript she mentioned a recipe I would find interesting on page 99. A one-hundred-dollar bill was Scotch-taped to the middle of the page. This seemed proof of her intention to look, for the moment, the other way.

The same question was asked later, in a much different way,

long after I had left the doctor's house and kissed the golden girl goodbye. I had made some hard choices since, had held down my share of demeaning, underpaid jobs, and was living in a comfortless apartment on the Côte. Marc and I framed a series of old book illustrations and repainted the ceiling of the bleak apartment a cool, ethereal blue. I bought a gilt-frame antique mirror in which I could see one-third of myself. I propped it on the floor or the washbasin, the windowsill, depending upon which third needed inspection. The apartment was as steadying as a nun's bare cell, although there were significant differences. I had met Marc as he was finishing his last year of studies and living en pension. We were both ready to leave Paris. We considered all that a move together to the South of France could imply. As it happened, there were a few oversights.

"I want to know who it was that answered your telephone. It is seven o'clock in the morning your time."

"It's the milkman, Mom. In France they bring it right on upstairs."

"This is no time for jokes, Lucy."

"Did you know that Agnes is the patron saint of chaste girls? According to legend she was forced by medieval governors to walk through an area of prostitution naked. God immediately covered her nakedness by having her hair grow to her knees. There's even a day dedicated to Saint Agnes—the twenty-first of January, I think."

"I did not phone you to discuss my name. Don't try to softsoap me with charming stories, young lady."

"Alright. The truth. I found him hanging on the wall of a museum and he was so gorgeous I put him under my coat and ran home. Mom?"

This steely veteran of the wisecrack just wasn't having any. My mother hung up on me. The next call didn't go any smoother.

"Lucy? Can you hear me? This is your mother."

"Perfectly. It's like you're sitting right next to me."

"Have you slept well since we spoke?"

"So-so."

"As I thought. We have had to appeal to a translator on this because it turned out to be rather tricky and we just weren't making ourselves understood. Lizzie Bile, you might remember her. She graduated from Cornell with highest honors. Not that any of that matters. Have a pencil handy?"

"Hang on. Yes."

"I don't know if I'm pronouncing this correctly: Helene Manotte. She is a ticketing agent with Air France. She is holding an open ticket for you in your name. The ticket is paid for and you'll need only to confirm the date with Miss Manotte. The ticket, I should add, is one-way. There is also a sum of money waiting for you at American Express, as I'm sure there are things you will want to ship home."

"Can you put Dad on?"

"Your father's out to dinner with some clients from Dallas."

"How is he?"

"Sunk in gloom. Yes, I think it's accurate to say he is sunk in gloom."

"Not because of me, I hope."

"Who could be unaffected? I'm afraid there's more, though. People are talking about converting a good piece of the Ouachita Forest to pine."

"So?"

"No more mixed forest. Your dad's in a dither."

"Give him a kiss. Tell him I'll be home soon."

I left the money at the American Express office, but I did accept that ticket from Miss Manotte. She had exceptionally red hair on the day we met.

"Ah, so this is Lucy Lerner. But you look like such a nice girl."

"I am a nice girl, Miss Manotte."

"You know your parents are so worried about you. You make their hearts break."

"That's why I'm going home. To reassure them I'm alright."

Miss Manotte looked at me for a long time, then at Marc, who was standing just behind me with his hand on my back as if he were propping me up. He was wearing his favorite sunglasses, the kind that throw your own reflection right back at you. She didn't look convinced at all.

"Well, here is your ticket then. My first name is Hélène. You call if you need me. Manotte has two *t*'s."

Around that time I was careful about some things, less careful about others. I had a job as a waitress in a rather bad cocktail lounge. It was not a bar where tourists tended to go. One night a man threw a match at me to see if I would go up in flames. I did, if only for ten or fifteen seconds. He thought this was very funny and so did his friends. Pierre, the bouncer, pulled him out of his chair by the earlobes and led him out to the street.

Sitting in my mother's kitchen, I pulled off black leather gloves Marc had bought for me on a trip to Florence and laid them carefully on my lap. They were wonderful gloves, suppler even than my own skin. There was plenty of explaining to do. First, the burn on my right hand. Then, the bright gold band on the left.

Her back didn't touch the back of the chair. We had been shouting and were now sitting at the negotiation table, though there was little to settle. I would be flying back in three days. Miss Manotte had written the return ticket unwillingly, sucking on the inside of her cheek with one eyebrow raised. We had paid for that ticket in cash.

"I have become a believer in outlook, Lucy. It's our outlook that has to change, because clearly events won't. How long have you been married to this boy?"

"Man. Five days."

"Five—Wade, will you hand me a cigarette? And it's your intention to stay married?"

"Well, I thought I'd give it a shot. Five days isn't much of a yardstick, but things seem to be working out so far."

"If we are to establish a dialogue, you will need to keep that mocking tone out of your voice. As I understand it, you married this boy as a security measure, to make sure you would get back to France."

She paused and looked past me to the kitchen window. Two

hummingbirds were floating by the feeder. Rubythroats. It had taken her several months to lure the pair in. Now they'd grown pesky, hissing at her when the feeder was empty.

"Lucy, let me ask you a question, and I want a straight answer out of you. Are you in some kind of trouble?"

I somehow managed to get back on that plane three days later. My father drove me to the airport because she said she couldn't sanction my decision. She gave me a sharp, dry kiss as I left and asked me suddenly if I would be coming home for Thanksgiving. And then all the implications seemed to hit her at once, as my father and I loaded the car in the garage. Did I intend to celebrate American holidays, supposing there were passport complications? And what if there were a state of national emergency? Did I have the consulate address?

"Babies, Lucy. Your babies. What will they be?"

"Agnes, I think you're getting a little ahead of yourself. Come on now. We'll miss her flight."

My father leaned over me and closed the door gently. He promised to stop for milk on the way back from the airport.

Economy class was purgatory. I was pulled into service by a young woman traveling with three children under five. I function well under pressure and rocked or sang much of the way back to Paris. The woman had made a serious mistake and swallowed a Valium before getting on the flight.

"Mommy, tell us the one about Higgledy Piggledy."

"I won't fasten my seatbelt. You can't make me."

"I have to make a pee-pee."

She turned to them dull-eyed and got Higgledy Piggledy all mixed up with the story of the little red hen whose friends believed in all work, no play. I knew card tricks. I had picked up money during high school by being Miss Pockets, a great act I performed at birthday parties all over South Tulsa. This was the kind of trouble I knew something about.

I was the last passenger to deplane and by then Marc had already given up. He sat collapsed on a bench by the luggage claim.

"You looking for someone?"

"Lucy, I thought—"

"You thought they weakened my resolve. No more wife, maybe."

"Tu sais."

"Oui, je sais."

He looked at me warily. My husband was nourished on stories of gravediggers and magic spells. He remains a great lover of science fiction. He would not have discounted a macabre switch. It took him days to really welcome me home, to wish me well. Days before he was sure I was actually Lucy.

"What's this?"

"Cadeau."

I recognized the wrapping. To celebrate any event, minor or major, the gift exchange tended to be the same. Our apartment then sat atop a lingerie store. In the morning we could watch the parade of women from the washbasin in the bathroom. There was sometimes a pram parked outside the door to the boutique, a tiny occupant staring up at the three whirling pedestals, a forgotten bottle or pacifier lying off to one side. On display below the apartment were three sets of stockings that never changed, regardless of season. The three stockings were impressively cut out to reveal handsome muscled buttocks or a bare plastic crotch. Framing the window was a length of gold tinsel. Mothers filed out of the store wearing elevator tennis shoes stitched with gold and silver, their purchases discreetly wrapped, wedged in a panier between a baguette and a proud fan of swiss chard.

They were wonderful black stockings, fantastically sheer. Nothing in my closet could possibly live up to such stockings. I had returned to a shabby, weatherless day. We took the coast road home and a water skier would occasionally pierce the dirty fog, or a simple fishing boat, three or four poles listing out from the boat at cock-eyed angles. There was no visible horizon. The gray water and sky seemed to converge, forming a solid chalky block. France looked dingy. I recognized this as a mild form of regret.

"Marc."

There were snapdragons on the table and the smell of cooked meat hung in the air. Our neighbors were having dinner.

"I think we'd better try to make more friends. Maybe get out more."

He set down my suitcase, the box I had packed full of old photos and some textbooks I thought I might one day need. He looked more tired than I.

"I mean, I think it's just too stark the way we've been living."

"Comme tu voudras."

For a long time after that trip I became a great joiner. I did a brief stint with the American Women's Club in Menton, sitting through meeting after monthly meeting. I served punch at organ recitals and rushed to evening astronomy-club meetings at a village youth center. Marc frowned and reached suddenly for my hand when I told him I had joined a group of neighborhood vigilantes. We posted warnings about animal droppings and urged local shop-owners to be more stringent about barring dogs from their premises. My butcher, out of gratitude, began producing boneless chicken breasts. He had read somewhere that Americans liked the dry, white meat. He would hold them out to me, cupped in the palm of his hand. I left my job in the bar when I found out I could make more money tutoring English to terrified students preparing for the baccalauréat. I also gave lessons to a quiet, middle-aged couple who tremulously told me they had once seen the Grand Canyon.

My mother's eventual sanctions came in the form of Tupperware. It arrived in installments—lettuce crispers and celery savers. I paid twenty-six francs at the post office each time and marched dutifully across town back to that airless apartment.

October 8, 1975

Dear Lucy,

I have recently been reading about the refrigeration problems in Europe. Be careful how you open and shut these. Otherwise you'll break the freshness seal and they become just like any other plastic container.

Her anxiety for me was highly focused. It had to do with various forms of decay.

January 21, 1976

Dear Lucy,

I just came across something in Richard Schmidt's column that might be of interest to you. A woman wrote that she and her husband had just returned from Europe and she suspects that they might have eaten HORSE MEAT. *Mr. Schmidt replied that you can always tell the difference between the two [horse and beef] by the unusual bright redness of horse meat. I would think it would go bad faster than your ordinary beefsteak.*

I eyed my mounting collection of Tupperware, some of it filled with bright green sockettes, my antidote to a cold stone floor, and all the hopeless frippery Marc purchased from the shop downstairs. Later my mother sent four pots of moisturizing cream she had made up by a friend who lived in the Ozarks. With the moisturizing cream she seemed to psychologically tie off her fears for me, like a finished row of stitches on a piece of canvas. Still, not one word about Marc. Stalwart, she continued to address her packages to Lucy Lerner long after I had officially become a Laugier.

May 1, 1976

Dear Lucy,

There! Do you remember Maxine, my friend in the Ozarks? I drove over to spend a few days with her and we discussed your skin type and conditions over there. The air is very dry where you live, as I have shown Maxine some photos I have cut out of magazines. Those women, she said to me, look like walking handbags. Please think enough of yourself to use these creams, Lucy.

And here it is May.

I relaxed a little after the cream came, rubbing it into my skin each night in the tiny circular motions she advised. Gradually my memberships in everything expired. I missed four consecutive astronomy lectures and was quietly blackballed. Marc and I accepted a doomed family contract and moved out of that apartment into a restored livery stable on his parents' property. We would come to La Belle Eléna much later.

7

It was April of 1981 when the fact of my pregnancy was confirmed. The doctor's office was in an apartment building in Antibes, on the fourth floor. I had one look at the metal elevator that stood open at the entry and thought of the dumbwaiter in my cousin Ella's house. It could probably handle a tea service but not a pregnant woman. If I shouted Au secours! in this shadowy building, who would save me? There was a cleaning woman down on all fours, scrubbing the floor. Her daughter sat on a bench, working a crossword puzzle and snapping her chewing gum. I took the stairs.

The sign said to ring once, twice if you were entering without an appointment. I rang and pushed the door open, finding no one. It was a marble-floored, circular room with open windows on one side. The dense, leafy exterior threw a cool green cast on the walls. There were three possibilities and I chose the middle door. There was an escritoire to one side of the door. Someone had begun a letter with a real quill pen. The middle room gave onto a glossy waiting room. There were no footprints on the tile. Women sat in pairs. I was the only lone woman in the doctor's office. There was no chair free and I stood by the glass door. I watched two pigeons outside on the small balcony searching each other for lice. I stood until there was a chair free. Then I folded my hands over my stomach, like some of them were doing.

"Madama Laugier. Entrez."

The doctor smiled through the examination and talked about his trip to Spain. Didn't stop talking, in fact, or smiling. I thought this technique was apt for mental patients, but for me, rational and happily expecting a first child, it seemed queer. He had not asked me a single question about why I had come. His full, pink face was stationed over me, but his hand was not. He had run warm water over his plastic glove.

"Eh bien. Vous êtes dans le troisième mois, n'est-ce pas? Et ça va?"

Then he asked me questions as I dressed behind a screen painted with blues and greens. There were women and fawns in a wooded park on one side of the screen, angels on the side where I stood naked, stepping into my skirt. That mix of personal and professional worked. I relaxed as I studied his diplomas, the pottery he had brought back from a trip to Africa. I later learned that he was a complete alcoholic. He owned his own clinic because no bona fide hospital would have him.

"Vous avez quelqu'un ici, Madame Laugier? Votre mère, par exemple? De la famille en France?"

Things were not going smoothly in the stone courtyard. My mother-in-law, in a symbolic gesture, had stopped watering the marigolds I had brought her, the marigolds we planted by the stone puits in the court. The tiny gold heads drooped in a straggly, abandoned row. When she learned I thought I was pregnant, she watered them. By then it was too late and they toppled over into the mud.

"Mon mari, Docteur."

Every month he asked me the same question, looking up from his desk suddenly as if he'd just remembered the key question. Famille en France? I saw the same mothers and daughters in the waiting room. The resignation was awful. The swollen daughters dressed in the same sober tones as the mothers. A single gay ribbon was a violent cri de coeur in that place. Two months before Sam was born one girl issued a total surrender and gave up reading. Her eyes closed, she listened as her mother-in-law read mockingly about Brigitte Bardot and her attempts to modify canine destiny, man's cruelty to dogs. Sam was so active. You could actually watch his movement through the heavy cotton dresses, my belly suddenly careening left or right. I had inexplicably developed morning sickness and was out of sync in nearly every way.

The doctor's delivery clinic was set far enough back so that you couldn't see the lycée, but the sound of it seemed to seep in through the windows. You heard motors gun at noon, then again toward late afternoon. Friendly insults floated through the open window the nurses insisted on each morning. One five-minute airing was all we got, then they were slammed shut for the rest of the day. The place was stifling. I didn't notice the entrance until it was too late to wonder about implications. As we drove through the gates I saw two granite balls, one placed on each gatepost.

"Funny sculpture, Marc."

"Un peu froid."

There was no St. Francis, scattering seed to the sparrows, laying a gentle hand on an unfrightened deer. No image of the Virgin standing in a quiet alcove. This was the doctor's clinic, utilitarian and no-nonsense, marked by an outsized pair of granite balls. I would suck the air from outside as eagerly as if I had been trapped underwater.

Sam, despite months of punching and kicking, was in no hurry. Labor was induced and I was hooked up to an IV, Pitocin dripping slowly into my arm. I watched Marc out of the corner of my eye. He was terrified.

A nurse was with us, her back turned. She explained she would phone the doctor, who was minutes away. She seemed awfully busy with something, then stepped back as a flame leaped up. She poured a liquid over a large tin plate that looked like a roasting pan. The Pitocin was having its effect. There was a deep low pressure as if someone were making a fist in my belly.

"Madame, si je peux vous demander. . ."

She mopped her forehead with the back of her hand and looked at me. I must have been staring at that fire.

"I sterilize you instruments. How you feeling now?"

The doctor didn't have time to take his coat off. Marc told me later his breath could have knocked an elephant over. The bastard, he added, didn't even wash his hands. Our son came hurtling down the birth canal and roared even before he was struck by that drunken doctor.

"Merde."

He had stopped smiling, studying me. This would take concentration. Perhaps even sobriety. The boy had burst his mother apart. He looked at me with derision, for I had ruined his afternoon. I thought of a recent supermarket drama—I had reached for the wrong mango and brought five or six crashing to the floor. They lay split open and exposed in a pulpy mass on the dirty floor. I felt embarrassed and mentioned episiotomy. Then, finally, he smiled.

"Eh, oui, ma fille. Mais c'est un peu tard."

The battle lines were clearly drawn between me and my mother-in-law in that birth clinic. First, of course, the name. We only gave him one, where her father had no less than five. She felt herself slighted with a mere two—Martine Pascal. What was it anyway, this strange shout of a name? Sam! That was how she said his name, turning it into an exclamation. The fury over that name subsided, however. It gave way under the pressure of an hysteria I didn't know she was capable of. She was made for the role. I think she lost all self-awareness in that place, righting her wig suddenly after a tirade or scratching her backside briefly as she looked out a clinic window. She contemplated her grandson's mutilated future. Her son's wife was a butcher. I wanted Sam circumcised. She stood out in the hall with Marc, for she couldn't confront me directly. Yet she raised her voice to such a pitch that after visiting hours were over, women would wander to my room asking about the outcome. Were we going to cut or not? I would pretend to sleep if I were too battle-weary to respond.

Marc was puzzled. He didn't understand my ardor any better than I did. The decision felt monumental, central to our child's future welfare. I felt Sam's hot breath tickle my neck and stripped off his cotton pyjama to come closer to him. The truth was I was in over my head. My oversight was so elementary I couldn't bear to talk about it with anyone. I had never pictured our son in anything other than an all-American setting. First-string football, wrestling tryouts, a kid to pack the bleachers in any gymnasium. Would Sam be subject to locker room derision if I failed to act? I grew shrill and dead right. My own short-sightedness stunned me. Thus my first maternal decision was made. We cut.

"Marc, let's call a rabbi. This is foolish. In America . . ."

"This is not America. We aren't calling a rabbi to circumcise my son. A surgeon will do it. A competent surgeon. You are both making me crazy. Foutez-moi la paix!"

We were all under strain. Sam was to be completely anesthetized for a simple matter of foreskin. I couldn't feed him and held him all night as he howled. They were hot, dry screams. The tears that soaked the pillow were mine. My mother called. I couldn't speak, for Sam had just been hooked up to a machine and a cardiologist measured his heartbeat.

"Honey, don't even try to talk. If you want to just cry it out, go ahead. I'm content to just listen. Your dad and I—we'll call back when you're feeling peppier. God bless you, Lucy. A boy!"

When Sam survived, we started from scratch with a cautious civility. I complimented her dress, for it was pretty though too girlish for her. She asked me what she could bring, for I was obliged to stay the full ten days after delivery. We were women. Why shouldn't I tell her what was bothering me? The food was indigestible and I was getting more uncomfortable each day. I could settle my troubles with fresh fruit and raw vegetables. She nodded solemnly when I asked her for prunes. Each day thereafter she brought me a cooked chicken or a wedge of pot roast. The final assault was the boudin, that black blood-sausage even children know better than to touch. I enjoyed the game and thanked her tenderly for each offering carefully covered with a freshly ironed dish towel. I lined the stuff outside my window on the ledge, and ten days later when

I was dressing to leave, the smell had begun to make its way into the room and down the corridor. I had a start on arriving home, for in Sam's nursery lay a small pine coffin.

For reasons my mother-in-law has never cared to discuss, her own mother worked for the post office. Her father was an artisan. If pushed further, she will tell you that he made coffins. That her mother worked as a postal clerk for twenty-five years is a brutal, humiliating fact. Her father's profession, by contrast, is remembered as genteel and distinguished. Il était discret, she will repeat with a kind of wonder, recreating his atelier and the modest showroom, the smell of pine needles that clung to the long, pleated skirts she wore as a girl. His workshop was high above the national highway on a woody hectare. That was long ago, when there were only three or four serious glassblowers in the village. There was something compatriotic in the two skills. The glassblowers borrowed ideas from each other and traded styles until a kind of conformity developed, a loose suspension of trapped air bubbles and comfortably thick stemware that would become synonymous with Biot. Her father's sturdy coffins with a sudden explosion of wood carving fore and aft seemed as discerning and tasteful to my mother-in-law as those rose-tinted goblets. It was a natural playground for a little girl. She didn't go to school until she was six. She brought her coloring books and hand puppets to her father's workplace on rainy days. On sunny days she collected pine needles for an eau de cologne, soaking them in a water and oil solution in empty yoghurt containers. She played hide-and-seek in the reception area, calling out Trouve-moi, Papa! from inside one of the coffins standing upright along the wall. The glassblowers called her father the King of the Dead.

Sam's nursery was upstairs. Once it had served as a loft for hay bales, and there was a low support beam that cut through the middle. We put in a low line of heavy leaded windows. Those windows gave us a natural light source. Still, it tended to be a melancholy room, the showy tin soldiers and furry, bright-eyed animals unconvincing. Now, with a pine coffin against one wall . . . I turned to Marc and didn't bother asking.

"It was my toy chest. Oui, oui, je sais. Morbide."

I opened the lid and found it full of Marc's old toys. An old bow and arrow, with careful rubber tips. Back copies of *Tintin.* Pinocchio and two sets of noses. And firearms that weren't toys.

"What are these?"

"Ils ne marchent plus. They were my father's. He stopped hunting when I was small. Tiens! Elle a gardé tout ça."

I wondered if I should empty the toys before I heaved the thing out the window. Or if it would make more of a statement left as it was, the broken toys and shattered wood lying in a pile of rubble. It could have been postpartum depression. Any number of things. But despite the murk in Sam's nursery I was enjoying the clearest vision I'd had in days. I saw our future, drastically modified now. I didn't apologize or hesitate. I bent low to show Sam the view from his new digs. He had just been fed and was placid, screwing up his face slightly in the milky light.

"I want that thing out of here now. I don't even want it in this house. Remind her you married an American. Our culture doesn't recognize aging and death. Bury that thing."

It made a mournful bumping noise as he dragged it downstairs. I never asked what became of it.

It could be the exorbitant price of land here, but I don't think so. I've seen the phenomenon too often to believe it. The tradition of the family compound must strike some deep chord that an outsider is too tone-deaf to hear. I've seen young prosperous men and women go off to Paris or Brussels during those hardworking middle years. As soon as they have the means to do so, they start construction on their family soil, talking vaguely of retirement. The estate is modest or grand as circumstance has it, but the result is the same. Maman, Papa, and sons and daughters. Bickering, sharing the precious sunlight on the same scrap of soil. I tried, really tried to settle into that system. The land on the hill slanting west was already being leveled for Marc's younger brother. Unmarried, a student still and leaning dangerously toward an interest in comic strips. He was free then, but one day the bell would toll for him as well. Marc's father is an electrician. He is successful and has won nearly every sizable city contract for the last fifteen years. They are not gifted, he will say, thinking of those two seditious elements. Photography and comic books? He shrugs his shoulders, looks up to the sky as if searching an answer, and finding none, mounts the driver's seat in his big red truck.

With some maneuvering I didn't have to see my mother-in-law every day. Rain or shine, she walked to the market at 8:00 each day save Monday. On Monday she mounted the big red truck, Mr. Laugier taking her hand as if she were made of porcelain. She stepped daintily into the truck to go to the commercial center on the road to Digne, and returned at noon with sacks of detergent and canned foods, a cotton dress or shirt purchased for less than the price marked on the tag. But what I could not avoid was that seven o'clock reveille. Up and down all through the night with Sam, I was standing at the kitchen sink the first time I saw it. I was so tired all I wanted to do was crawl back into bed, not make coffee and change diapers. At seven that morning I saw Martine thrust her wigless head from an upstairs bedroom window to stuff her eiderdown coverlets outside for that deathblow to germs. She did this each morning. A glance up from my kitchen sink and I saw a shock of bare scalp and those two coverlets that looked just like lolling tongues.

We had an odd encounter once. Oddly pleasant. We stumbled upon a sort of solidarity. Marc was spending all day in Cannes, struggling with a delegation of Italian hairstylists. Later, there was a power strike scheduled by the communist union. The strike organizers would answer questions and pose for pictures after the blackout. There was nothing to eat in the house. I asked if I could ride out to Digne. It was an intoxicating ride. Sam gurgled and laughed. We were so high above all the Renaults, the British Minis. Children in passing cars were delighted by our bright redness and the commanding size of the truck, the extension ladder that folded into itself like a grasshopper's leg. They pressed their faces into the back windows of their cars and waved.

And then we shopped. Perhaps it worked because we were

standing at an unlikely intersection of two conflicting worlds. But it was fine, my father-in-law holding Sam as we proceeded with women's work. He stood off to one side, bemused and nonessential, as we stuffed sacks.

"C'est une bonne idée. On attaque?"

It was fairly complicated. Two grocery carts, minute plastic sacks unequal to this type of buying, which was unabashedly American. Aisle after aisle, fantastic abundance and relative ease. And yet to do this kind of buying unschooled, an outsider could be a goner. There were no smiling bagboys. The cashier punched in prices as we loaded and unloaded, then struggled with checkbooks and cash. It took teamwork, and old misgivings disintegrated on the road to Digne. We often made those shopping excursions before we stopped speaking.

8

It is not Roselli's death but her dog's attempted suicide that captures the imagination. She didn't have time to unfold her red beach towel or summon her children. She died in bed, her feet wrapped in two plastic supermarket sacks. Did she anticipate rain on the day she died? Or, sensing death near, did Roselli envision the next life as shrouded in mist and perpetual damp? These questions aren't asked. All speculation focuses on the dog. Was his leap from the window a call for help? A canine au secours? Or the act of a beast in mourning for its master? The daughters, seeing her cold, bare feet, wept and prayed for the old woman and covered her feet with their half-finished shawls.

The dog, a yapping pest, has now become a kind of deity. Long toothless, he was by far the most vicious animal allowed to wander unleashed. To compensate for his toothless plight he had developed a low-headed butt, which when aimed at a shin caused considerable chagrin. He could catch a hem in his muzzle and was responsible for torn slips and skirts, and innumerable upended market baskets he charged with a bull's precision.

He established his noxious place in the community and no one ever thought to complain to Roselli's children. Certainly not to Roselli herself, too senile to understand. Those who thought of it would break off a long switch from a bush before passing her house. Others would carry an old riding crop or a flyswatter. But now the dog rests in a wicker basket in a sunny corner of the courtyard and one neighbor or another honors him every week with a substantial veal bone or pig knuckle. The character of the dog has not changed and he remains a mean beast, growling at whoever approaches. He achieved celebrity by casting himself from Roselli's bedroom window. His deathwish contains more interest than an old woman's soundless tapering off. Her needs have not ended in death, only changed. It is not her rickety gate, down again, but her crippled dog that brings us to the dark, shuttered house. A butcher lives nearby and we don't have to buy food for the thing. He stops grudgingly at noon with a shaved-off bit of meat he used to save for the gentleman who lives in a rented room above his shop. The meat is kept in a blue basin under the cash register. The dog, not Roselli, is often in our minds.

The last act of recorded violence in this gnarled web of rutted streets and blind alleys was in 1963. That was the year Esmerelda Garcia was charged with assault when she went at her husband with a length of frozen sausage. The Garcias had not owned the deep-freezer for long. It represented autonomy and stability at the same time. Mrs. Garcia liked to show people her deep-freezer, filled with wild game and poultry and lamb from her mother's farm in the east. She was a proud woman and wrote her butcher a crisp note saying she would no longer pass on Thursday for they had bought a congélateur. It meant they would never live in a trailer again. She could finally enroll her children in school and expect them to finish out the year. That she went after her husband with what amounted to a sacred object titillated the entire village in 1963. It would be months before anyone bought a saucisson d'Arles without a round of laughter aimed at Mrs. Garcia. It may be pure coincidence that domestic violence has once more boiled over, this time on the heels of Roselli's death and the dog's attempted suicide. The notion of suspect soup did not die with the old woman and her broth allegedly made of bad boys.

I first discovered Gaétan's flightless birds at a village fund drive for victims of natural disaster. The collective conscience is in good working order, and at the onset of flood, fire or earthquake we set up stands to aid victims everywhere. Among the crocheted pot holders and leather belts purchased by the lot, jars of blueberry jam and lavender honey, are perched Sélections Gaétan, top-heavy whittled birds that fall over if not steadied by books or paperweights. Gaétan guards a property on the Cap d'Antibes and his days are long and still. He is the caretaker for a sculpted woods accessible only by water and a closely watched private drive. He whittles to stave off sleep, wandering down to the water's edge to flash his security badge at the swimmers who negotiate the rocky harbor fronting the property. He gives them a minute or two to catch their breaths on the granite steps before sending them back into the water, chatting about a scene from a movie that was once filmed on the spot where they stood. I have too many of Gaétan's birds in the house. Because of their repeated presence in the kitchen, over the fireplace, wherever books are found, they've lost their power to astonish. I bought them to remain in his favor, for he was teaching Sam to whittle on occasional free Saturdays. That a victim of misfortune may be helped by the purchase is only an afterthought. Sam returned home after each session with a bandaged thumb or forefinger, his pockets clogged with feathery bits of wood and golden glass eyes.

Gaétan was old enough to be his wife's father. Her behavior at the local pizzaria often drove him to bouts of indignation and wrath. The proprietor of the pizzaria was an old friend from his wife's lycée. That he slapped her on the rump or gave her a bold kiss on the lips when she burst through the curtain of purple beads surprised no one. No one, that is, except Gaétan. They had always cavorted like young animals, everyone said. Just as unpunishably. To frustrate their teachers and delight their classmates the two had perfectly mastered sign language. They chattered away silently straight through terminale. Then they both failed the baccalauréat and went their separate ways. Laétitia started a quick round of marriages that ended with Gaétan, an acquaintance of her uncle's. She entered his house with a full set of children as her dowry, proud of this proof of fertility. Her last husband had left while the smallest was still breast-feeding. Gaétan watched as she wearily drew a full, blue-veined breast out of her housedress to insert into the child's mouth. Speechless, Gaétan lit his young wife's cigarette and watched as she blew smoke over the baby's soft cup of a head. The oldest child was invariably dispatched on food-getting missions in a red, woolly bathrobe and slippers. No one batted an eye. They knew it was just fragmented, thoughtless Laétitia's child. Gaétan, aware of a new flush of contentment that spread straight up from his loins taught Laétitia to clean his guns. He said quietly that he always did like a bowl of soup on Friday night. Just soup, he said. Which, as it developed, suited Laétitia fine.

Gaétan's birds were flightless, carefully riveted to a flat piece of laminated wood, but his young wife was not. I knew of Laétitia's comings and goings because of her appetite for American jeans. Gaétan was old-school on the subject and wouldn't have them in the house. She cited their utility, their popularity, to no avail. She wheedled, whined and carried on like one of her own children before the clothing store in town. The longer she continued, the more intractable he became. One day, watching Sam whittle away at the kitchen table, dropping shavings all over her kitchen floor, Laétitia changed tack suddenly. She made him a voluptuous snack at four o'clock, a portion of baguette the length of his forearm, covered with unsalted butter and jam she had put up herself. She brought him home, the confiture still on his mouth. Her appeal was very direct. She assumed a solidarity as we were both young women and mothers. She wiped Sam's mouth clean with water from the pool. There were certain things we could say openly to each other.

"J'ai envie de me mettre en jeans, Lucy. On s'habille comme on veut, n'est-ce pas?"

I went upstairs to fetch a pair of jeans and watched as Laétitia struggled into them by the side of the pool. They were a good size too small. She wore her perpetual high heels. She lit a cigarette nervously, her color high. Cigarette ash drifted down on her breasts as she walked up and down, as if on a modeling ramp.

"Ils me vont vachement bien. Qu'en penses-tu?"

"Superbe!"

"Tu me les prêtes?"

"Je te les donne."

"Tu es un ange."

She folded the jeans tenderly into thirds and patted the contraband into place in the trunk of her Renault, under the rubber flap that covered the spare tire.

La Poulette escapes classification. It is not a nightclub, although there is a dance floor. Nor is it a restaurant. Ten tables are laid, though rarely occupied. The plat du jour never changes. It is coq au vin, summer or winter. Blood is used as a thickener for the sauce and the faithful clientele of La Poulette steadfastly beg off. The place is unrelievedly innocent. La Poulette was once a poulailler, a simple chicken house in the hills above Nice. The owners have invested heavily in cuteness, and seduction is difficult at best. Erotic intentions tend to wilt at La Poulette. There are rubber chickens everywhere. Bowls of hard-boiled eggs are desultorily consumed and refilled. People jockey for a position on the tight dance floor and leave the place hotter than they were before, their lives otherwise unchanged. Laétitia's assertion that all she wanted to do was dance, had she danced anywhere other than La Poulette, would hold no more water than a straw hat. As it was, she danced every Friday in the old chicken house and her assertion was generally believed. She climbed into her Renault around midnight quite alone. She only stopped when she was several blocks from her home, where she would shed her American jeans as a snake would shed his lifeless skin. She would let herself in soundlessly and rouse Gaétan from where he sat, slumped at the kitchen table beside his plate of soup. He had no memory of that table-to-bed transfer. Thereafter he slept sounder than Laétitia's children overhead.

Gaétan began to stumble. His afternoon whittling sessions with Sam stopped because of eyestrain. The Relief Committee for victims of the earthquake in Naples replaced Sélections Gaétan with a table of brown, hand-thrown pots that didn't sell. He finally consulted his physician when he fell off his bicycle. He pedaled Sundays, rain or shine. By his own estimation he lay in a grassy cradle by the side of the road a full forty minutes in a sleep so deep it took the rude, unmuffled roar of a band of bikers to rouse him. He wept uncontrollably in the doctor's office. To think he had discovered Laétitia one year ago and here he was, still flushed with love, dying certainly of a brain tumor. Bitter tears fell again when the results of the lab test came in. He wept mostly for the silence he feared would swallow him whole. The silence of the woods he protected. The silence of his house when Laétita and her band of children left. For Laétitia would have to leave. If she could put barbiturates in his soup every Friday, every week for a year, she could do anything under the sun. This time the victim of disaster was Gaétan. He drove unsteadily to the gendarmerie in Vence, pulling his car over frequently to stare at the doctor's signature on the paper.

Laétitia's sentencing was hard on the village. The children were placed in foster homes and the sight of the oldest wandering the streets in her nightclothes was sorely missed. The pizzaria closed indefinitely. Some people said he went to the mountains. He had a ruin near a village on the French-Italian border. He worked on it sporadically, retreating into fits of masonry that could last days or weeks. The village consensus felt it best not to leave Gaétan too much alone. Invitation followed invitation, but conversation was difficult even when enthusiasm for Gaétan's tragedy was at its highest peak. He sat wrapped in silence, gratefully accepting seconds on everything, depleting the family store of Calvados and Armagnac. The invitations stopped gradually and the village let him go home. The scandal, in time, faded to incident.

Facts were slowly recast. Business at the pizzaria dried up, for wagging tongues had it that Laétitia [quelle salope] and the patron of the pizzaria had acted in concert. What he could sprinkle into a soup he could sprinkle on top of a pizza. Interpretations changed again when American jeans were discovered rolled up in the trunk of her car. Public opinion tipped in her favor and Gaétan's character began to take a beating. Imagine depriving her of jeans! What foolish, old-man notions of propriety. My jeans became a leitmotif as fiery as Madame Garcia's frozen sausage.

There are times when you are too much of a villager or not enough of one. It isn't clear which. Times when you suffer a little shortness of breath. I know quite a lot of women who are content to drink their way through these periods, waiting for whatever it is to pass. Others who steadily reread literature they've always loved or who spend days on the telephone, calling old friends. It's not depression. It's a distraction so deep it pays to heed it in whatever way seems fitting. I just might, during these times, go sit for a couple of hours in Eliot's dusty bookshop, taking over the cash register to give him time off. Or I might cook up an excuse to go stand on line in the American Express office, soothed by the comfortable hum of Americans hashing things out.

"'Hal,' I say to him, 'You are asking for it now. Watch how many of those you drink.' 'This itty-bitty thing?' So he drinks another and then another. Then I see the expression on his face change quick like he's having an attack or something, so we call the hotel doctor. The same thing happened to us in Mallorca. He drank six coffees there, too, and thought it was his heart. I swear."

"You can bet a thing like that wouldn't happen in Memphis. You never see things like that in Memphis. They'd hose a person like that off the sidewalk in Memphis."

"You want to know what's bugging shopkeepers around here? I'll tell you what. Take a look at their shoes, why doncha. I guess I'd be out of sorts, too, if I had to stand around in those things."

More often, though, I just telephone Chan. Leslie-Chan Stubb is as pure as an applied principle and the shortest route to the mythical Southwest I know. She buys imported beans and chile by the case from Hédiard. She has more than once referred to the mayor of Nice as a little pissant. Before becoming Chan she was simply Leslie Stubb from Lubbock, Texas. When life at La Belle Eléna is too importunate or when homesickness is more tangible than a hunger pain, I long to see my friend. I phone her for lunch to combat my feelings about Laétitia's sentencing.

"Your skin looks great. I see you took my advice."

"I get plenty of ribbing, but yes. Sam won't come out of his room when I put that mask on. It's terrifying."

"Well, it paid off. I swear I see a difference. Are you hungry?"

"Starving."

"Great. Let's split a big piece of meat. Do it up right. Wave at that little guy and let's us order."

The waiter, obsequious and clearly blinded by my friend, finally approaches. He holds his pencil high in the air, as if about to conduct a symphony orchestra, and takes our order.

"I've missed you."

"I stayed in Riyadh until I couldn't stand it one more minute. We almost got thrown out. Those people aren't kidding."

She sighs and twists one of the rings she's wearing. Chan's great skill is in the use of her hands. I met her years ago in Paris when I was still in the doctor's house. She was living with a Chinese gentleman then. They demonstrated plastic plates in department stores. He taught her to open her hand like a silk fan, as she wooed customers away from traditional porcelain. Then he hung the name on her like a warm cloak and left. She doesn't like to discuss the origin of her name. A broken nail can still set her way back, even though the Chinese gentleman has been gone for years.

"Cheers, Lucy. Here's to the Lone Star."

"To the Lone Star."

"What's Sam up to?"

"No good. He's a bit of a discipline problem at school. He incites the others. Won't eat cheese, either, which is a capital offense. He's a handful."

"Bless him. He's a little boy. What's he supposed to do? Sit around and play dolls? My brothers were all like that. Sam's a pistol, that's all. Lucky he's got spirit."

"I don't know. Sometimes I look at the other little boys in his class. So clean. They call me Madame and their clothes always match. Remember I told you about that time Becky sent me on child development? Sam is nowhere to be found. Or, rather, he's everywhere. Part of his behavior can be found under what is typical of an eight-year-old. Then for some of his acting out I have to turn back to age three."

Chan leans forward and takes my chin in her hands.

"So, write your kid in between the paragraphs. Stick him in the margins, where most kids fall anyhow. Just don't lose your faith. Not now. It's them, not you. And from what you tell me about your sister-in-law's daughters, they don't fall into such neat categories either. You're a gold-star mommy, I mean it. I was looking at the *Nice-Matin* yesterday and saw a picture of a whole bunch of women who call themselves Les Mères Admirables. Marc took the picture? Anyhow, I thought immediately of you."

Despite Ali's fleet of smoke-colored limousines and the suite at the Hôtel de Paris that stands open for their use all year round, Leslie-Chan Stubb remains indisputably from Texas. She and Ali fly friends in from Athens and Rome. She owns two apartments in Monaco and knows not a single neighbor. She finds my life strange and Lubbock-like. She treats all my anecdotes as if they were beamed in from another planet. I tell her all about La Poulette.

"She poisoned the old guy's soup? My God. Those jeans make you an accomplice or something, don't they? You know my mother sends me back copies of the *National Enquirer.* I eat that stuff up. Guess what? You may be looking at the next Mary Boone."

"Who's Mary Boone?"

"You are such a peasant, Lucy. Mary Boone is this terrific art merchant in New York. Well, you just ruined my presentation. I'm opening a gallery in Nice. Ali is signing the papers next week. I don't know how much money it took to get space out of that little pissant."

"Which pissant are you referring to?"

"Our beloved mayor of Nice. He's got his hands in everything. The space I want for the gallery is part of a corridor that's dear to his heart. Anyway, we got it. Congratulate me. You will not find any rubber chickens in my gallery."

Midway through dessert Chan hits me with some very solemn news.

"Guess what. Spot exercising doesn't do a damned thing. Sit-ups, for example, don't burn up abdominal fat like you'd think. I almost died when I read that. I've done fifty sit-ups every morning since high school. You're not going to finish that? Pass."

"You feel like a walk afterwards? I brought my boots. Unless, of course, you've read something slanderous about walking."

"No, no. Walking is still highly regarded. Brisk walking, though. Strolling does absolutely nothing."

There is a slight, crescent-shaped stretch of sand near the Cap d'Antibes that is barely visible from the road. Some evenings toward five o'clock the sea stills with a light rise and fall perfect for children and nonswimmers. I've driven Sam over at this uncommon hour and found the beach filled with Arab fathers and daughters. Not far from the beach there is an apartment complex that stimulated a furious debate on the Côte when it was first built. Some saw in it a huge fortress, cold and impregnable, that seemed alien to the gentle coastline. Others claimed to see in its design the sinuous, curving backside of a sleeping woman. The most vociferous group of all said it resembled another HLM, the government-sponsored housing projects not notable for their fine architecture. I think these men wander down to the beach from this building. They coach their girls with animation, standing barefoot in the sand. Chan invited us to this beach once. Ali had ordered up an elaborate picnic lunch. A few of his guests had never been to a public beach and there were great exclamations over what the tide brought in—a lone ballet slipper and a tangle of seaweed cradling an impeccable peach-colored shell. We left when the afternoon descended into a business meeting. The only woman that swam was Chan. She was suited up in a mauve Speedo. She swam out to the point several times, dropping all her jewelry into a plastic cup. Ali stood up with a great show of displeasure when we left early and hugged me tightly, extracting promises to meet again, though after that afternoon Chan and I didn't attempt any further get-togethers with Marc and Ali. We fell into a series of rendez-vous more fitting for illicit lovers than for girlfriends.

I pull on muddy boots stuck under the seat of her car. Mine are mariner green, meant to weather land, sea or air. Chan inserts delicate, pedicured feet into a pair of hand-tooled lizard cowboy boots.

"My heart has stopped. What did you pay for those things?"

"Aren't they wonderful? Touch. That's a real steel instep. Let's see if we can't find the same trail we took the last time. The one that lets out right at the gorge. This is the best part of the day. What do the French call it again? I can't ever remember."

"Crépuscule."

"Listen to what they've done to twilight."

Despite the drawbacks of strolling, we walk slowly, not talking. The park has kept nature in tow. There are hiking trails and huge grassy fields bounded by parking lots. It suffers a biannual mutilation on the First of May and the Fourteenth of July. The traffic jam in the park on those days surpasses the most legendary Parisian embouteillage. We have the park nearly to ourselves at this hour. Nearly.

Hard, bright stars come out overhead just as prostitutes begin to appear on the trails. As we pass them they fix their stares at some point over our heads. They smoke slowly or examine a nail. They lose their toughness in the woods. Single men begin to appear on the trails, holding a hat or gloves in their hands.

"Aren't we getting uptown? Just like the Bois de Boulogne, only nicer somehow. Prostitution in the provinces."

We only leave when the woods become so secretive and closed that we feel like intruders. When we reach the gorge and turn back, the women have left their posts. Presumably they're doing business somewhere inside the black line of trees. I feel a little edgy and eager to be gone.

"I'm not crazy about twilight. Makes me think of lost children."

"Yours specifically? Marc picked Sam up, didn't he?"

"Oh, yes. But if Sam were out playing, this would be the time I'd turn frantic. I'd start howling for him from the terrace right about now. I get that way around thunderstorms, too. Just before the sky cuts loose, when it's that awful shade of gray. I want everybody I love around me."

"That must have something to do with the old frontier, don't you think? I mean it. This sounds ancestral. I can see you standing inside a circle of covered wagons beside a campfire, staring towards the horizon. Just like you see in old movies."

"Old B movies."

"Bet you think about Cody, too."

"I said lost children, not grown men."

Chan breaks her nail opening the car door and gives a little gasp of disappointment. I look at my own hands, the nail polish as chipped and scarred as the paint on my car. Then, of course, I think about Cody.

9

Our postman has his hair cut in a checkerboard design on the back of his head. He is shaved in bald, alternating squares. Postcards never get past him. We once reported this, but dropped our complaints when more important correspondence started to disappear. It may be that he uses postcards to replace wallpaper or collects them under plastic sheets like stamps. I don't know. I hear his moped sputter up the hill. He braces it with his feet spread apart, for the rutted gravel road is rough going. He likes me. We talk a lot about rock and roll, what all the music means. He hands me the mail and mentions a certain rock group that is soon coming to Nice.

What he feeds me through the iron gate is not a letter from Mexico. It's a letter from my cousin Ella, special delivery. I look at the return address. She has written 0000 Wits End, Vinita, Oklahoma. The zeros are marked in red ink and seem to spill off the edge of the envelope. There is a state mental hospital in Vinita.

Dear Lucy,

When we were little Wo He Lo meant love. Work, health, love. Do you remember that oath and the cute uniforms? Only I can't think if we were Bluebirds or Campfire Girls. They brought some kids in here the other day on a tour. They were all dressed alike in dark blue uniforms and small hats.

This is the worst it's been. If I ever get out of here I'll come for a visit.

Smell this before you throw it away.

Love,
Ella

She has poured vanilla extract over the letter. It has blurred the writing a little. I fold it twice and put it in my back pocket. It was Ella who gave me my finest farewell when I announced I was leaving for France to work as an au pair. Ella whose imagination rose to the event. The night before I left, my mother threw a big party. She invited all the cousins she swore she'd never speak to again. Ella led me out of this room filled with plates of cocktail cheese and olives, the vague congratulations floating through the room. She took me into the guest bedroom and cleared out a space for us on the coat-filled bed. The air smelled like sweet perfume and animal pelts. She breathed softly and looked down at her hands.

"Do you know the truth about 'encore'?"

"What truth? It means again."

"Yes, but the origin of the word. Okay, close your eyes and listen. There were these two lovers in France centuries ago, not Abelard and Heloise, but two others. She suffered from insatiable appetites and he was hopelessly in love with her. They locked themselves in an attic chamber and began to make love. Each time when he was finished she would whisper 'encore,' until he could no longer continue. At that moment they set themselves on fire."

"Ella, I've never—"

"Look, it's true. Another truth is that the average Frenchman knows sixty-five ways to do it."

Cody and I were remorseless in our teasing. We managed to underscore what was off-center in Ella through our constant joking about Vinita. All aboard for the express train! Nuts and fruits travel free. This coincidence is too close for comfort. I sit down on the steps for a while, marking the progress of tiny red ants. Sam loves to crush them because of the deep red stain they leave on his finger. I think back to one family gathering in particular. I must have been nine or ten years old.

My aunt's cook sang in a church choir and when she screamed, in delight or dismay, it had the height and pitch of good gospel music. She was howling and the sound of it ricocheted around the dining room. It could have been Thanksgiving or Christmas, for turkey was served on both holidays. I remember a big twenty-pounder on the table. She had forgotten one of the white paper crowns she usually fits over the drumsticks.

"Mrs. B. Come have a look at this! Somebody in here gonna get his behind warmed good."

Ella was an ideal pigeon. She would walk through fire for Cody and me. Ella would always test the limb, the water, the hollow side of the log where snakes could nest. She had no notion of consequence and loved us both unconditionally. She went scarlet as soon as Churchy started wailing.

My aunt led Churchy out of the dining room. When she returned to the table she patted her lips several times with her napkin. I had already put the whole incident behind me. The planning, the execution was over and there could be no further pleasure or fear. I looked at Cody, perfectly composed and poker-faced.

"Well, you children might like to know that Churchy had the impression she was going to faint. Was that your goal, kids?"

My mother's voice was tense.

"What's he done? What did Cody put on that tray?"

The dumbwaiter in Ella's house had fired our imagination for years. We heard it start with a lurch and then groan as it struggled up from the first-floor kitchen. Churchy was a wonderful cook, but even if she'd been merely mediocre, the notion of a dumbwaiter would have added allure to whatever she prepared. The dumbwaiter was the former owner's doing. Billy Tuck had read about a French count's château connected to a separate kitchen by underground tunnel. All this to avoid cooking odors in the château. In a fit of pique, Billy had a dumbwaiter installed and moved the dining room upstairs. I don't remember why we chose to defile this. But the three of us spent the whole morning reconnoitering cow dung as the grown-ups assembled. Cody and I put on gardening gloves, screwing up our noses as we collected the hardened paddies from the pasture. The cows were the only witnesses, stroking sulpher blocks languorously with their pink tongues. We ditched Churchy's cheese pastries under the sink as she served the adults their sherry and carefully recovered the tray with the white linen towel. Ella pinched her finger closing the door of the dumbwaiter.

"Young lady."

Ella, coughing loudly, was summoned to the head of the table. She had been careless and the smell of our adventure had gotten into her hands and hair. A bar of soap was produced. Churchy withdrew her demission with some cajoling. She said she felt like taking a day off, just the same, to fish. Our plates were scraped with much ceremony and our dinner was fed to the bird dogs who were kept in a cement run outside.

When we fought on the long drive home, it was to draw blood. The echo of our hollow stomachs was the day's only repercussion. A snow came down that melted into sleet as it hit the windshield and driving conditions were bad. The treacherous state of the roads underscored the escapade. My father swore as he swung around curves and ordered us to hold on tight as we slid helplessly into the looming backside of a blue Oldsmobile stalled at the end of a blind corner. He snapped the door hard when he got out. A woman in the parked Olds frantically locked her doors as he marched toward the car. She opened her window a bare inch.

My mother turned in the seat, clutching the headrest.

"As far as pranks go, it was very second-rate. But on one level you made a terrific hit. Sadie will be able to pass it on to Eunice. Eunice will naturally phone Bobby. And that ought to keep them busy for a while. Then Cody, my pride and joy, you'll have to think of another way to dishonor me."

The point was never the act itself but the amplification our aunts would give it. They all wore their hair in the tight, lacquered cones of the day so aptly called beehives. Cody heard on the evening news that a woman from Skiatook had finally succumbed to a spider bite. The spider had been nesting unnoticed in her hair for days. The broadcaster urged women to dismantle their beehives each night to avoid similar hazards. We instantly dubbed Eunice and Bobby the Black Aunts. This incident was one more proof that Agnes Lerner didn't have what it took. Oh, she might know how to play the piano by ear and she read a lot alright, but look at those children! Aunt Sadie was an innocent teller of tales. Later the Black Aunts, their beehive hairdos immobile despite the excitement, milked those tales for all they were worth, their hands flying up to their mouths in horror.

Uncle Rob was a wildcat oilman before the market went. Sixty percent of his wells came in. He had built-in indicators. Things on his body that throbbed as he was sinking a well so that the results never surprised him. Dry or a gusher, he knew in advance according to what hurt. One very good year he bought a stud and started Ellworth Ranch. He bought several fillies and geldings so he could have entries in the New Mexico races. But his heart wasn't in running horses. The stud was his pride. Conquistador Treasure, sired by Black Ramon out of Waco, Texas. Say, Wade, he would say to my father. I'm shipping some semen out to Denver this week. His eyes shone. He sucked on the end of a cigarette, daydreaming about stud fees. His knowledge of horses and men overlapped. He was superstitious about having another stud on the ranch because he thought it would demoralize Conquistador. What a goddamned life, he would say as he leaned on the fence, stroking the horse's rump.

We drove out to Ella's place often. The house was a sagging, creaking wonder. There was always something to do. My uncle had bought the Tuck boys' house. No one really knew what the old bachelor brothers did way out there besides work on the house. It was full of their crazy enthusiasms and they added on or remodeled when it pleased them. One of the Tucks saw a picture of an old man going up a bannister on an electric chair. At the time he was only thirty years old, but he planned to die in the house. Preferably in the bed he had bought from the Persian gentleman passing through Oklahoma with a furniture catalogue full of unspeakably beautiful items. He ordered an electric chair. He modified it and made it a mobile throne with a groove in the armrest meant to secure a drink. Only one of the Tucks used it. The other was afraid of electrocution. The Persian gentleman's bed was gone when Ella was growing up but the chair still worked. We rode up and down the stairs until the adults complained about the noise from the motor. Then we ran outside, strutting like the peacocks that freely roamed the property. It was a dumb trick that never worked. If they ever spread their tails, it was only when our backs were turned.

The house was linked to the barn by a dirt footpath that cut between a grove of elder trees. You couldn't reach the barn unobserved because the trees were too sparse. When Conquistador Treasure was working we were instructed to steer clear of the barn. Gus was alerted and ran us off if we appeared. This ain't for kids, he shouted. Now git! The news of the mare's arrival rocketed through the fields. Conquistador bellowed as we bent over plates of food in the kitchen. If we were playing outside we could hear the mare kicking the metal sides of the U-Haul, issuing high, nervous whinnies. We were nervous ourselves. We tried to decode horse talk.

"She's scared, poor thing. Listen."

"You dummy. When they make those kind of grunts they're happy."

For once I was on an equal footing with Cody. He was baffled and had no answers either.

"I mean, what does Gus do with that big stick?"

Only Ella was quiet as we tried out theories. She sucked a loose tooth or pulled her hair.

"Let's have a look. You two keep quiet so Gus won't hear us."

We were always discovered, scared off like crows. We went home when our parents could hold no more coffee, the best gossip all spent. There was an edge to the long drive back. Our disappointment was keen. The peacocks consistently refused to spread their tails and the tantalizing elements of horse breeding remained out of reach. Ella did not return to neat city blocks and neighborhood gangs. Her whole growing up was pierced with those cries. Each year she drifted farther away from Cody and me.

We all had theories about Ella. My own was that my uncle might have just taken Ella's small white hand in his own and led her down to the barn, despite the flies, the heat and the racket, to unravel that first mystery. Maybe right then in that dusty corral her personal history would have been adjusted. But that never happened. I stopped spending the night out there when her sleep became seriously disordered. She woke up under the bed or on the closet floor and found marks on her body the next day. All the teachers' notes indicated that she was falling behind. The school gave my aunt the name of a woman called Mrs. Briggs. Mrs Briggs was not quite a psychologist. She had "a way with kids." She gave Ella chicory coffee with so much milk it was nearly white. She put a plateful of packaged shortcakes on her kitchen table and put her own kids outside to play. Then she had Ella finish stories. She would introduce a character in the worst kind of trouble and Ella would have to get her out of it. The trouble was never Ella's own kind and she did very well. But when the stories got closer to Ella, she went back to waking up on the floor.

Conquistador Treasure didn't live to a ripe old age. He died a cruel death in his ninth year. Someone put poison in his watering trough and they found him lying swollen and stiff-legged in his paddock. He looked like a huge, unwanted pool toy, not the proud descendant of Black Ramon. My uncle had been involved in property feuds all his life. He couldn't file a complaint because there were too many possible malefactors. His interest in horses lapsed completely after the murder. We were allowed to ride his purse-winning quarter horses bareback and without supervision. We could swim them if we wanted and did so, clinging to their manes, which had grown long and tangled. We urged them through the muddy water of the pond on his place. They were natural swimmers and we struggled to stick on their backs as they cut through the water. Nothing could prevent them from rolling in the dust afterwards. We shot off them just in time to avoid being crushed.

My uncle's mud-caked line of quarter horses sprouted unlikely potbellies. We developed a makeshift kind of horsemanship that my mother later corrected with lessons, as one would brace a limb that refused to grow properly. You'd better ride something growing up in Oklahoma. If that can't be, because of forces beyond your control, a tractor or football float, well then, a horse. Whether we were sabotaging the dumbwaiter or mindlessly gliding up and down in an electric chair, these visits to Ella's gave me my first notion of place. Place that had nothing to do with city blocks and numbered streets. I think Ella's farm prepared Cody and me for wonder. That it may have fostered eccentricity, then a kind of madness in my cousin made absolutely no difference.

The red ants have converged on a sliver of sticky fruit candy someone has spit out on the sidewalk. Are ants as sugar-mad as humans or would the same roiling mass form over a bit of bread or cracker? The steps have grown cold and I feel stiff and tired. Sam and Marc rush at me, talking simultaneously. Sam is hot and has leaves in his hair. I must look as if I don't understand, for he raises his voice and takes my face in his small hands.

"Maman, j'ai gagné. C'est moi cette année. J'ai vu le lézard!"

The lizard so soon? It's our loony symbol of hope and renewal. Whoever catches sight of the first lizard sunning himself on a flat rock or skulking over a wall wins. There is no prize, for this is not a sweepstakes or lottery. The victory is in forecasting summer. Marc and Sam race to take off their clothes. Marc hops around on one foot, struggling with his jeans, while Sam sits V-legged on the pavement. They're out of their clothes in an instant, squealing at the shock of cold water. The widow is drawn to her window by their shouts.

Cody is gone. So is Ella. But I'm not alone on this earth after all. There are two bodies, naked as blades, to prove it. After a while I walk inside to hunt for a volume of Flaubert, her favorite French author. I can't rescue her from the nuthouse, but I can copy down a passage from "Un Coeur Simple." And assure her that Wo He Lo did and does mean love.

10

Sam walked when he was seven months old. He flew through space before he could speak, his short legs pumping until we lifted him off the ground or until he fell. We were afraid he would damage his spinal cord. I had constant nightmares about a cracked physiognomy, warped bowlegs and a duck's webbed feet. He lost interest in food. There wasn't time. We locked his door at night, because he stormed around in the dark and we were afraid he would fling himself down the stairs. One day my mother-in-law brought over Marc's old leash. I blinked hard. She threatened any day to dissolve into total caricature. No wonder her second son loved comics. I felt a smile threaten and bit the inside of my lip.

"Martine, vous pensez vraiment qu'il nous faut ça? Cela me semble un peu—"

"Certainement, Lucy. Sinon il sera impossible!"

I made a big show of gratitude, folding the leather leash and putting it in a corner of the panier. She seemed relieved, seeing that. It was true. I didn't manage well in the market with Sam and returned with the oddest hodgepodge or two kilos of a single vegetable or fruit. I paid with Sam locked between my knees, my change forgotten as I rushed after him. But a leash? Each outing was breathless. My resolution was a pair of tennis shoes I wore for a full year, sprinting after him until he responded to a sort of dressage. Arrête. Avance.

When I thought we were both up to a long plane ride I phoned Miss Manotte. It was 1982 and I was about to bring my son to America for the first time. That year she was a platinum blonde. She'd put on a bit of weight since we'd last met and when she held Sam he pulled hard on her fleshy cheeks. She met us at the exit gate the day of our flight, introducing us to an Air France steward. At the last minute Marc dug around in my purse, claiming to have misplaced a key. He pulled a stray hairpin out absently and put it in his pocket. That was a touch of airport voodoo, to make sure we came back.

"You don't have to do that, you know."

"Do what?"

"I'm coming back. I always do."

"You make me feel like a leper."

"We've talked about this a hundred times. I'm not ready. Please don't read things into this, Marc."

I promised not to have my hair cut in America, though he looked doubtful as we pull away from him. Then he shrugged.

"You're lucky I'm a nice guy. If I beat you perhaps we'd all be happier."

Sam eventually fell asleep, one stiff leg thrown into the aisle, his head cocked back. I brought him up to date and whispered a few cold facts.

"You're going to meet Grandma and Grandpa and Uncle Cody and Aunt Becky. Look out for her, she's a real snake in the grass. Then there's Cousin Eleanor and her baby sister."

I looked at Sam's hand, open and turned up expectantly.

"You'll love Cody. You two are just alike."

The movie started badly. I took off my headset and closed my eyes. The airline passengers cackled suddenly at some joke, then there was no sound at all. Only the occasional swish of stockings brushing up and down the aisle or a snore that sounded like the roll of a kettledrum. I found I was able to sleep wrapped around Sam. I only woke when the window shades began rudely snapping open. Sam opened one eye as we were circling Kennedy for the third time.

"Hey, pal. Welcome to America."

If it was an inaugural visit home for us, it certainly didn't feel like one. Where was the fanfare? I had produced a magnificent boy since I had last seen my mother. I felt slightly swindled. I was shortly to discover, however, that my mother's quiet acceptance of Sam could not have been otherwise. She was abstract and distant, as focused on an attendant upheaval as an animal beginning labor.

"Pass me another dairy product, please."

I poured and poured, Sam sucking delightedly on the empty container, then stashing it in a pocket.

"What's become of half-and-half? Or real milk?"

"Can I get you folks a refill?"

"Do you have any real cream back there?"

"Real cream? Gee, I don't think so. Plenty of Dairy Lite, though. That be all today?"

My mother and I peered at each other. The surface of her hands had changed since I had last seen her, and she had switched tinted sunglasses again. This time she was wearing a deep green shade with a small rhinestone on the right lens. They were nearly as opaque as Marc's but without the gleam. Each time I looked at her, it was like staring into an aquatic surface. She was there somewhere, but I hadn't found her yet. Her reserve was new.

"Why do you ask, Lucy? He's all boy, that's for sure. This uncertainty is unlike you. What kind of a question is that?"

"Well, you and Becky are so up on child development. I just want to know if you think he's normal, that's all."

Sam was under the table unlacing shoes. He came up for air and a lump of sugar, then went back to work, humming happily. We were both a little winded. We had been to the park.

"You let him eat sugar like that? This is all so unreal to me. To think he doesn't understand when I talk to him. It makes me feel, I don't know . . . helpless maybe. Why don't you speak English to him over there?"

"I do. But I don't get anywhere. At some point I always have to start over again in French."

My mother seemed a little shell-shocked to me. Too pacific. This was not the odyssey I had hoped for. We were just passing time.

"I think red pants might settle your problems. Bright red pants and you wouldn't be so likely to lose him.

We bought the pants together and strapped him in with a pair of striped suspenders. She was right about those pants. Sam, running faster than ever in this strange new land, was identified over public address systems in two shopping centers as a "little lost boy who won't tell us his name." We could hold him in our eyes longer, talking with our attention pinioned on that bright red vanishing point. I knew just when I had to stop talking and break into a dead run. All of my mother's intricate theories, then, boiled down to a single pair of pants. I knew I could get her to talk if I could get into her bedroom. I wasn't having any luck.

"Oh, this is such a mess. Let's go sit in the kitchen."

"I'm just about dressed, Lucy. Give me five more minutes and I'll be out."

My mother changed interiors every five years. There was some unwritten contract between her and an interior decorator to "freshen things up" every five years. That meant frantic slipcovering and curtains up and down until a decision was made. Fabric samples were strewn around for weeks before a new order emerged. The changes were completely hollow. Paisley or Liberty prints were chosen, the change effected, and the five-year timetable honored. It was changed and expensive, but never very interesting. My mother wouldn't let Bea Adams into her bedroom. Because that, in fact, was where she lived. At the chipped, scarred desk piled high with unpaid bills and newspaper articles clipped in a moment of true energy and discovery. There were grocery sacks in one corner filled with presents that would reach their destination late or not at all, potpourri that after months would lose its scent and grind down into a kind of musty powder. The decorator didn't step foot in there. Because it smelled bad, like soot and neglect. Because the fabric on the loveseat was faded from years of sunsets. And because the room contained her whole messy life. Bea took charge of the careful outer world and made it a place where my father could bring clients. He could pour respectable, middle-class cocktails and lead them to a card table upholstered in cowhide.

The light never changed in there. It was something tactile. I tiptoed in. She was putting on makeup in her bathroom for some proposed outing. I came armed with coffee and cigarettes. There was no routing me. I sat cross-legged on the bed and offered to zip her up. She frowned into the mirror.

"Damn. I bungled my lip line. Lucy, don't you knock? I'll be out in a minute and we can talk then."

"We can also talk now. Look, there's coffee."

"I don't want Sam in here playing. It may not look it, but I know just where everything is and I don't want it disturbed."

"Sam is with Big Bird. Perfectly happy. Don't keep running me off, Mom."

When I was a child, I established myself as a mountain climber. I crawled up and up her long body for a kiss. She was never one of those small, available mothers. She didn't wear frilly aprons to cook, she wore a torn men's shirt. She didn't bend down to kiss you. You had to climb straight up until she submitted, laughing.

"Am I? Am I running you off?"

She came into the bedroom with a mascara wand held lightly in one hand. One eye was done, long-lashed and brilliant. The other looked smaller, but bright and beady as a bird's. I had brought photographs. Marc's and my own. They were like cue cards in our new language, which had to cover time and distance and blistery old wounds.

"This woman?"

"Martine. Remember, I wrote to you about my mother-in-law. A thesis, if I remember. Here she is in living color."

"What is that she's holding? Looks like it would reap hay."

"It washes floors. It's a kind of rubber scraper you cover with a special rag. I use good old American sponge mops. She really hates that."

"And why?"

"It's a metaphor, I think. She only functions on that level. A sponge mop has to be replaced because the sponge part wears out. The special rag cleans on and on. My mop represents waste."

"Ah. It's lovely there. The old and new. Does that lemon tree bear?"

"Not since I've been there. She's made the most out of that fact, too. I've got to get us out of there."

"I see your point. I can certainly understand that."

"Who's this guy?"

"Dr. Robert Schuller. A minister out of California."

"You keep his picture in your bedroom?"

"Oh, just until I can find the proper spot for it. You know how I am until I get organized."

"Here's a picture of Marc. He's taller than that picture makes him look. Bad angle."

"I don't believe I care for those sunglasses. Although he's a very nice-looking man. But those glasses make him look almost sinister."

"He does it on purpose. You really can't see through them."

"Do you want to stop speaking in code, Lucy. Why do you always speak in half sentences?"

"Sorry. What I mean is that Marc doesn't give himself away very easily."

"Deadpan. Like you. Well, birds of a feather."

". . . And I think it's a habit he's picked up from work. He claims he gets better results when he wears a mask. When people see that a photographer is affected they get self-conscious. It botches everything for people who aren't used to exposure."

"And what else?"

"What do you mean?"

"I mean what else about your husband? There must be something awfully distinctive about him. Irresistible. After all, look at the trouble you went through to marry him. *Tell* me about him, for heaven's sake."

I'm surprised to find myself hot. I look into my mother's full-length mirror and see I'm red. My mother is leaning forward. She's eager to hear about the superman I have netted, now that emotions have died down and her worst fears for me have not been realized. But I haven't married a superman or a Don Juan. Would she like to hear about an old-world gentleman or a hot-blooded Latin type? A struggling photographer. An easy, natural father. Un bon copain. Would any of these descriptions satisfy my mother's appetite for details? I stammer.

"Why don't you just draw your own conclusions when you two meet?"

"And when will that be?"

"Maybe next year. That Schuller reminds me of someone. But not exactly someone. He reminds me of several people. Kind of unnerving. Almost like he's a composite of a lot of different people. What's Cody doing in Louisiana?"

"Next question."

"You mean you don't know."

"I mean I don't ask. Cody is incapable—oh, don't let me get started."

She is an elegant, accomplished smoker. She lights a Lucky at exactly the right moment and never lets it degenerate into a mere nicotine habit. She's smoking now, indicting my brother in a deep, disconcerted inhalation.

"Of what? Incapable of what? Her Hallmark cards indicate all is well. She sends me those idiotic cards every other month."

"That's typical of Becky. Thoughtful of others. Which is really what breaks my heart. She bears up so beautifully with the girls. She even has time for volunteer work and voice lessons. She is always alone. Every weekend he's off to Louisiana or Texas or some other place. Talking investments all the time. He could line up investments here in Oklahoma, couldn't he? Your dad thinks—

"Oh, we don't know. We just don't know what he's up to.

The more he's on the go, the more we see these girls change. Especially Eleanor. Children are sensitive alright. She makes a beeline for men, she'll do anything for their attention. Becky spoke to me about it the other day. Eleanor's searching her daddy, that's clear. And Cody's gone. Even when he's here, he's gone, if you get me. Haven't I said enough?"

There wasn't much time. I had just until the end of her Lucky. She always smoked them all the way down to the filter.

"Maybe Cody's just preoccupied with their financial future. I mean, she does tend to spend. I made Sam stay outside yesterday. Their place is like a museum. White wool carpets—all the silver she's got could fill up a Sotheby's warehouse. Cody probably has to invest."

"That's all from Catch and Anita. Don't let this leave the room, Lucy. You hear me? I think your brother has a little babe stashed away somewhere. And he doesn't even have the good sense to be discreet about it. Why don't you go check on Sam? I could just bite my tongue."

It was evident that something was cooking chez Becky and Cody. And clearly that brew, bubbling and spitting above a dangerously high flame, would shortly boil over.

I watched as "The Hour of Power" unfolded.

"Wow! What is this?"

"Crystal Cathedral out in California. Magnificent, isn't it?"

"So this guy is a faith healer."

"Sssh. Wade, turn up the volume."

"He's a born-again, right?"

"Well, of course, Lucy. Hush now. I can't hear what he's saying."

Dr. Schuller looked happy. He smiled on and on and opened his address with an anecdote about how he had visualized his church years ago. He had read an article about Philip Johnson, the architect, and contacted him about designing a building for four thousand people. He wanted it to be all glass. The architect registered shock and Schuller felt called upon to explain himself and his dream, which dealt with the riverbanks in

Iowa and the desire to worship once again under the open sky. He made a joke about stock in Windex after the Crystal Cathedral was completed.

"He's so—actually, he's funny. Is he a real minister?"

My mother handed me a pencil and paper.

"This is very frustrating, Lucy. Write your questions down since you're so deeply interested. Please be considerate of others. Oh, I love this couple! They sing the nicest duets."

The boy's name was Lonnie and the girl's was Carol. They sang a zippy song about Jesus, and people started clapping their hands. My father left the room to make coffee and Mom sat tapping her foot. Then Schuller introduced a football player from USC. The football player brought the audience down. His song was gentle and soft. Again about love of Jesus, but in a different context. Where were the underachievers on Schuller's show? The poor, the sick, the troubled? Schuller's young and old looked sharp and sassy. Affliction was hard to imagine given the general look of well-being. Schuller reappeared, to issue prayers for individual members of his congregation. Some of these prayers were in response to poignant letters from television viewers. After dispensing a panacean prayer, great enough to cover all the types of suffering described in the letters, Schuller seemed ready to grapple with all the issues. Which today were worrisome. Financial. And headed toward the Crystal Cathedral like a U-boat straight on course. He urged believers to use their good sense and good faith. Then there was a parable from the Old Testament and more guest stars. At the end an address flashed up on the screen.

"How thoughtful of him. So even if we're not sitting right there in the congregation we can do our part. What are you doing?"

My mother was copying down the address at top speed, even though it remained on the screen for a full four minutes as a church elder discussed other matters.

"Mom?"

"What's a hundred dollars when you think of it? I ought to

send in more. I certainly get my money's worth out of this show. There's never a moment when it's too abstract or sophisticated. Bob Schuller is about everyday living. He's practical and handy as an iron nail."

"Why don't you ask the iron nail how to fasten down someone like Ella? Certainly for a hundred dollars, you'd think he could offer a little—"

"I don't know where this comes from, Lucy. This tendency to belittle things that are of value to others."

"I mean it, Mom. The man answers his mail. On behalf of the whole family you could write just a couple of lines for Ella's well-being. You wouldn't have to go into detail. Look at the size of his congregation. Multiply their prayers by the number of television viewers and she might wake up a rational person."

"This kind of derision is just like you."

"I'm sorry. I'm just not accustomed to this new approach. It's so jazzy, sort of."

Her eyes were wide and shining at the airport. My father stared out the window at a line of saplings a maintenance crew settled carefully into the ground. She handed me one of her favorite books by Bob Schuller, *Tough Times Never Last, But Tough People Do!* I finished the last chapter in Orly Airport, waiting for an airbus to Nice.

Every once in a while a needle-nosed garfish will rise to the surface of an Oklahoma lake, seeking light, fellow fish, an easy feed. It is likely that he'll be bumped by a skier or clubbed on the head by a beer-brave boy crouched on the deck of a fiberglass Crisscraft. His smooth, white body and others like it float on the calm lake. The inexperienced, pontoon-boat element on the lake wonder what a swordfish is doing in the middle of America. Big damn thing, isn't it? I don't figure you'd want to eat one of those. I just knew this lake was contaminated.

Cody, dumb as a gar, has surfaced in Oklahoma City. One of Catch's men laid eyes on him. I get a sort of UPI release from my mother.

September 4, 1983

Dear Lucy,

Cody was spotted at 2:45 at a downtown intersection in Oklahoma City. He was driving a white Fleetwood convertible with red upholstering. The plates were from Texas.

In the photograph Catch brought over (it is very grainy, you can't see your brother's face, but it's Cody alright) he is touching the girl's shoulder lightly. As if he is asking her a question. She looks like a prostitute but I know your brother better than that. He would never pay for what someone's giving away free.

Becky is trying to move ahead with divorce proceedings, although the girls still think Cody is in California. We have been seeing a great deal of Becky, taking whole cooked meals over. This is mainly my initiative. Eleanor telephones me once a day. She says that Becky is no longer selective about what she eats. Dry cereal for dinner, etc. We have noticed a new bitter edge to Becky and expect it is the awful strain she's under. She cannot possibly mean what she says.

Bob Schuller ran away from a tornado. He started a church with five hundred dollars. He lived through the amputation of his daughter's leg and his wife's struggle with cancer. He says, and I believe it, that every problem has a limited life span. I guess I can handle this little bit of dirty business. Catch's men lost Cody at a busy intersection so we cannot tell you more. But I expect with the license plate number in hand, news of his whereabouts will be forthcoming. We are not surprised by this and have generally put Cody out of our lives. Your father is outside more and more with this tree project of his I mentioned. I expect this is his reaction to Cody's actions and do not mention that his constant hammering and sawing is worse than a jammering woodpecker. Trees, trees, trees, I want to say. What about Agnes?

I do hope things are fine where you are.

In deference first to his mother, then to his wife, my father finally climbed down out of the trees. The quiet, prosperous owner of a pipe supply company would have chucked it all at one time to be a forest ranger or a treeman. Arboretum? You want to take me to an arboretum? Don't forget I'm underage, Wade Lerner, my mother said when she was seventeen. She smoothed her velvet skirt over her knees with a wounded air, wondering whether a decent toilet could be found in a pool hall.

He learned to content himself first with his own grove of bonsai. Then, over the years, the dwarf trees saddened him inexplicably and he gave them away to a church that was holding a rummage sale. Before he hauled them off in the flattened backseat of the station wagon he took an old Windex bottle filled with rainwater and misted them. Cody and I closed our eyes and bent our heads over the miniature forest. The smell was intoxicating, better than anything that had ever drifted out of the kitchen. After the bonsai collection was gone he planned a family pilgrimage to the Redwood Forest. We entered the forest as if it were a chapel. He had Cody and me lie down at the foot of a sequoia, instructing us to look straight up and just breathe. We straddled trees to discover their girth, to understand a little of their immensity. We didn't remain reverent for long. It's big alright, Daddy. Can you turn up the radio, please? Are we almost out of the woods, Dad? Jeez, it's sure dark. And finally we drove him down to sea level, canceling our reservations for a log cabin rental. We made for southern California. Now this is more like it, Wade! My mother put on seven pounds because of Mexican food. I turned darker than a leather saddle while my father endured what remained of the vacation under a beach parasol, playing crossword puzzles and swimming only when it was absolutely necessary. Then Cody cut the trip short by almost drowning. My father was smug on the way home, the rightness of the Redwood Forest confirmed by the mishap. No harm had come to our family under those stately trees. Later his approach became more sedate, more scholarly. He wrote an article called "The Metaphysics of an Oak," a very personal tract that was rejected by eighteen natural science magazines and country journals. He conducted a Sunday redbud tour at a northside nature study center until the center closed because of funding problems. That he has succumbed once more to trees is no surprise.

I brought Sam home a second time when he was nearly three years old. My parents pronounced him long and lean. Calmer, though still apt to demonstrate emotion in movement, rather than speech. And when speech did occur it remained incomprehensible to them. In short, they loved him, but knew not what they loved. My father leads him into the trees.

"It doesn't hurt, Dad?"

"A little. But it was a simple break. Hasn't held me up, as you can see."

"Can Sam sign your cast? He's doing a series of hieroglyphics he claims spells Sam."

"I'd be honored. Well, what do you think of it so far?"

"I wish I were his age again. Why didn't you think of this when we were little?"

"I don't know. Too busy making a living, I suppose. Some ideas take time to evolve."

The grove of oak trees, despite the threats by my mother to reduce the whole eyesore to firewood, has survived. The diseased or dead oaks have been removed. The thinned grove of healthy forty-year-old oaks appears deeper and fortified, like a head of newly trimmed hair. The skunks have been evicted from the decrepit doghouses and the briar bushes yanked out. A neat footpath now leads down to the trees. Long rods of sunlight make their way to the base of the oaks. My father continues work on the project despite the broken arm. Lucky, he says, that branch broke my fall. Otherwise the collarbone would have gone, too.

"Biggest problem turned out to be the coons. There was a whole colony of them down here that turned aggressive once we started work. I called the city after a worker got bit. You should have heard them hiss. Damn nuisance."

"Is this a community service deal, Dad?"

"A gift to the city. Every kid should spend time in a tree

house and most never have the occasion. Ever take a look at the public parks here? Pathetic. One-hundred-degree summers and not a shade tree on the place. The mothers don't even get out of their cars come June. They set the kids out there to broil and then they hightail it back to an air-conditioned car. We are a city that refuses to dream. A city of basement-dwellers and flat-thinkers, if you ask me. It's been years since anybody around here looked up. Except Oral Roberts, of course. And he doesn't have time to build tree houses."

"So if it's a gift to the city you get a tax write-off, I suppose."

"Well, you shock me, Lucy. All grown up and thinking about loopholes."

"Who gets to come here?"

"Why, anyone. Anyone at all."

"Neighbors happy?"

"Screw 'em."

Sam is dazzled. He lies immobile on a high platform, one boot caught in his hand. I've never seen him like this, unfocused and dreamy. The tree community is ambitious. Catwalks link every tree house and the construction is anything but simple. Some of the treehouses are unadulterated platforms, with nothing but a guardrail surrounding them. Others contain different levels suitable for a single child or several. There are isolated crows' nest and Dutch doors. Nooks and shelves deep enough for a favorite book. I grab my father's good arm.

"I'm so proud of you. Of this."

"Beats selling pipes."

"Who built all this?"

"A country boy named Abe Masterson. He let me hand him tools every now and then. We had a hell of a time. What do you think about this stain we chose? That was tricky. Incorporating the wood . . . I want those kids to think about trees, not carpentry. Say, I got a little note here from a child psychiatrist who lives in New York City. His mother sent him a copy of the article in the Tulsa Tribune. He told me there's a ginkgo right outside his office. He mentioned that if he could set up his practice in a tree he would. I felt I was on the right track after that."

"How about if a kid falls out of a tree?"

"Why don't I set up a meeting with my lawyer while you're here? The parents have to sign a release and there has to be an adult present for small children. Any other questions? Lord, you're sounding like your mother. I'm sure glad you're home."

"I take it she's not thrilled."

"You just ought to listen to her. 'I've raised kids of my own. Finally, just when I'm about to have a little peace and quiet, you invite the whole city over to play.' You can't even see the tree house from the back door. You could run the Grand Prix down there and never hear a sound. What I want to know is where all this positive thinking is getting your mother. It's Schuller this, Schuller that. Maybe if I could get an endorsement from Schuller she'd let me alone on this thing."

"Go easy on her, Dad. The woman's in mourning."

"If she weren't so goddamned flinty about Cody, she'd be better off. You're right, she's written her son off for dead. Which is way off because Cody's not dead at all. In fact, I'll bet he's more alive than he ever was here, supervising miniature golf and unloading the trunk of his wife's Mercedes. Please don't quote me. I've got my hands full as it is. How are we gonna get Sam out of that tree? Has he ever heard of a Tootsie Roll?"

The roads have improved since Oral Roberts took over the southern end of town. At one time the only reason to drive this far was to visit an eccentric seamstress or buy fresh corn and tomatoes from a roadside stand.

"He should have built a mountain under it."

"You can't build a mountain. Mountains just are."

We've reached the City of Faith, Oral Roberts' medical complex. My father is right. Oral Roberts is neither a basement-dweller nor a flat-thinker. Three eerie golden towers lift up from a mirrored base. The towers contain twenty, thirty and sixty stories. There is no preparation for the City of Faith. The shimmering, futuristic structure has no relation to the miles of level land that surround it. It rises splendid and whole as one of Oral's visions.

"A modern-day Oz. You're going to have to stop this, you know."

"Stop what? I've smoked for years."

We are parked in front of the sculpture of the praying hands. Students, smiling, weave around it without looking up. They all speak to each other as they pass. Or if not, they nod in greeting or hold up a single flattened hand.

"All this promiscuity. Make up your mind. Who's it going to be? Oral or Bob?"

She snorts in laughter and shakes the cigarette ash from the front of her sweater.

"Very funny. You're the one who wanted to drive out here. Word is, he's going to come out alright on the deal. It's been a very dark time for him. The community mocked him for the longest time. It got so bad people weren't even discussing him at cocktail parties like they used to. Like Schuller says, every problem has a limited life span. The last I heard he was going to provide services for the indigent."

"To fill up his empty hospital."

"No, to serve the poor, Lucy. Do me a favor. Be a little more discerning. Schuller and Oral Roberts are both men of God. But they're not the same man of God and I wish you'd stop lumping them together."

"You're right. Oral has logged far more visions than Schuller. Twenty-one talks with God so far."

"Lucy!"

"What did it cost to construct this thing?"

"One hundred and fifty million. His operating loss is running at about one million dollars a month."

"And you say the dark time is over?"

"He's sounding more optimistic. More like himself. I swear you come here to research the flora and fauna, Lucy. Most people return home just to visit. But oh, no. Not you. You fly in, collect a little data, and disappear for another year. Seen all you care to?"

Kyle Lark is clearly small potatoes. Visions around here come in at a fast clip. As Oral tells it, God first spoke to him with reference to the City of Faith seven years before its construction. He instructed Oral to build a medical complex that would combine the best medical care and research possibilities with the healing power of prayer. In 1980, funding hit an all-time low. Then one night, Oral told his television viewers, a nine-hundred-foot Jesus appeared on the construction site to offer encouragement. When Oral was operated on for nasal polyps sometime later, both an angel and Jesus appeared in his hospital room. He said the angel was as tall as the room and three times as wide. Oral dispatched the angel to bring in patients to save the City of Faith. I guess it was around then he began offering free services to the indigent.

"It's weird."

"What?"

"When I come back here I feel like I live out of God's range of vision. Or He lives out of mine. I mean, do you think these guys really summon angels?"

"No one can summon an angel or a vision of God. What nonsense. God appears. Or one of his messengers. Period."

"Is Oral a prophet?"

"He's a preacher. A man of God whose job is passing the message on."

She prods her temples furiously. Then she eases out each deep frown line with an index finger.

"Honestly, Lucy. You talk as if this is all some new language to you. Like we're all talking Zulu around here. The message is love, damn it. And don't play innocent with me. I know that behind all your questions is mockery and disdain and that's what gets me so riled. The Christian message is beamed through the Iron Curtain. God's news is being broadcast throughout the world and my daughter acts as if she's been in a coma for the past decade. As if she doesn't understand a word of what's being said. The message is love."

"Is the message forgiveness?"

"It certainly is."

"Is the message tolerance?"

"Of course. Now just where is this leading us?"

"Mom, why are you pretending Cody is dead?"

My mother lays on the horn. It's not a short, friendly toot.

It's a furious blast. Heads around us turn and the car in front moves at last.

"We can turn right on red now, though people still need reminding."

I wonder if she's heard my question. Perhaps part of the message is turning a deaf ear.

"Since you're so free with your questions, maybe you'll let me ask you a few."

"Shoot."

"I want to know why you won't bring your husband home to meet your family."

"I—"

"Are you ashamed of us or ashamed of him? Is it Ella you're worried about? Under certain conditions your cousin functions just fine, thank you. But then, there's no reason for them to even meet in the first place, if you're skittish about it."

"I'm not ashamed of anyone."

"Are you in some kind of trouble over there?"

"Of course not."

"You take me for a very backward woman. That's it, isn't it? Strictly corn pone. Well, Miss La-ti-da, I've written off one child. I can certainly write off two."

And then my mother cries. For want of a better site we pull into a Git 'N Go parking lot. Sam stands frightened in a corner of the backseat. He bangs me once on the head and retreats again. I wave away the store manager and a curious construction worker who shuffles toward us in iron-toed boots. It's alright, I assure them, shooing them off.

I finally go inside to buy Kleenex. The manager corners me at the dairy case.

"Anything I can do for you, lady? Personal problems you two having out there?"

"You might say. In fact it's so personal I think I'll just pay for this Kleenex and be on my way."

"Here's your change. Take this and try to have yourselves a good day now."

"Here. Complimentary Visine. Smile at him or something. He's frantic."

My mother lifts the bottle of Visine as if she's proposing a toast and smiles. She opens a compact and starts repair work.

"Just look at my nose. So the problem is not shame?"

"The problem is pride."

"I don't get you. Pride?"

She is more attentive than a schoolgirl, wide-eyed and ready for instruction.

"Sort of."

"You burn me up. Listen to me, Lucy. You've got your nerve. You write letters more inscrutable to me than the Dead Sea Scrolls. You come home year after year, root around for a little local color and then shoot off again with a grandson I barely know. You don't even have the courtesy to teach him proper English so I can talk to him. The husband you keep stashed away. You mutter nonsense about pride and imagine that will pacify me. Well, get this. I'm not old, but I'm not young either. I could die tomorrow and never know the truth about the way you live. How long do you intend to keep this up? If you've got problems, let's tackle them. If you don't, then bring your husband in so I can get a look at him. This is unnatural. I think you need to stop and x-ray your motives, young lady."

This is Schuller's Alphabet for Action. He advises moral and spiritual x-ray.

"I don't think I have any motives, Mom. I'm just not ready is all."

"You've been gone for—"

"It hasn't got anything to do with time. I don't want to go through the decoding is all. I don't want to sit and make sunny conversation in a charming French restaurant. I don't want to translate the menu or the milieu or my husband. And I don't want to bring Marc here either. I can just see it now, the shutter clicking away a mile a minute. All the gun racks mounted on pick-up trucks. The endless shopping centers and Sunday mornings with Schuller. The point will always be missed. Explanation kills everything. My true life wouldn't bear up. It would all turn into a curious village chronicle."

"Selfish. You just want to hoard all the candy for yourself."

"We were safer talking religion."

"It seems. You're a funny person. I don't know where your ideas come from sometimes, Lucy."

"I don't summon them. They just come."

She's about to parallel park. The space is made for a smaller car and she'll never make it. She hikes her skirt up and starts to angle in anyway.

"Don't count on me for summer vacations when he's older. I don't run foreign-student programs."

"I won't."

"Does he call me anything when I'm not around? What's grandma in French?"

"Mamie. He doesn't call you that, though. He calls you Agnès."

She brakes and looks at Sam for verification, one eyebrow raised.

"Rhymes with princess. To think I've been flinching over my name for all these years, when it could have been so—how am I doing in back?"

"Fine, Mom. I think you've got it made."

11

When Sam began nursery school I composed a glossary of epithets. The most striking were food related. Patate crue! Grosse nouille. As he grew the glossary changed. There was a transition period filled with the stuff of nightmares. The fat and the aged, the hairy and downright demented all figured in that language of insult. Now that Sam has discovered the power of language there is no stopping all this boytalk. I think Rabelais was the first to use "faire chier" in a literary sense. That it is being reapplied in the schoolyard or shouted from a landing at La Belle Eléna says a good deal about the continuity of language. When I was called into the office of the directress, I assumed it was about Sam's use and abuse of la langue pure.

"Madame Laugier. Prenez une chaise."

Sam's principal is a contralto. She started her school thirty years ago in Africa. When her husband died in a plane crash she moved her school and her faithful five to the Côte d'Azur. Of the five, two have died and two have deserted. There remain, then, the directress and her right arm, Liliane, who discreetly leaves the office when I arrive. Liliane is responsible for the particular veneer at Sam's school. She changes the roses in the office. She takes charge of the lunchroom, force-feeding carrots and semolina when necessary. She releases the cage of homing pigeons at the end of the year for the graduating class and dispenses tissues to weeping parents. The directress, Madame Sarl, leads her graduating students each spring into the Périgord, where they will spend three days discovering the caves and rivers of the region before lurching into sixth grade. The spirit of a safari permeates these excursions. She wears the same high leather boots she wore years ago as she marched her students across a wide savanna. It is often the vision of this eventual débarquement that keeps students enrolled when the tuition makes its annual jump.

"May we speak to each other in English?"

"Please."

News of Madame Sarl's nursery school English has spread through the IBM community like wildfire. She has a steady following there among families who are in and out of France on two-year contracts. Work on the elusive English phonetic system starts early, when children are, as Madame Sarl patiently explains, language-porous.

"Sam. Worries. Me."

I'm wearing a suit on permanent loan from Chan. I can't help stealing a glance at my knees. I am unused to the sight of them in this context. They seem to belong to someone else. Madame Sarl wears woolen knee socks and sensible shoes. Her own knees are hidden under the folds of a long plaid skirt.

"I realize he is rough with other children."

"He's a boy. We're equipped to handle little boys."

"His language has become very vulgar."

"We expect to hear that. It is all in the context of his age. We're equipped to handle Sam's language."

In the pause between this cat-and-mouse game I begin to envision armored tanks on a hill. Long-range artillery and a series of trenches.

"Madame Laugier, I must be frank. I think your son is a deeply puzzled little boy."

"Puzzled? In what sense?"

"I don't think his position in the world is clear to him. His relation to the world. Le point fixe, for a child, is of tremendous importance."

"Are you talking about his self-esteem?"

"No, I don't think his self-esteem is at risk. It's something more intangible I feel about Sam. On the agenda that was distributed at the first of the year you will recall La Petite Heure de Raconter. This means very simply a free time when one child stands up to tell a story about his family. We intentionally have this hour scheduled for Monday. There is always a great deal to discuss after a weekend spent with the family. Sam, much to our chagrin, has never spoken during this period. When he is called upon, he slips into myth. Not storytelling, Madame Laugier, but *myth.*"

"What sort of myth?"

"Personal myth. Sam recreates himself and his world in terms of personal myth. In most children's stories there is a hint of what they watch on television. Or hear on the radio. Most certainly the parents figure in this. Their disputes, their preoccupations. We hear none of this in Sam's talk. Sam's stories spring from . . . Well. I think there is great confusion in Sam's mind as to where he fits into this world. When asked to describe this confusion he retreats into very elaborate tales involving self-transformation into a fish."

A plastic Neanderthal man is crouched on Madame Sarl's desk. She runs her finger absently down his back. Her light eyes rest on a small map of Ethiopia.

"Sometimes . . . often children of divorced parents are prone to this type of . . . self-definition. Children suffering a sudden rupture or change of direction. May I ask if—"

"My husband and I are not divorced, Madame Sarl."

"Do you have family living on the Côte d'Azur?"

"My family lives in America."

"And your husband's family?"

"Here. On the Côte. But I have broken relations with my husband's mother."

"Ah, I see. Ah, yes. Does your husband continue to see his mother?"

"Oh, yes. Every Sunday, in fact. He and Sam have Sunday dinner there."

"Does Sam have the occasion to know your parents?"

"Oh, yes. We travel to America at least once a year."

"The three of you."

"The two of us. Sam and I."

"Mrs. Laugier."

Madame Sarl shakes her head from side to side. She seems saddened by the news.

"A child must have continuity. This notion is ideally contained and carried on by the child's grandparents. Children thrive on the notion of past, present and future. According to what you have now described I would say your son has a dwarfed notion of the world. I would say you have failed to provide your son with certain very important concepts."

Les Mères Admirables meet three times a year. There are awards and special citations. Certain admirable mothers stand up to give testimonies honoring other admirable mothers. They have had lunch at the Négresco Hotel for the past thirty years. I look at my knees again. One is bruised from a fall.

"Mrs. Laugier, you have the extreme good fortune to still have living parents. Your husband's parents are right here on the Côte. Can you not overcome your little differences, whatever they may be, for the sake of your son?"

Madame Sarl stands up and moves to the window. She holds her hands behind her back as she looks outside. Her office looks out on the playground for the youngest children. We both watch as they make their way in and out of lime green tunnels. The girls struggle their way through, weighted down with patent leather purses or long skirts that trip them up. When the younger children move out of the labyrinth of tunnels Madame Sarl has constructed, they will not only master physical coordination and a fledgling English. They will master La Morale, a two- or three-sentence moral lesson that changes week in, week out. In many ways, it prepares them for the eventual expedition into the Périgord.

Her voice is low, melodious. Much of her success has to do with delivery. I wondered earlier what was wrong with myth.

Now I know myth is a thing to be reckoned with. I stand up, too. Madame Sarl taps vigorously on the window at the two boys slugging it out over a sand shovel.

"We must, as parents, bury many of our brutish instincts for the children. Part of our métier, Madame, is to be exemplary. To the extent, that is, that we are able."

She begins to move me toward the door. I feel winded, as if I just finished a fast sprint.

"Votre sac. If I might suggest a project. A family tree might be a wonderful thing for you. Apply it to a door somewhere in your home. Consider it a tool for our Sam, an aide-memoire for him. This is a complicated world, don't you agree, Madame Laugier?"

"Thank you for your time. I think . . . yes. I agree that this is a complicated world."

I watch the younger children in the courtyard for a while. One of the teachers gives five short blasts on the whistle and playtime is over. Two little boys fetch rakes and begin to smooth over the gravel. Two girls gather all the sand toys, stopping occasionally to ogle a treasure half-submerged in the sand. All work in the court is done in pairs and some kind of competition seems to be in the air. Four more sharp blasts on the whistle.

"Plus qu'une minute. Dépêchez-vouz. Sabrina, Emilie, lâchez ça tout de suite!"

Two girls are involved in a struggle over a cleaning rag. A tug-of-war has begun.

"C'est le mien!"

"Espèce de tomate!"

"Donne, donne!"

Sabrina wins the right to clean only momentarily. She pushes her opponent in the face, knocking the little girl flat. She rubs the table in fierce circles until the other girl is back on her feet. She heads for Sabrina with her mouth wide open.

"Vous deux. Au coin!"

An uneasy peace ensues. The girls head upstairs to sit in a corner, as they have been instructed. Surreptitious pinches are exchanged on the way. Sam is somewhere inside that pink building, chewing a pencil. Puzzling, no doubt, over his truncated, dwarfed view of the world. I think on the way home of Bettelheim and his examination of favorite children's tales. Then I run over what I recall of the repertoire of Toto, the infamous bad boy in France who was immortalized in an early Truffaut film. Toto and his attacks on church and state still have a wide group of followers. Italo Calvino, then, in translation. It isn't until I'm in the parking lot of Quickburger that I remember it was me who dreamed up the notion of Fishboy.

Quickburger is the hub of the universe. In the parking lot I see license plates from Hungary and Italy. A station wagon, fitted out with equipment for every possible water sport, is from Denmark. You can place your order in French, English or Italian. Marc is sitting in a sunny corner, his head bent over Le Monde.

"Salut. Tu veux un Quick, Lucy? Ou une salade?"

"Quick et frites."

The Quick hostess is friendly. She is the woman who distributes balloons and settles happy paper hats on children's heads. She passes toward the end of each meal to ask questions about service and the quality of the food. I hear her telling American customers that she won fifty dollars once in Las Vegas.

"Five-cent pieces come all falling down. You like you Quick?"

Marc returns with our food. His shirt pocket is stuffed with packets of ketchup for Sam.

"What's up this afternoon?"

"Une photo de groupe. Croix Rouge. Soon the ball, remember."

"Tu as l'air fatigué."

"You know that I dreamed about the ball last night? I dreamed about the Red Cross Ball."

"Bientôt, Marc. Something has to change. I feel it. Oh, God. Look at your shirt."

One of the ketchup packets has burst and a red stain marks his pocket. I think of the cleaning bill because of the suede trim. This is becoming a joyous lunch. I switch the subject to Madame Sarl.

"She thinks Sam is confused."

"About what?"

"His position in the world. She says when he is forced to describe himself he slips into myth. Whatever that means."

He glares at me and continues eating.

"She seems to think he slips into mythmaking when he tries to describe his confusion. The uncertainty he feels about where he fits into the world."

A little boy next to us is feeding french fries steadily off the edge of the table. He is hunched low and slides each one slowly toward its fate. He shouts BAH! when the fry hits the dirty floor. His mother watches with amusement until the Quick hostess works her way to the table, then they scold the boy in unison.

"And what did you reply?"

"Not much. I explained I had broken off relations with your mother and then she asked me about our trips to America. It all seemed to make perfect sense to her. I mean, I suppose this is where Sam's confusion comes into it."

Marc begins folding all the paper on his tray into precise little shapes. Fast food origami. His body is very still. All the movement is in his hands and face.

"So now what?"

"Well, Madame Sarl suggested designing a family tree. Something we could tape to the bathroom door, for example, to give Sam—"

"Are you serious?"

"Why not?"

"You really think our problems can be resolved by making an exercise like this? Don't be ridiculous. If we offer Sam a half life, then we must accept the consequences without remords."

"Remorse. It's not a half life, it's a good life. And the best we can do."

"You're lying, Lucy. You don't have to be my mother's companion. But you could reach an accord for the sake of our son. You've made it clear I'm not part of your summer travel plans.

But your reasons, if you know them, are only clear to you."

"Are you through?"

"Stop crying."

"I'm not. Allergies. Are you saying that all of Sam's troubles are because of me?"

"I'm saying things could be improved. 'The best we can do.' Just don't use that phrase."

"You're all the same."

"Who?"

"The French. So damn certain of yourselves. Cartesian. You're drowning in logic. What would dinners with your mother accomplish? We're enemies! I stole her son. What would united summer vacations do for Sam's outlook? My brother is missing. My mother is a religious fanatic and my father is hiding out in a grove of trees. What good will it do?"

The spot of ketchup has begun, grotesquely, to expand.

"You can put a tomato plant out in a patch of bad soil. If there is sunshine and enough water, it will grow. But turn the soil about, spread fertilizer on it and water it generously. You get tomatoes from both plants. They'll both yield. You know the difference in the results as well as I do."

"Good. Agronomy. We're not at work on a vegetable patch. We're trying to raise a little boy."

"Don't complicate what is simple. And don't lie. Just don't lie, Lucy. We're not giving our son a rich life and it's beginning to show."

He stands up to go.

"Oh! Hang on a second."

"What's wrong now?"

"You forgot to take your tray."

"As usual, you have it backwards. *They* forgot to take my tray."

The Bluebird or Campfire Girl always resurfaces at times like this. I take my tray dutifully to the designated area and glance back at our table, messy now only on one side.

"I don't see why you just don't follow the rules. I mean it. Cleaning up after yourself in a fast food joint, not littering, for God's sake. Standing on line. These are the only moral imperatives we have left. Marc. I'm assaulting your character. You could at least pay attention."

He isn't. He has entered still another combat zone and is bickering with a black African a few steps ahead.

"You're very tiring, Lucy."

"Maybe. I'm also right. It's so much easier to just follow the rules."

"You follow your rules and I'll follow mine. I spend a word or two on Sam and you become hysterical."

The African has marked us as tourists, for some reason. He suggests an ivory bracelet, hand-carved by a hungry mother in Africa. If not that, then, a handsome men's watch in real gold that is completely shock-resistant. Then he just offers to take our picture for twenty francs. He is persuaded we've just come from some other place.

"I do speak English, you know. You wouldn't be dragging around a dumb, silent tourist."

"You speak tea cozies and summers in England. You're a shining example of bilingual pilot schools. But it doesn't apply there."

"Are you referring to deepest, darkest Africa or your own Oklahoma?"

"Very funny. You're going to be late."

"Je m'en fiche."

Our postman is eating lunch by the pool. The checkerboard is gone. He seems to be wearing a crown of laurels, though it's only what's left of his hair, clipped into the soft shapes of leaves. He hands me a box marked with Sam's name. Ordinarily he should leave me a slip saying I have received a package. The trade-off for this first-class service is apparently a poolside lunch. I stare at the box.

"Qu'est-ce que tu as?"

"Rien. Tu prends un café?"

I make him coffee and watch as Madame Leconte scares off some birds from where they roost on her roof. They have an eye on her ripening tomatoes. They rise suddenly in a black cloud and whirl overhead for several seconds, seeking direction. Finally a leader emerges and they set off toward the village.

The postman chatters about the Sting concert in Paris and I pretend to listen. He glances at his watch and rinses his face with water from the pool. He asks me if I wouldn't mind throwing away a stack of flyers advertising a fitness club. The flyers show a muscle man hoisting weights with a good deal of effort. He is surrounded by topless admirers on a sunny beach. Some of the women clap with joy. When the postman pulls on his cap, the crown of laurels is hidden. With the hat on he looks like any other compliant, good-natured postal worker. When he's gone I set to work on the box. I'm not mistaken about the handwriting. It's from Cody. He's written out Sam's name with a blotchy blue pen. Inside is a robot. Or an airplane. It might be both. I read the print on the box.

> IT IS A DANGEROUS WORLD. THINGS ARE NOT AS THEY SEEM. JOIN THE ROBOTECH TEAM. AT ANY GIVEN MOMENT YOUR ROBOTECH CAN CHANGE, BECOMING A TRADITIONAL ROBOT WITH A FIRST-RATE DEFENSE SYSTEM. PULL YOUR ROBOTECH INTO PHASE TWO POSITION AND TAKE CONTROL OF YOUR MISSILE-FIRING ACTOJET. THE CHOICE IS UP TO YOU. TRANSFORM YOUR WORLD ACCORDING TO YOUR PERSONAL DEFENSE NEEDS.

The price tag, half on and half off, comes from a big toy outlet that could be anyplace at all. There is no return address, but a post office stamp reads 'Biloxi, Mississippi.' There is a letter inside the package written on the back of a piece of gift wrap. There are smudges all over it, as if from a sheet of carbon paper. There is no Dear Lucy. It just starts out, as if it completes a conversation Cody and I have already begun.

And so here I am. I wonder if Sam has any of these Robotechs. I put myself in his shoes to buy this thing, but since I'm out of contact with little boys, I wonder if I've made the right decision.

I am trying to reestablish contact with my girls but dialogue is difficult at present.

I have had my highs and lows since you last saw me. I plan to return to Oklahoma in the next year. Right now there is no exact place where you could reach me.

May the Lord's blessings be with you. My best to your family.

Once Ella and Cody and I were sitting in the sun-room the Tuck boys added on in 1949. It was the last thing they could think of to do to the house and it just clung to the third story like a parasite. In the winter it was pleasant to sit there, for it was essentially three big plates of glass that seemed part of the sky. My aunt wallpapered the ceiling with something meant to imply a thatch hut. Bits of straw were always dropping down from the ceiling. Churchy vacuumed laboriously up there, predicting doom.

"This room gone go up in smoke one day. This room here is the end of the line."

There wasn't much to do up there. The warm sun put you to sleep as soon as you opened a book. There was a radio, but the antenna was broken and the only station you got was country. The day I remember was a Sunday. The funnies were strewn all over the floor and Ella and I were fighting about the crossword puzzle. Then one of the dogs we had up there bit into a lamp cord. We were sure the animal was dying, though it was dying without a sound. It backed around and around in circles, with its jaws open as if it were choking on a piece of gristle that wouldn't go up or down. Ella's screams filled the whole room and part of the sky that seemed in there with us. I couldn't speak or move or do anything but look. It was Cody who grabbed Ella and got her to stop. He yanked her hair once and in her surprise she stopped screeching. Then he caught the dog by its hind legs and held it until it stopped trembling and flapping its jaws. The dog was still for a minute in his arms and seemed calm. Two days later it ran off howling and never did come back. I don't know why I should think of that awful day now.

12

We are trying to manage lunch. But it's warmer outside than anyone suspected and the insects have joined forces against us. There is also the disturbing sight of Sam lying face down in a flowerbed.

"Lève-toi. C'est pas très malin. Debout!"

"Oh, Sam! Ça suffit. Get up this minute."

Eliot and Marie-France have no children. Sam is their drawing board. The theories sink or swim with him. Sometimes they keep him for the weekend. He is unused to a small apartment and at the end of his visit they look pale and exhausted. Months will pass before they try to conceive another child again, Marie-France swallowing gallons of an alleged fertility potion made up for her by a herbologist in Toulouse. Playing dead began in their apartment several months ago. When Sam discovered he could create such a furor by lying contorted on the ground by an open window or in a heap at the bottom of the stairs, he turned playing dead into a kind of art form.

"Look at us. This is exactly what he wants. Let's back off

and play it cool. Finish lunch, for instance."

We cast a last look at Sam, who's flung himself into the pansies alongside the garage.

"Pity about the pansies, though. That boy of yours."

Most of the food is left to the fat black flies who walk untroubled across our plates. We exchange theories about five-year-olds and nibble at the raw vegetables that are fast drying out in the sun.

"A bid for your attention."

"He has our attention. Most of the time it's undivided. I don't buy it. Sometimes he lies there so long, he just falls asleep right where he is. The last time he pulled this—remember, Marc?"

"She called me at work. Hysterical. He was curled around the base of the olive tree."

"They do this at school. It's a very big game right now for little boys. He's just carrying it a little further."

"Maybe this is some kind of depression."

"Eliot! My God, he's five years old."

"Depression is not strictly limited to those over thirty, or haven't you heard. You're intelligent, Lucy, but not highly évoluée. Which continues to be a problem in the way you handle Sam."

"It's a game about control."

"Could be. But don't discount what I said about depression. As embarrassing as it may be, your son could be asking for help."

From the kitchen window I watch Marie-France lift Sam off the ground to pick a ripe fig from a tree. She lifts him bent-kneed, her muscled thighs taking the brunt of his weight. She grew up in Marseille and has wide arms from a life of hoisting sails and scrubbing down ship decks. Her father ran a charter boat business and tried, unsuccessfully, to put her in a convent school in Aix when she reached adolescence. She howled so, put up such a brawl, he was summoned to the school and Marie-France remained on board, picking up a sketchy education in the public schools around the port. Sam nuzzles her and they sit down in the gravel to begin construction of a feudal village. He is excited and decidedly alive again. He begins to collect plastic soldiers and horsemen that lie scattered near a sandpile. Eliot has followed me into the kitchen with a tray loaded with dirty glasses and empty bottles.

"More on Sam?"

"That's a subtle form of vanity, you know."

"Eliot, I love you dearly. But you wear me out."

"To assume you're the only one with problems is, I maintain, a form of vanity. A kind of self-centeredness. Lucy, I don't know who else to tell about this."

"About what? Tell me."

He turns to me in some anguish. He's brought over a copy of Graham Greene's *J'ACCUSE,* a quiet indictment of niçoise politics. It has disappeared from regional bookshelves and he has actually wrapped the little volume in brown paper. He looks over his shoulder as he hands it to me.

"Well, you know Mother is coming next week. This is really difficult for me. . . ."

"Go on."

"Could you talk to Marie-France about . . . or could you possibly lend her, uh? It's so hot and close in that apartment. With Mother sleeping on the daybed . . ."

"Antiperspirant? Eliot, could you possibly be talking about antiperspirant?"

I've met his parents at his bookstore, that peaceful little junction near the Anglican church in Nice. He had an open house for them last year. His mother is active in the Philadelphia DAR. Her father had once met Will Rogers, she told me brightly upon learning I was from Oklahoma.

"It's true, Eliot. I may not be terribly evolved, as you put it. But I know a wimp when I see one. This is unconscionable. Your wife's underarms are not your mother's business. If she's unhappy about French hygiene, put her up in a hotel. When are you going to stand up to your mother?"

Eliot sniffs, mutters a kind of apology and wanders off to find Marc. He will mope for a while, most likely, and hunt through his shelves until he can find something that applies. Some literary corridor that will connect the two conflicting elements in his life. The confusion of the unwitting expatriate sometimes tends to be the same. Eliot and I—sometimes even Chan—sensitive to booby traps in this unlikely life, pass solutions back and forth as eagerly as if these solutions were the water of Lourdes.

Many of our conferences about Sam take place at night, by his bedside as he sleeps. When he was younger, I used to crawl in beside him to contract a little of his untroubled sleep. No more. Recently, Marc and some friends built him a special sleeping unit, with a carefully disguised guardrail lest he consider the bed a crib. It is sturdy as a fortress. There are narrow slots for comic books and a special section for toys and clothing. Sam sleeps with robots now. There are four stationed at the foot of his bed and sometimes I have to rush in at night to shut them off, their arms and legs waving wildly. We have covered one wall with fluorescent stars and comets that glow softly in the dark. I open the door and find Marc already there, staring at the planets.

"Stargazing?"

"Comment?"

"Tu regardes les étoiles?"

"Notre fils, plutôt."

"Did you finish those prints?"

"I couldn't concentrate. Après."

We listen to him breathe for a while. He sleeps belly up for the moment, with his chin tipped to one side. An arm shoots out suddenly and he rolls to the side of the bed, as if dodging a punch.

"You worried?"

"Putain. Playing dead. Qu'est-ce que ça veut dire? I never did that when I was a child."

"Who says? We never remember ourselves accurately."

"My mother remembers for me. I never played dead."

"Let's get some sleep."

In this thick-stone echo chamber that is our bedroom Marc's breathing rises and falls miles off. Though we're lying down side by side we could be divided by a transcontinental highway.

La Belle Eléna is like a crumbling bulwark, full of faults and fissures, a misleading sonority. I toss and turn, finally jamming my clock in a drawer to muffle its ticking. By one in the morning it has become as imperious as Big Ben.

Sleepy-eyed representatives of three generations are standing together in the shower stall. It's barely 7:30 A.M. Sam, still in pajamas, stands between Marc and my father-in-law, Sauveur, with a bit of pant leg in his fist. Maintenance problems here tend to fall into two categories: mortal and minor. The presence of an electrician near a water source at such an early hour suggests this is a problem of the first degree. I yank Sam out of the shower stall and smile at Marc's father.

"Petit déjeuner sous la douche? Bonjour, Sauveur."

"Maman! Devine! Il ne faut pas se laver. C'est très, très dangereux."

"Marc! Comment ca se fait?"

"Un truc à régler. Tu nous fais un café?"

"And just how am I supposed to make a coffee?"

"Vittel pour le moment."

I work alongside Sam, who prepares his grandfather's tartine all by himself. By the time coffee is ready a solution is at hand. Sauveur beams as he describes the adjustment he'll have to make. The need to eventually rewire—the whole house? I blink, thinking he's lost me on a technical detail.

"Bien sûr. Ils ont fait n'importe quoi ici. Vous risquez beaucoup. Heureusement je suis là. Vous faites un bon petit café, Lucy."

We take time having breakfast. Sauveur makes a list of intended modifications. Marc frowns and tells him how many units we've been given by the utilities company.

"Pas suffisant. Attention aux coupures de courant cet hiver."

The discussion escalates. They go on to discuss the heavy demand on the little electric heaters we've installed throughout the salon. The necessary energy cutbacks once the tourists flood in in the month of August. I serve Sauveur another coffee and Sam brings him a brioche, unevenly sliced in half and dripping with jam.

"Tout ça pour moi? Viens ici, toi."

"Et notre douche?"

"Vous pourrez la prendre ce matin. Tu viens me donner un coup de main, Sam? Il est temps de travailler."

The morning passes without further mishap. Sam tails Marc's father like a pup, whistling repeatedly the one note he has mastered. He proudly passes him tools from the shiny metal box. Was the faulty wiring in the house installed by one of Eléna's admirers or a handy customer short on cash when it came time to pay for a meal? I mull over the possibility of a long, damp winter spent wrapped in our overcoats. Sauveur emerges around noon and announces with a laugh that we can take a shower without fatal consequences. He steams ahead with further ideas for repair, and I should feel relieved, but I don't. I feel warned. In a jinxed house one problem usually signals another. I brace myself, figuring this won't be the end of it. It isn't. In this way, our next visitor's appearance has been heralded.

The man who steps off the train several days later is hot and weary. He swallows before he speaks and his voice breaks in the middle of his sentence. Marc doesn't have the heart to turn the man away. There is dust all over his shoes as if he's been walking a long time. He is not an old man. In fact, he was born in 1938. José, the grower of grapes and bottler of wine, is back, seeking Eléna. He nods his head slowly when I show him the empty bottle retrieved from the disordered grenier. He wears a light summer suit that has known many seasons. The lining has come loose from the jacket. That it droops out behind gives him the look of a bumbler. The kind of man who is sometimes the butt of practical jokes. He has a leather purse that hangs from a shoulder strap. He digs for a piece of paper and when he finds it at last, sighs with relief. It is not a love letter, but a lunch receipt. Ah, voilà! he cries upon finding evidence of another time, a decidedly different Belle Eléna. On the day in question José ate a roasted chicken, garnished with spring vegetables. For dessert Eléna prepared a clafoutis. Ostensibly the wine he drank was his own.

We seat him and explain Eléna's absence. I offer to prepare lunch but he isn't hungry. We repeat everything, uncertain whether the sudden lurch forward at the end of each bit of news is disbelief or deafness. When the chain of events is finally clear, he becomes distressed.

"Mais, Eléna?"

"On ne sait pas. Nous ne savons pas, Monsieur."

"Mais elle est toujours dans la région?"

"Nous ne savons pas. Désolés."

Clutching his bag tightly, José asks if he can see the house before leaving. Marc pushes past the cypress trees and holds a branch back for the man. The trees need cutting back. The two men stand together over the fissure on the terrace for several minutes and José measures the depth of the crack with a measuring tape he pulls from his sack. He shakes his head over some damaged tiles and, nearly beside himself, points to the bubbling earth outside the kitchen window, a sure sign that the septic tank is clogged again. I hear doors opening and closing inside the house, exclamations by the fireplace and then a lowering of voices as Marc and José return to where I'm standing by the barbecue preparing hamburgers for whoever will have them.

Marc takes the spatula from my hand and begins turning his hamburger.

"Aren't we nonchalant. What's going on?"

"I've asked him to stay."

"What?"

"Just until the house is in order."

"My house is in order. What do you mean by that?"

"I'm only talking about small repairs. He wants to do work before he goes back. Le pauvre type est fauché. His son went to work for Renault and the other is a chômeur. No one is left to work in the vineyard. I'm sorry for him. I think he spent everything to get down here to see Eléna."

"Brother."

"Comment?"

"You always accuse me of being so soft. You're a real bleeding heart. So where does our friend sleep?"

One thing we do have is bedrooms. Dusty and neglected, unheated in the winter. But bedrooms and a study that quick-changes for unexpected visitors we do have.

"This is not a mission."

"Five days. Five days and you get all the bushes cut back. He's got plans to organize a woodpile and move all the rubbish blocking the grenier."

"I don't care. We never use that space."

"He noticed the door that's mounted incorrectly in the hall. I showed him the radiator that doesn't work in the upstairs bedroom. He'll get the refrigerator to stop making noise and clear out the birds nesting in the chimney. He's a gentleman, Lucy. Sad gentlemen should not be turned away."

"Promise just five days. Odd. I always thought of Eléna's admirers as having big, suntanned chests draped with gold chains."

We explain the concept of the hamburger to José, whose appetite has returned. He seems bothered by the fact that you have to touch it to eat it. I wonder how such a dainty man will fix all that's going wrong at La Belle Eléna. I wonder if his wife is dead and how much his son earns at Renault. And if that suit of clothes is all he's brought with him. He draws a comb from his pocket frequently to smooth back his hair. He speaks when spoken to, like a child. He is so soft-spoken I hardly know there is a stranger in my house.

Reviving a memory, restoring a dream is work that takes place out of time. José's steady pace was hysteria, thinly disguised. When he rose at seven o'clock it was already too late. He would drink his coffee standing at the kitchen sink, not having the time to dawdle with the rest of us. We begged him to take meals with us before they got cold or lost their flavor. He sat through it politely, wishing he were elsewhere, mixing cement or bracing a heavy tree limb that, unsupported, dipped lower and lower each year. Every day his desperation increased. His love for Eléna was manifest in the work he fought to complete but the object of his love was far from him in an unknown place. She could be suffering in some cold, wet climate. How she hated the cold, he confided in me one day.

When winter set in she suffered from crying spells and cruel moods. He showed Sam tiny catprints in the tile hidden under the stone bench in the entry hall. He bent to show him where the mason had signed his name in the fireplace, perhaps overcome by the beauty of his own work. He showed me how I could swiftly organize a meal for fifty on the barbecue, reciting meals past and how Eléna cooked and served as her happy guests looked on. He mopped his forehead steadily with a handkerchief doused with cologne and washed his hands outside at the completion of each task. Eléna's husband was never mentioned in the stories, never implied. Any brawls or drunken scenes had long since slipped beneath the surface of things. What remained was a string of untarnished events lustrous as a strand of pearls. The only time panic about finishing the work diminished was when José could actually speak of her and special Carnaval dinners she served, the masks and the music. Or the way she encouraged dancing and singing on warm evenings. Once he, José, had danced with a famous chiropractor's wife. It was August 1959. That kind of social democracy only existed in dreams. Eléna!

José made a dramatic discovery four days after he arrived. Les odeurs, he would mumble, checking our septic tank system for the second time. He began asking questions about the property backing the Belle Eléna. I explained that the unsightly briar patch belonged to an avaricious young woman from Cannes. She wanted a maison de campagne alright, but had refused to participate when neighbors undertook private roadbuilding some years back. Property owners gradually choked her with the construction of two new houses. Now that she had no access to her own property, she made no effort to maintain it. It was impenetrable. José borrowed some fishing boots from Marc and waded in slowly, sniffing more fiercely than a bloodhound.

He returned around lunchtime, shaking his head. A wily neighbor had been quietly routing his sewage into the property for years. He had concocted a discreet sort of Alaskan Pipeline that disgorged its contents practically at our feet. Kind Raphael was the perpetrator. He offered Sam bubble gum from a blue glass candy bowl at every occasion. It seemed impossible. All this was hidden under a thorny blanket of yellow brush and dying apple trees.

"Quel malin. Il a dû faire ça il y a trente ans."

The presence of embarrassing odors was explained, if not rectified. If we wanted to complain to the proper authorities, it meant a tangle of red tape, numerous encounters with the unsmiling staff at the mayor's office. I thanked him for his persistence and he went on to other things—caulking for a series of shabby pipes. The investigation of tiny, precise mounds of dust under a wooden beam that could signify termites.

Before he left, he produced the birds' nests he had dug out of eaves and inside the chimney. There were three of them, lice-free and tightly constructed. He lined them up on Sam's windowsill, just as he had done for Eléna's boys, and filled them each with a round, pink stone that seemed a perfect egg. His promise came true. Two weeks after he was gone, a merle did come to peck on the window, dead set on having those eggs. Whether the bird was a bereaved mother or simply curious, we never knew. She fussed and hammered on Sam's window until her presence became a nuisance. We put them on a shelf instead and they're still there, sharing space with a wooden Pinocchio and flag-bearing soldiers from seven nations.

13

When Marc was ten years old a disconcerting discovery was made. He broke an ankle in a fall, and because of his behavior in the clinic, the doctor mentioned to my mother-in-law that her son clearly had no threshold for pain. This straightforward, medical proof of an intolerance for pain marked his youth. Rough sports were not encouraged. He developed a wide range of board game skills—attentiveness, a shrewd willingness to sit tight and play his cards while his partner lost patience and grew bumptious, knocking over glasses of grenadine syrup and water Martine would serve to young guests. Any grimace indicating physical discomfort was a harbinger of drastic importance. The doctor's offhand remark became a document my mother-in-law used throughout Marc's growing-up years. It gave rise to a sensational amount of hocus-pocus.

"Marc, you're being ridiculous."

"Fais ce que je te dis."

"C'est ridicule. I'm calling a doctor."

"Va voir Maman."

Maman.

"You have a simple stomach virus. Aren't you ashamed of yourself? Sam has more courage than you do at the moment."

Marc turns his head on the pillow and I see the case is closed. When he turns his profile to me there is no further discussion. I read that African royals used to do that before the continent sank into uprisings and internal disorder. In a gesture loaded with presence and power, they simply turned their heads to display their profiles. An olive-tree branch drags back and forth against the window. For a while that's the only sound in the room, the leafy drag on the window and the bursts of sound coming from the wind.

"What should I ask for?"

"Just tell her it's my stomach. She'll propose something."

On the way over, I find it helps to think of the jeep we used to have before we settled into the conventional closed car we have now. Sam and friends had plastic telephones in the back. There was important chatter and singing wherever we went. At Christmas we decorated the inside of the jeep. Disapproving mothers melted when they saw me drive up for their children. A lot of what we did then was for effect. In a spasm of guilt we bought an ordinary car and strapped Sam into a seatbelt.

It can't be easy for Martine. If she stands outside on her balcony she can drink in the sight of the whole valley. She can see the house where her mother was born, now a storage space and garage surrounded by a carnation grower's greenhouses. She can also see the village cemetery. The tombstones stand as erect and pale as frightened young soldiers. Martine has known her husband since she was five years old. When we lived there and were still speaking, I would sometimes accept a cup of coffee from her when she hadn't slept well and couldn't burst off to market. She confessed that sometimes she woke at night unable to breathe. I always thought those periodic struggles with asthma came from a life too tightly circumscribed.

The house is not visible from the road. Visitors are heard before they are seen as tires bump over the grate at the entry. An odd thing happens as soon as the grate bangs. If she is not in the garden, I can see my mother-in-law streak past one of the five windows fronting the house. I've often wondered about this. Maybe she sits around without her wig, comfortable at long last. It happens again today. I spot a dark blur upstairs that is my mother-in-law rushing by.

There is no portcullis, that sliding grill of iron you see in medieval fortified palaces, but there is a small square carved into her oak door, covered with a metal plaque for a modern measure of protection. I've opened this myself and it's a remarkable thing. You're not unobserved, as with a peephole, nor are you completely exposed. Quickly opened it allows a sudden blast of whatever's out there. You feel a swift rise or fall in temperature, maybe the sight and smell of red roses someone's kindly thought to bring. Today it's me. I knock and hold Sam up in front of the little door so Martine won't open fire.

She is not the first one to speak.

"Coucou, Martine. Dis bonjour, Sam."

"Coucou. Ouvre la porte. Tu ne vois pas que c'est moi?"

The door opens, only because it absolutely must. I stand outside and wait to be invited over the threshold. I can't remember what our last words were, but I think it wasn't the sort of conversation you can, in any way, retrieve.

"Martine, Marc est *gravement* malade."

I add gravement as good measure. She bites the inside of her lip and considers.

"Vous devez faire quelque chose."

"Qu'avez-vous mangé?"

"Rien d'extraordinaire. Mais je vais vous le dire et vous pourrez décider."

The studiousness suits her. She frowns and massages her forehead in concern as I tick off the things we've eaten recently. Salad last night. With garlic? She spits out possibilities —moules, porc? We reconstruct everything consumed over the past three days. She offers me a chair and Sam follows her to the kitchen, where she begins concocting. Of Martine's brand of doctoring I know very little. Many remedies are family-held secrets that I didn't prove worthy of knowing. She is not long in the kitchen. She looks self-satisfied and Sam's holding her potion in his hands. It's contained in an old jelly jar. The label,

Bonne Maman, is still very much intact. Sam shakes it repeatedly and peers at the swirling liquid. He has several plastic paperweights in his room and he might be hoping to catch sight of a cheery Père Noël or Florida Sunshine billboard once the motion subsides.

"Quatre fois par jour, Lucy. Du pain sec. Que du pain sec."

"Et à boire?"

"Faites cuire du riz. Jetez-le et donnez l'eau de cuisson. Le mal sera passé après-demain au plus tard."

We shake hands and she bends to kiss Sam. Two of her buttons are undone at the back of the dress.

"Vous n'avez rien oublié, Lucy?"

"Non, non. Merci encore, Martine. Je vous dis ça du fond du coeur."

She watches as we trundle off, and I can feel her sizing up my hairstyle and the cut of my pants. Sam is freshly bathed and his hair gleams as the sun strikes his head. I wonder on the way back if that's how old warriors operate. Peace could well begin with a long, sidewise glance at a shining metal breastplate or a string of wooden beads.

Marc's mother has chosen metal plaques, iron grates that announce the presence of an outsider with a bang. She lives her life behind bars. And my mother? Hardly. I rarely bother to call, for she's almost never home. The recording on her answering machine is simple. THIS IS AGNES LERNER. I AM OUT. The caller is not invited to leave his name or number. Perhaps this reflects her impatience with such a gadget in the first place.

Instead she phones now from public pay phones. I think this is because of my father's successful tree project, though I don't mention it. All the telephone jacks in our house are at the back of the house. This is no oversight. It has something to do with her scorn for people who spend time talking on the phone. She keeps a plastic timer in a kitchen drawer by the wall phone. Her friends don't know about the red plastic timer. They just assume Agnes Lerner is a mighty busy woman. But now, standing in the kitchen or one of the back bedrooms, the eye is logically drawn to the window and the seductive line of oaks. Children of every shape and size dangle from the limbs or lounge on circular platforms. They holler. They make bets and wage child wars. Sometimes at lunchtime, one will slip past a monitor and knock on my mother's back door, asking for the mayonnaise their own mother forgot to spread on a dry ham sandwich, or a cookie. There is no compunction in these requests. They stare balefully at her, spreading the sandwich open as living proof of the forgetful nature of all mothers. Her voice is tinny over these pay phones, but I don't mind. It's like a call from a roving reporter. She never frequents the same booth and begins every conversation now with a view from where she happens to be.

"Lucy, it's me. I thought I'd phone from a pay booth to save us both some time."

"Hi, Mom. How does this save me time?"

"Well, not you exactly. You'll never guess what's going on here. A group of heart patients is walking the mall. That's what they do for exercise. A whole bunch of people, too. They walk briskly. You just ought to see. Around and around."

"How are you, Mom?"

"I am just fine. Of course, I—can you hear me?"

"Sure. Go on."

"I wanted to phone before I left."

"Where are you off to now?"

"To California. I'm going out to California for a couple of weeks. Your father is not joining me."

"A singles vacation?"

"A pilgrimage. I'm going out to see the Crystal Cathedral for myself. I'm not traveling alone, of course. Your aunt has asked me to take Ella along."

"A quick change of venue. What did Ella pull this time?"

"It was insignificant, really. A small episode with some construction workers. They certainly baited the wrong young lady. Sadie feels a little trip might be restorative. There are quite a few spiritual shareholders in town and we—"

"Whoa. A spiritual what?"

"Shareholder. People who follow Schuller and give to his

church. We've organized a charter bus. I had thought I'd wait for the Leadership Training Center to be built. But I feel the need to go on out now. Lucky me. We've got forty-five members of the Eagle Club alone who are as anxious as I am to actually see the Crystal Cathedral."

"You want to tell me about the Eagle Club?"

"People who give five hundred dollars during the calendar year. Awfully good people. I guess that's not why I'm calling, though."

"Do you feed coins into the machine?"

"Credit card call. You all don't have that there? I'm calling, I suppose, because of your brother."

The rise and fall in her voice is muted because of the acoustics in the pay phone, but I can still hear the slight catch on the word brother.

"Has he been in touch with you?"

"Yes. He sent Sam a wonderful toy. A nice note to me, too. Vague, but nice."

"Phase one is toys. Don't fall for it, Lucy. Becky and I have spoken about this onslaught of gifts. Because of your brother's stealth Becky has not been able to stem this flood of things as she would like. He sends packages to their friends so they waltz in at odd hours with Cody's presents. He thinks of everything. Even payola for the gift-bearers. Wristwatches and expensive trinkets to insure fidelity and continued service. Too much, as I have already told Becky. My son is too much. Not that there is any risk, because Becky wouldn't let him step in the house."

"You mean Chico wouldn't let him in. New rooster ruling the roost I hear. And the new one sounds pretty possessive, the way Becky talks."

"I don't ask questions. Becky's life is her own and more power to her, I say. I am only telling you this because I want you to be on your guard. Your brother is sniffing around after all this time. He wants back in the flock. That much is clear. And after all the damage and heartache he's caused."

"So you advise me to harden my heart against my brother."

"That is not what I said. Please do not distort what I said."

"Be on guard."

"It's easy enough to play poor me until everyone forgets what happened and life just picks up where it left off. Easy."

"Mom? Have a wonderful time in California. Really. Gifts of the spirit. Why doesn't Dad go with you? Women only?"

"Hardly. As soon as I mention Bob Schuller, your father—you'd think he was jealous. You know, these heart patients are picking up followers. Now it's not only heart patients. It's children and old folks. I see some obese individuals now walking the mall. That's something to remember. How one small group of people can generate something much bigger. Oh, I'd estimate there are fifty people circling the mall. Do you have dates out there, Lucy?"

"Dates? Yes. From Tunisia."

"I thought I might just send out a package of California dates. I'll have to think of something else. . . . Kiss Sam for me. Tell Marc bunjer for me."

"Bunjer?"

"Hello in French. Tell him his mother-in-law says bunjer."

I know a woman who lives in Venice. Her vision of the apocalypse is not the city sinking finally into the Adriatic, but rather a Venice completely covered with abandoned shopping carts. Here is a vision to equal her own: the ailing, the aged and the overweight mindlessly circling shopping malls, picking up silent recruits as they continue walking.

She calls several weeks later.

"Lucy? I'm calling from a public phone in Garden Grove, California."

"You made it! Where are you standing? In a mall again?"

"I am standing in the parking lot of a Taco Bueno. But not at all like the Taco Bueno at home. There is bougainvillea in full bloom and you eat your taco in a trellised garden terrace. Lucy, I have seen the San Bernadino mountains. The tops were snow-covered. But of course I knew they would be."

"And the weather?"

"Bliss. But of course I knew it would be."

"You're sounding beatific, Mom."

"And why not? That's the title of his latest book. Or almost. It's called *The Be (Happy) Attitudes*. Am I taking you away from something important?"

"Not at all. Go on."

"Not only have we been able to visit the Crystal Cathedral and the facilities here. Once Bob Schuller learned a group of shareholders was on its way, he arranged for a meeting with us. Imagine a man like that putting things on hold for a bunch of people from Oklahoma."

"What shouldn't he? People from Oklahoma, people from Idaho and Iowa and Kentucky are what keeps the Cathedral afloat. I read in that pamphlet you sent me—what was it? Fifteen million dollars in airtime alone in 1985."

"I want to put aside that kind of discussion for the moment, Lucy. Money matters, naturally, but there's something else. Something important I'd forgotten about Bob Schuller."

"What's that?"

"That he ministers. That his primary skill is still the ministry. He autographed my books for me and I said with my heart in my throat, 'Bob Schuller, can I have a private moment with you while I'm here in Garden Grove?' And, Lucy, he found twenty minutes for me. On January twenty-first at two-thirty he found twenty minutes for Agnes Lerner. And he opened my eyes to many things. We spoke primarily of brownouts."

"You and Robert Schuller discussed electricity?"

"Emotional power failures. You can blow a fuse anytime, anyplace. It could happen to you and it's important to know the difference between a burnout and a brownout. The two are not to be confused. With God and prayer you can be immune to burnouts. A burnout, according to Bob, is a permanent resignation. A brownout, however, is a temporary shortage of energy. Lucy, the lights can come back on in your home if God is present. Lucy?"

"I'm listening, Mom. I just—"

"What Bob and I managed to put together in our talk is that I'm in an arresting phase in my faith. Which is probably why I felt this urgent need to *get to Garden Grove*. There's been nesting, testing, investing alright. And here, sure enough, comes the arresting, which if I hadn't caught it in time could have hung me up for good."

"You know, this is so methodical. Do you really think—"

"Let me finish, Lucy. This arresting phase is crucial. Do you quit or give up? Keep that measure of faith or let go? Bob convinced me to move through this arresting phase, to just grit my teeth and pass through this trial in my faith until I get to the cresting phase. That place where your faith is rewarded. Where the sun shines."

"Did Schuller spend time with Ella?"

"Ah, Ella. Well, that didn't quite . . . your cousin didn't make it out to California."

"What happened to her?"

"I called Sadie from Shamrock. She came on down to get her in a private plane. The trouble and the expense that girl puts her parents through is enough to make your head spin."

"You haven't explained what actually happened."

"It's what stopped happening, Lucy. I sometimes wonder if it isn't simple belligerence in that girl. One minute she's photographing migrating armadillos, the next minute she's totally immobilized. That old respiratory rigamarole."

"She had one of her asthma attacks, then."

"If you like. In, out, in, out. What could be simpler than just breathing? No, her asthma is a pretext. I say Ella's mad as all get-out at someone, but you know your aunt. She would never accept that kind of hostility in her own daughter. What were you doing when I called?"

"Planting bulbs. Better late than never."

"They'll want a cold snap."

"Don't worry. They'll get one."

"I love you, Lucy."

"I love you, too. I'm glad you're having a good time."

"A good time. Well, I hadn't thought of it quite that way. But I certainly am. Sometimes I think I could spend the rest of my life this way. Traveling on buses and crossing towns at night. Sharing experiences with others."

I get back to work and wonder what these midwinter plantings will give. The earth is packed and muddy after several days of rain.

"I'm not sure I believe in optimal conditions. Do your best, you guys."

I'm always at a loss as to what to actually say to plants, though everyone concludes they respond to human speech. It's as absurd and essential as talking to babies. I find myself excusing circumstances (inadequate sunlight or poor soil) and explaining, when it's possible, why things aren't going to be smoother for them. The important thing is to keep up the babble.

Sometimes I pick Sam up early. I like to do this, jamming my pockets with cookies and cars, then swinging by for him. It's like springing an inmate. From four o'clock to four-fifteen is Le Silence. This is a difficult time for him so I bail him out when I can. During this period of silence the children sit in two long rows, cross-legged on the floor, and are forbidden to speak or move. There is fifteen minutes of this every day. They call in an assistant and the teachers slip out in the court to smoke a Gauloise. One of the teachers has long, black hair. The others weave her hair into a thick tress as she tells long, convoluted tales about the Canadian French. Croyez-moi, she says. Ce sont des cochons. She issues this testimony from the depths of a miserable three years spent in Quebec.

"Sam!" I hiss as soon as I get him out of the building. "Let's go to the ocean!"

"Pour de vrai? On ne fait pas de courses?"

"No errands, sweetheart. Let's go look at big boats."

Marie-France has told Sam that when he is eight he can sail with her to Corsica. She drew this number out of a hat, I think. Each time we are in a marina, he reminds me of her promise and describes the voyage in great detail, as a way of stilling his fears. He knows that the crossing requires sleeping one night on the sea. It must be very black, he tells me. Not that kind of black, he insists, pointing at my pants or a cat or the thick letters on a billboard advertising a residential community. Plus noir que ce noir, he repeats, his eyes very large.

Clotheslines are strung on the decks of certain boats, shirts and shorts flapping wildly in the breeze. Music blares from the cabins and men and women work in T-shirts and jeans. On other boats we see stewards in white jackets serving wine or pouring coffee. There are bouquets of flowers on these boats that say *Cape Horn* or *London*. Some of the boats seem to have developed genders that respond to their names. There is *My Love*, for instance, with cabin windows cut in multifoil design. The banner **Mike** hangs from a streamlined boat, outfitted with only the barest essentials.

"Maman, il se trouve que tu n'es qu'une molécule. Enfin, beaucoup de molécules."

Sam has just learned about molecules. In this case molecules undermine just about everything.

"Well, I'm made up of molecules. But not only molecules. Un être humain, c'est beaucoup plus que ça."

"Et une molécule, c'est invisible. Une chose qu'on ne peut ni toucher ni voir."

"Oui."

"Je te vois."

"Oui."

"Je te touche."

"Eh bien, oui."

"Je trouve que d'être une molécule, c'est con."

One of his shoelaces has come undone and I stop to retie it. Sam's dark thoughts concerning physics lead to equally gloomy conclusions about geography. We walk the jetty all the way out.

"Tu m'as dit que l'Angleterre, c'est par là-bas."

He points in the general direction of England and I nod.

"Et aussi que la Corse, c'est par là."

"Right."

"Tu les vois, Maman?"

"Non."

"Comment le sais-tu?"

"I just know from looking at maps. D'après les cartes."

There is a gathering of cats at the end of the jetty. An old woman operates several fishing lines. She tests the tautness of her lines with a forefinger, then returns to the cats which are mewling and batting empty tin plates with their paws. Sam watches for a while, then pulls me down beside him on a wide, flat rock.

"Je vais te dire une chose. Entre ici et la Corse il existe une île inconnue. Avec des gens très sauvages et très vicieux."

Sam goes on to describe a terrible island on the way to Corsica where people fight all day long. Their swords are made of steel and since all they do is wage war, there are no tourists on the island. The community bears an uncanny resemblance to the scattered facts he has picked up about our predecessors, les hommes préhistoriques. He looks as if he's been sentenced to the gallows.

"What a miserable island, Sam. What an awful, unhappy place. Mais, attention. Quand on fait le passage la nuit, on doit certainement la cogner. You might just run into that place on your way to Corsica."

"C'est ça."

Tears are near. He opens and closes his fist several times and studies his feet, then the cats which are feeding now. Anything but the wide blue sea.

"I can't let you go on the trip, Sam. Je parlerai avec Marie-France. Désolé, mon lapin."

We finish our walk in peace, Sam hugging my leg occasionally. Seeing the lamps rock gently inside the ship cabins, he speaks suddenly and with great longing, of home. He tips his head back and sings.

When we get back, Marc is packing suitcases with scissors and wireframed sunglasses, metal cups and every screwdriver we have in the house. He packs them carefully, in rows, as if each of these mundane objects had an inordinately high value. He separates them with rows of cardboard and tissue paper. Dissatisfied, he takes them all out of the bag and starts again. The suitcases are worn and scuffed. He stops and scratches his head in agitation.

"A few weeks ago my mother said to tell you bunjer. I forgot until just now."

"Comment?"

"Agnes said to tell you bunjer, which is Oklahoman for bonjour."

"Lucy, tu n'as pas un peigne?"

I draw a metal comb out of my purse. It's a long-handled comb that ends in a metal point. I've often thought it would make an excellent weapon in case of attack.

"Marc?"

He wedges the comb decisively between a steel mousetrap and a pair of pliers.

"What on earth are you doing?"

"Arché is going to x-ray it all. We'll do it Sunday when nobody's there. Then I'll see if I can pull a clean photograph from it."

"Then?"

"I don't know. I want to see if the image is as crisp as what you see on the screen at the airport. This is for me, not the *Nice-Matin*. I can't stop thinking about it."

"Why Arché? He's completely crazy."

"C'est un marginal. Crazy men are not partners in x-ray laboratories."

A poet steeped in the tradition of Rimbaud, Arché pastes up his poems inside the public shelters meant to protect bus riders. He is meticulous with his poems, spending weeks on each stanza. He always pastes a blank sheet of paper next to his poems, for comments. The comments range from scathing to banal. His public wonders why his poems contain no color and why he talks so much about flies. Others, the offended ones, tear his poems off the wall and write *Merde!* and *Quelle Ordure!* on the blank paper provided. Arché wonders over these comments and returns sadly to work Monday morning. He writes for his public. Sans public, je suis un zéro.

Arché collects damaged surgical equipment as a hobby. Perhaps he could be an ideal collaborator. I've been wrong before. Marc draws a dull scalpel from his pocket to show Sam, thus launching an energetic chat about dissection. The same scalpel is later featured in a photo Sam tapes on the wall next to his bed. Suspended inside a filmy block and sharing space with a compression coil, the scalpel seems toylike and quizzical.

Under Miss Manotte's patronage, Marc has become a member of the airport underground. The Chef de Service offers him a rough handshake and claps him on the back. He is on excellent terms with the customs agents and was one of the first to know, in 1978, that a major personnel change was in the wind for the staff at Hertz. Marc can now read an airport security pattern like the lines on the palm of a hand. Key members of the police force call him by his first name. They see him standing off to one side of the x-ray machine used to check baggage for hidden weapons or explosives, and look the other way. They understand, from what Hélène Manotte has kindly explained, that with his wife and young son airborne again, this is a young man in strictest mourning. They don't dare run him off.

He doesn't remember now what caught his attention about the images that came up on the screen or why he continued to think about them. The clarity of the forms, he thinks. And then their frivolity. The hidden life in the suitcases slowly seduced him—hair rollers and all kinds of beauty aids for the women, what a child judged to be essential for a long trip. All the garbled paraphernalia travel implied. He knew just when to retreat. He stood staring eight to ten minutes and then retired to the airport bar or the men's room, where he would mark down a juxtaposition of junk that pleased him. A spray of paper clips scattered in a plastic sack. To the side he inserted a question mark. It could have been a magnet game for the little girl tugging on the woman's hand. A box of fishing tackle. He leaned closer and withdrew. Longer than ten minutes and someone would complain to the sleepy security guard.

They lie stacked in the darkroom for several weeks and then he runs out of space.

"Lucy, would you mind if we put them in the salon?"

"Wherever you want them."

It's finally clear just who's living here. The pictures go up all over the place. They become slowly less facetious, and more singular. A few of Arché's limp poems also appear. Things continually turn up missing now and I'm reminded of Ella's pet racoon. This was supposed to be therapeutic but the racoon was a scoundrel and the whole thing backfired. A treasure trove was discovered in his backyard cage. One of my aunt's dinner rings. A whole set of garage keys and a few cast-off horseshoes. Marc's inventory is as varied as that dead racoon's.

It is decided that Marc must have a show. Chan's gallery is open and plunging along on Arab cash. Her ideas now pass as expertise. Eliot, erudite in such matters, grows whiny and insistent the more Marc retreats. There's something wrong, too formal in this. We circle the living room with drinks in our hands and every remark is more self-conscious than the next.

"Soyez pas ridicule."

"No one is being ridiculous. These pictures are good enough to be seen and should be seen. They're not doing you any good propped up against the walls of your home. What are you so nervous about?"

"I've asked him the same thing, Eliot. You ought to see how he hustles his work otherwise. The way he heckled that woman with *Paris Match*. He knows no shame. Yet now, when he really has something . . ."

"They're not derivative."

"For God's sake, Chan."

"I mean it, you-all. Somebody mentions derivative and it's the kiss of death. Afterwards, nobody's buying. I'd buy them myself, but my clients aren't mature enough. If it's not real big or gold, they're not buying. Marc, what's this here? Looks like one of my dad's Black and Decker drill bits. Is there a subtext to all this, do you think?"

"This one here. Look at how the light fills out everything but that child's toy in the center. And this one. It contains all the stillness of a womb."

"Shows how much you know. A woman's insides roar, you fool. Bloodflow, heartbeat. Things."

"I am speaking of a quality of suspension, Chan. A figurative silence."

"Nom de Dieu."

Marc steps into a corner and presses the tips of his fingers to his forehead. He scratches the back of his head.

"We've made him nervous."

When he is exasperated, Eliot's diction becomes very Philadelphia. He prunes every word and tightens his lips around each sentence.

"I think there's something slightly *oily* about hiding talent when you're lucky enough to have it. Why are you insisting we stand around like this persuading you that you have it?"

"'It' is what?"

"'It' is what makes you something other than a staff photographer for a small-time newspaper. 'It' is a good idea, in this case, and the clean execution of that idea."

"Interesting that a professional photographer can still blush like a flattered schoolboy. Eliot, lay off."

Eliot hands me his empty glass for a refill and brushes back his longish hair with a world-weary, patrician sigh that dates all the way back to the American Revolution.

"Je cède. Marc, my friend, do what you like. What's this?"

"My father's wire gauge."

"Fabulous."

The vernissage takes place under a driving rain. Most of the guests don't seem to mind. There is shelter. There is animation, with several pretty women and lots of long-haired men who advance every sentence with "A mon avis." There is even wine, red or white. Marc's first show is at Galerie Quai Dix, near the train station. It is a very few steps to an actual quay and many of our guests are on their way somewhere or, indeed, have just returned. Chan is disappointed, though not surprised, that none of her fifty invited guests have turned up.

"Chan, they're not the type of people who would ever, under any circumstances, come to a train station. Except for deportation under a new regime."

"My champions of art. Shit. I'm so sorry, Lucy. Here was something I could finally do for you and nothing came of it."

"Your relationship with Médecin got us in here. You helped persuade Marc in the first place. Cheer up."

"Let's get security to help with the old guy over there. He's asleep or worse. I don't guess you die sitting up, do you? Lord, he's slumped right over!"

"Don't bother about the guard. I'll go help him. Circulate, Chan. You're too glamorous to stand in one spot. Spread a little of that around."

I sit next to the man for a few minutes, thinking of what to tell him. His grip is still tight on a crumpled brown bag and a small valise that once moved on rolling wheels. As I begin to speak, he straightens suddenly, recovering some of his dignity. The general effect is of a little wooden toy, ordinarily in the form of a donkey or goat, that collapses at the press of a button, then reanimates stiffly when the button is released. He blinks quickly and I continue, explaining that my husband's photographs are being shown here. As the old man squints at the photo straight ahead, I explain what he is looking at. A valise, like his, filled with the stuff of travel. I offer a tentative profile of the traveler. A worrier—look at all the stuff he's included in case of disaster. Although the old man is unshaven, he has certain ideas about elegance. He's wearing three silk scarves, two knotted at his neck and a third acting as jaunty red pochette. He hugs his things tighter as I stand up and steer him to the door. The wheels on his valise are all broken and he holds it to his chest. He seems afraid someone will point a camera at his affairs and expose him, too.

"Do you get my drift? I'm not sure if you get my drift."

"Let me introduce you to my wife. Lucy, this is—"

"Arthur Glad. Lucy, pleased. Very pleased to meet you. I was just explaining to your husband my vision of how things ought to proceed from here on out. Trouble is, he's a modest guy and modest guys always have a tough time promoting themselves. Thank God, or I'd be out of business."

Arthur Glad looks like a seventeenth-century fop. He is wearing a burgundy velvet jacket with shiny black pants. The velvet jacket opens and closes with a system of yellow metal latches. The shoulder padding is worn and buckled and Arthur Glad's right shoulder rises higher than his left. The metal latches suggest he is hopelessly trapped inside this costume.

"I love American-French couples. They provide me with a lot of my business."

"What exactly is your business, Mr. Glad?"

"Art promoter. I know how to build interest in art. I know how to sculpt a career. I take the good and make it palatable to the public. The public doesn't know what to make of art without a context. As I see it, Lucy, we've got to take your husband on the road. This is a traveling show. I say, let's take it all the way."

"Could you be more explicit?"

"This—" Arthur sweeps his arm around in a scornful circle "—is a phony piece of shit. I mean all these *people* standing around making nothing pronouncements and drinking wine. In particular, the blond Chinese who claims to have a gallery on the Promenade."

"Careful, Arthur, she's a friend. All openings are the same. You can't do without a certain amount of baloney. A man in your line of work can accept that."

I try to lower the tone a bit as people begin to stare. Arthur has broken out in a light sweat and continues to talk. His hair falls in neat, long waves and he's put something on it that makes it glint like certain kinds of volcanic glass.

"That's just it. I can't. I can't accept any of it. If I had some kind of official mandate or something, you know what I'd do first off? I would detonate the museums and the tidy little galleries. I would bring the art into the street for people to touch and smell and feel. I would figure ways for all forms of viable art to move into the bloodstream. I'd get rid of the smoothies and the cool art-people. The only way to understand art is to mainline it!"

"Marc?"

He has winced at Arthur Glad's last proposal and touches his eye.

"What do you suggest for us, then? Could you get back to your vision about my work?"

Arthur drains what is left in his glass and purses his lips, studying Marc.

"Right. As I see it, this show has no business in a gallery.

Take it from one train station to the next. And I don't mean dillydally either. I mean the actual platform in the actual station. We do our own little Tour de France. The only thing I would change would be one thing. Mind you, I'm just suggesting."

"Go on."

"A little glitz with the presentation. I think you got yourself a framer with small ideas. It's like he took five minutes off from doing medical and dental degrees to frame your things. I'm going to give you my card now and let you think over all the things I've said. You contact me when you're ready. Lyon, Marseille. We hit the provinces first and then storm gay Paris. Let me tell you something."

Arthur Glad mutters something and then, as if to stress his own conviction, looks straight into Marc's eyes.

"I believe in combustion. I believe an art person can take off, given the presence of certain important elements. I want your work out of here, Marc Laugier. I want your work down there on the platform where traveling people can get a look at it. You tell me you had the idea from standing around the Nice airport. Take it back to the source and we explode. One last word?"

"Of course."

"Dump the technician. A nice guy, sure. But a real deadweight. His poems stink."

When Arthur Glad is gone, we seem to be standing inside some sort of cavity. The empty space he's left is tangible.

"A bum. A hustler. Did you see his pointy shoes? What does his card say anyhow?"

His address is printed with appropriate glitz. The paper is thin and cheap. It would cut your finger if you grabbed Arthur Glad's calling card too fast or at the wrong angle. He lives on rue Voltaire in Nice.

"An artist alright. A con artist. It's a shame we're going to have to work with a creep like that."

"Tu es d'accord avec moi, alors. Quel rigolo."

"Of course I agree with you. Combustion. Mainline art. He's a slimeball with terrific ideas. Why do you keep doing that?"

"Doing what?"

"Touching your eye. You realize the night is still young?"

"And?"

"Why don't we go out dancing? Savor the French Riviera for a change? This is such a glamorous place to live. Why is it we never, ever do glamorous things? Let's storm a nightclub."

"A ce point?"

"A ce point."

The rain has let up by the time we reach our destination. We park in front of a Middle Eastern deli. A leg of lamb turns on a spit as customers stand at the counter, smoking and eating simultaneously. A glass case is full of Lebanese delicacies. Tall jugs of marinated vegetables line the top of the display.

"This isn't exactly Jimmy'z."

"No."

"Nor Régine's."

"Patience."

"Marc, sorry to be a spoilsport, but just take me home, alright? I don't feel like eating any of this stuff."

He holds the door open and motions me inside. The owner of the deli nods and we pass through a swinging door in back and climb a flight of stairs. This is a different stratum altogether.

"Look at the tinsel in this place. I wonder if this is for the neophyte. Marc? How did you find out about this spot?"

"All the photographs of Kashoggi's girlfriend were shot here. Last August while you were gone."

"What else have I missed?"

The officiousness is light and airy. Appetizers are showered on us, the plates no larger than saucers. Grape leaves, delicately stuffed, and turnips dyed pink by a tart marinade. Olives and purées. I count fifteen dishes and we haven't ordered.

"So what else have I missed?"

"You should have missed me."

"I mean what, not who, have I missed."

"I understand your question; I just don't think it's the one you should be asking."

"Marc, for heaven's sake, I was visiting my family. I was hardly off sightseeing."

"Even so. I am your family. You haven't once asked what I've been doing out here alone while you and Sam were gone."

"What a conversation this is. You know I have complete trust in you."

"Trust sometimes feels like indifference."

"The Latin Streak. As infrequently sighted as Halley's Comet, but definitely present."

"You take a great deal for granted."

"For God's sake, were you here to shoot Kashoggi's girl or weren't you?"

"I was."

"Adjourned. Jesus. Pass the bread, please."

I swallow for a while in peace. Where does discomfort rank in the range of emotions? It lacks the decibel level of jealousy, rage and envy. Maybe discomfort is a preliminary operation, destined to equip us for our struggle with one of the big three. I glare at Marc for a while, trying to envision him with someone else. Then I accept another arak, fully conscious of the consequences, and begin to notice the dead seriousness of the clothing and jewelry in the place. People fill the dance floor and the small square is clotted with Armani and Montana. I spot a knock-kneed Per Spook.

"I would say some of these gals are overpowered by their clothing. Or too strongly identified by it."

"I think they look quite well. Lucy, you're jealous."

"Why are you in such a dour mood? You have just had a smashing vernissage. You may have hooked up with an efficient, albeit weird, manager, and you are giving your wife a horrible time. If I wanted one of those get-ups, I'd scrimp and save and get one! And I'm not the kind of woman who throws temper tantrums about who you see when I'm not around. Jealousy is a base emotion, Marc. A primal dud."

"Base or basic?"

"Do you want me to tear out my hair? If you want I'll go ahead and rip it out. Clump by clump."

"Calm down. Tiens, mange un peu de ce truc. Don't look

now, but a Saudi prince has just arrived. Which means they'll close up."

"What? We have to leave?"

"No, they just won't let anybody else in. They won't need to with what he spends."

"He's just gorgeous. Sure he's a Saudi?"

"Absolutely."

"Too damn bad about the woman, though. Is she at a walk, trot or canter? You'd think she'd put her back out moving like that."

"You know, Lucy, you expose yourself each time you see a real woman. C'est terrible."

"Oh! Now who's exposing one's self? And if *that* is a real woman, what on earth am I?"

"Je ne voulais pas dire que—"

"Stop while you're ahead. And don't switch to French when you're under pressure. Maybe we're better at body language. How about if we just dance?"

"C'est un champ de bataille. Tu es sûr?"

"Rise, my beloved."

We work our way onto the crowded floor. Marc looks apologetic, which makes matters worse. This is really no place to cut loose, but the arak has made me incautious. A tiny blonde cries out in pain as I crunch her slippered foot.

"Oh, pardon!"

"Lucy, fais attention."

I redress my movements and we dance carefully for a while. Marc looks dubious when the tempo changes.

"C'est un slow."

"Don't worry, I won't hurt you. Let's sidle up to the royal couple while we're at it."

"C'est sa petite amie."

"She's not his little friend. She's his mistress. Will you French ever call a spade a spade?"

Lost: sense of humor. Found: sore spot. I eyeball this archetypal real woman as we move stiffly around the dance floor.

"I can't stand it."

"Stand what?"

"The confusion. Are we supposed to look? Is her performance for him or for everyone else? She's petting him as if he were a puppy or a small boy. Also, it's such a cheat."

"Our night out is getting rather bloody, Lucy. Is this what is called ranting and raving?"

"May I finish? She's cheating because every woman under the sun could carry on in just the same way. But most don't. Most women opt for a little dignity. Look! Did you see that? The eyes upturned and head held just so. It's a feint and the exasperating thing is how well it works."

"Enticement and skill are age-old."

"Skill! What does that have to do with skill? Romance is very rudimentary. I'll take sex in a hayfield anyday. That woman would fall into a pothole and break her silly neck. Boy, do I hate ruse. It lowers the overall quality of my thoughts."

"I don't follow you."

"I'm just saying that stripped of her hifalutin clothing and jewelry and those femme fatale mannerisms, she would be in hot water alright. That kind of artifice drives me crazy."

"Continue. This is interesting."

"I can't. I'm too furious. Just drive me back home."

"You know that field you speak of makes me think of an English landscape painting filled with shepherds and milkmaids. You're such an Anglo-Saxon. That must be why I love you."

"Clever of you to skirt the issue by bringing up love. The hayfield was a metaphor, you know. Don't get any big ideas on the way home."

"Another question?"

"Why not."

"Do most American women consider Yves Saint Laurent hifalutin?"

"They may if they come from Tulsa. Drive, she said."

That night I assume my dreams will be full of wonderful portent. Maybe the little white train will rumble through, driven by that ambitious Arthur Glad, stacked high with Marc's photographs. They're not. They are tangled and confusing and I wake up repeatedly to drink milk and look at Sam. Finally at four o'clock in the morning I drink two glasses of grappa and listen to the radio. A woman is discussing bad love. She seems to think bad love is worse than no love at all. Next a man calls in to complain that he can't sleep for worrying about dogs. The other day I woke up at sunrise, he says. I look out my window and the first thing I see is a gentleman checking the soles of his shoes. Dawn breaks and an entire nation checks the soles of its shoes—the dog filth! He wants information on the dog population at present. The radio announcer, a woman with a raspy voice, admits she hasn't any figures for him, but if he'll call back tomorrow morning at the same time —the man keeps talking until he is automatically cut off. The problem is the half-breeds and bastards, he is saying. We have let the purity of each strain become infected and now what we have are these mongrels everywhere leaping at us from behind fences. In China, he asserts, the great leap forward was when they shot all the dogs. It doesn't stop there. Have you noticed how this country's jawline is changing? He is cut off and the next caller wants to talk about childbirth without pain. The grappa sets everything in motion and I have a little trouble getting back to bed.

I wake up once again and the clock reads 6:15. There is every kind of trouble in my dreams. Thanks to the man on the radio, there are packs of wild dogs running through the village streets. There is no noise in the dream and everyone opens their mouths in horror at the sight of so many uncontrolled animals, but no sounds come out. The widow comes out on her terrace to throw pots at the dogs below and they shatter one by one, missing the dogs. Somewhere in the tangle, my brother is lying on the street with his face exposed to those running dogs. He's alive but making no effort to protect himself and the dogs have left marks on his face. They could turn on him at any minute. That's what I'm shouting from an open window but there's no sound in my dream. Cody doesn't hear and the dogs tear past, cutting my brother's bright, upturned face. I'm afraid to sleep again. Instead I stay as close as I can to Marc. He wakes before Sam and brings hot tea to bed. I hear him explain outside the closed door that Mommy is sick and then they drive off together somewhere. I hear him turn the lock on the kitchen door.

I don't dress until late afternoon. I plan Cody's plastic surgery as carefully as if the nightmare were real, thanking God that the deepest cut was near the scalp. With that blue-black hair and a surgeon's skill, no one would ever notice. All the other marks were superficial cuts. They will fade first to slight, pale crescents before disappearing altogether. By five o'clock, when Marc and Sam get back, I'm eating dry cornflakes and feeling brighter. I nod when Marc tells me three photographs were sold and shows me the checks. Of course this is very fine. But the most welcome news is that Cody's upcoming ordeal, whatever that may be, won't kill him or leave him maimed. So that people later, when searching his face for some permanent sign of that struggle, will complain that they see nothing of it at all.

14

A curious war had broken out in the village. It began with the discovery that a lizard's tail, when severed, contains a wildly spinning life of its own. Depending on whether a sizable segment is removed or just the tip, the detached tail wags on and on by itself long after the victim scurries over a wall or under a rock. Bets are cast now on how many minutes or seconds the frantic movement will continue. Sticks of chewing gum and ice-blue marbles are lost and won and the fascination promises to continue as long as the lizard population holds up. The assault provides the lizards with a new peace. Bands of chattering boys recognize them as already mutilated and useless to their sport. Sam, too young to savor the thrill of this game, has captured six or seven victims. His elaborate plans to restore the lizards' tails involve light treatments, rest, and above all, calm. When he can figure out how to make them stick, he plans to apply cotton balls to the little stubs. Sam purses his lips when I brief him on regeneration and I can see that it makes little difference to his program. So far the lizards are waiting it out under Marc's halogen lamp. Leaves are showered on them daily, dead flies when available. The village boys, in bringing attention to themselves, will suffer a bout of redemption. Their cruel pastime has been brought to the mayor's attention by a delegation of outraged women whose clout rivals that of Les Mères Admirables. The mayor hires a youth coordinator named Habib.

Habib rolls into town on a Saturday morning. Desultory remarks about the "A Team" television series are made at a corner table in the Pause-Café. Another table seems to think Habib resembles a tall Texas sheriff, called upon to clean up a rough frontier city. Habib operates out of an American Motors van. Its passage through the narrow streets is difficult. Pedestrians flatten themselves against a wall or press up into a doorway. Small cars jump the sidewalk as he passes. On one side of the van a bare-breasted woman is painted. She is blond and advancing at top speed as well, her hair spreading out behind her. A psychedelic rose is painted on the other side. Rock music blares from the van. Habib passes through the village several times, announcing his presence. He finally parks in front of an apartment complex called L'Aurore.

He sets up shop next to the boule court, several days later. He swings open the door of his van and waits, lowering the volume on his radio for the sake of the old men who clap their hands over their ears and blunder the simplest plays. He is not hurried and files his nails until noon. He returns at two o'clock and opens the door again, resting a sandaled foot on the handle. He rolls up the sleeve of a white T-shirt, revealing a set of purple tatooed wings. By four-thirty, a band of boys is assembled near the park bench. They accuse each other of being homosexuals in loud voices and discuss what little gynecology they know. By nightfall they belong to Habib. They have entered the van and stroked the fur on his dash, chosen their favorite rock and roll station and finally run the old men off the boule court. Not one of them recognizes this as surrender.

The mayor lost face with the demise of the little train. He is determined not to lose a second time. He hobnobs. He buys the daily baguette in place of his wife, letting her spend an extra thirty minutes in bed. He frequents the Pause-Café himself, offering a pastis to an astonished sanitation engineer whose twelve-year-old son has been bringing home stories about Habib. He lingers in the aisle at Mille Choses, discussing his wife's hands, and selects a mild detergent for her. He mentions his pleasure at Habib's arrival in the village to the owner, whose own son is putting by money to purchase an American Motors van one day. He cites the case of a village to the west. Dying twenty years ago, he says as he counts his change. And some small auspicious thing happened and the village didn't dry up. That Russian dancer's husband died and she started giving lessons again, in the ramshackle building he owned for storage space. She started turning out prodigies. Sons and daughters of farmers took their place in professional companies and one of her former students now works for TF1. A small thing, you say? Ha! They are planning an autoroute exit for that town next year. The owner of Mille Choses sucks a mint thoughtfully and checks his watch as the mayor rattles on about Habib and top-quality youth.

In two weeks time Habib has a team of fifteen indentured boys. Each of the fifteen has at one time been called incorrigible by an outraged onlooker. They have successfully skirted first catechism classes, then judo lessons and even soccer. Finally all forms of approved group behavior. Their resistance begins to buckle under Habib's guidance. He casually mentions that he will be at the pool Saturday after classes and each of the fifteen loyally appears. They settle on benches with uncommon courtesy and watch as Habib cuts through the water with a well-defined, disciplined crawl. The purple wings tatooed on his arm flash. He doesn't give in to bursts of speed but maintains the stroke with monotonous precision. Casually, by twos and threes, the boys disappear and return in suits, to the lifeguard's amazement. He has yanked each of them from the pool at one time or another for frightening younger, inexperienced swimmers. Yet here they are, docile and willing to swim in their alloted lanes. The scruffiest troublemaker of all is a poor swimmer. He slipped out at night repeatedly on his uncle's tractor to raze entire fields of leeks and potatoes until his antics were discovered. And here he is struggling with a weak breaststroke. They return to the pool again and again, the lifeguard still disbelieving. For water, as pure baptismal rite, weighs heavily in Habib's program of redemption. Tired and soggy after a full hour of lap swimming, their collective heart and will is more easily won. They move on to other projects.

Charity becomes endemic as the plague. They repair fences and clear brush for a farmer whose arthritis is acting up. They capture a difficult filly and strap her into a trailer bound for a trainer in Toulouse. They transport medicine for the pharmacist whose car is in the shop. At any given intersection, one of Habib's boys may leap from behind a tree with a bucket of window-cleaning solution and a chamois cloth. None of them take any money. They duck abashedly when thanked and head back to Habib's van, still parked on the edge of the boule court, Saturdays and Sundays, their working week. Their wages are the right to sit in the van for an hour or two, smoking the cigarettes he dispenses freely. Girlie magazines are scattered on the floor of the van but the boys' eyes are mostly fixed on Habib, who avoids no questions. On Habib, who can tell them what it is like to live like a wild animal, with nothing but wit and instinct to help you survive.

His right hand, despite the missing finger, is shapely. His use of the deformed hand is graceful. He has choreographed different movements to disguise or highlight it, depending on his needs. When he speaks to the boys it is mostly on display. In Tunisia, he says quietly, stroking his upper arm, nobody batted an eye. It only seemed scandalous here, when we arrived in 1965. Swaggering home from school one afternoon, Habib stole a gold ring from a street vendor. Not a fancy ring, nothing to brag about. But the sun struck it in a way that made Habib believe that not having the ring would rival the cruelest kind of pain. He slipped it into his pocket. In the end it didn't even prove to be real gold. Still, when one of his jealous siblings tattled, Habib's father neatly sliced off his little finger with a kitchen knife. A good Moslem, he scrubbed the knife furiously and continued cutting up vegetables for the other children while the mother drove the wailing boy to a clinic in Tunis. His father drove a cab for a living. Hemorrhaging on the backseat of his father's taxi, his hand wrapped in a dishrag, Habib did not give in to compunction. Instead, as they jostled through traffic, he invented more elaborate crimes still. Crimes which left no trail. I'll tell you one thing, he says to the aghast company assembled in the van, it didn't wriggle around like those lizard tails. My father had a chemist make up a solution to keep it from rotting. Then he put it in a spice jar and covered it with a black cloth. Habib waits for their discomfort to subside before offering other stories. I lived in the desert for three months once and fed on snakes when the food was gone. I was in prison for three years.

"Dis donc, Habib. Qu'est-ce que tu as fait?"

He tells them he hurt a woman. But that was in Tunisia many years ago. The boys look at the glossy opened pages on the floor of the van and think of their own escapades, so pale and drained of life by comparison. Stymied in the face of real crime and real punishment they ask Habib to raise the volume of the radio. They strike awkward poses in the carpeted body of the van and listen closely to the song called "Troisième Sexe," seeking relief.

The mayor is burning the midnight oil, with reelection coming up. His neighbor, Madame Erte, ordinarily on the lookout for thieves and rapscallions who plunder her statuary garden, peers through her lace curtains most evenings simply to watch the mayor's bedroom, which stand directly in front of her own. He has taken to circling the bedroom now, going round and round in rings while smoking a pipe. Madame Erte watches as his shadow fades and reappears a third and fourth time. It is generally concluded that the mayor is planning campaign tactics. Wondering how to turn the reformation of fifteen boys into grist for his electoral mill.

We appeal to Arthur Glad only when it is clear that Arché has gone completely around the bend. He writes an incomprehensible ode to body hair and is arrested by the police, who catch him tacking up his work in a glass shelter just constructed to sweep dizzy tourists from a perfume factory in Grasse directly into the port of Antibes. They squint at the poem and, on the basis of a salacious stanza Arché labored on for weeks, haul him down to the commissariat. The lab falls into the hands of his partner, a small bald man who smells of strong soap. We explain our predicament to Arthur, who seems to have expected us. I'm breathless after mounting five flights of stairs. Each landing smells increasingly of garlic. His apartment is small but impeccable. Lace doilies are in evidence. I wonder what this interior has to do with a mainliner of art, until he wheels his mother out to meet us. She is a sweet-faced woman who waves at us from the seat of a wicker wheelchair. She is twisted and gnarled from rheumatism. Her right hand is curled shut, as if she has just caught something small and living that might fly free of her clutch.

"My mother, Minette Glad. Lucy and Marc Laugier, Mummy."

"'Jour, Madame, Monsieur."

"Too voo restay oh solay, Mummy?"

Minette's eyes flutter up. Arthur must apply her makeup, for her crippled hands could never achieve that surreal black sweep of eyeliner. It is fastidiously applied and finishes in a flirtatious tail. Her rouge is less artful. The two red dots seem clownish and artificial. He rolls his mother into the sun. She can see the swirl of busy pedestrians on the rue Voltaire from where she sits. In the building across from her is an older man, also wheelchair-bound. They carefully avoid eye contact.

"Minette's lover, though she would rather die than admit it. He is married, but his wife is in a maison de repos. He's pining for my mother. Nice, don't you think? Well, on to us. You've thought about my propositions?"

Arthur has done some homework and draws a large sheet of construction paper out of a hall closet. It looks like a scene to amuse children, a series of orange dots Arthur has connected with yellow lines. The dots are train stations, however, selected by Arthur according to his hunches. Which, he says, are faultless and have never let him down.

"In this business you have to be coy. Never solicit the big boys. Let them find you. There's nothing that thrills a Parisian more than a discovery in the provinces. If we were to directly approach Paris we would glitter and die in a day. Just like those bugs that mate and are dead by morning. They'll solicit us, don't worry. Oh, Minette's dropped her handkerchief. This woman keeps me on my toes!"

We settle the problem of replacing Arché as Arthur feeds his mother a bowl of stewed fruit. He chides her for poor appetite and opens his own mouth as he offers each spoonful, barking at her in their quasi-French. He pulls his silk dressing gown over his knees and shakes his head in mock frustration at Minette's admirer, who has drawn closer to his own window and given up all pretensions of disinterest.

"Out of the frying pan into the fire."

"Qu'est-ce que ça veut dire?"

"We have gone from Arché to Arthur. Do you really trust this guy?"

"Strangely, yes. And anyway, what difference does it make? I would just like to see a few prints."

"When are you going to take yourself seriously? Marc, I feel like buying something big and expensive."

"Tu peux préciser?"

"Our mattress is shot. My back hurts. I saw this wonderful trick bed the other day. It makes me think of my father's La-Z-Boy."

"Which lazy boy?"

"It's the kind of chair that reclines when you push a button. We call them La-Z-Boy chairs. The bed looks expensive."

"Tant mieux. On peut se permettre un lit, Lucy. On n'est pas encore dans la dèche."

"What is Arthur Glad exactly?"

"Un phénomène, tout simplement. Un phénomène."

We immediately begin a round of shopping, drifting from one commercial center to the next. The bedframe I like is white and low-lying. There are two slender twin mattresses, suggesting no horseplay and a guaranteed full night's sleep. It isn't a bed to tumble into, for you might break a bone on the way down. The support frame of each mattress lifts to a sitting position. We lie down side by side, then lift up to a mutual sit and stare at our images in the mirror facing the bed.

"So, what do you think?"

"I think we look like invalids in a rest home, that's what I think."

"Now that's where you're wrong, Marc. It's made to keep us supple and strong. Feel this, why don't you?"

"When I'm sixty years old. Mais pas maintenant."

"Is that a categorical no?"

"You could say that."

We spend the day prone, trying out beds. Flat on our backs, with Sam pressed in between, we work out a vaguely academic rating scheme, based on a scale of a possible twenty. We try them all and finally settle on something between my orthopedic preferences and Marc's, which stir up images of Vegas and wild, wild women.

"You're joking! But it's fur."

"I'm not talking about the bedspread. Look at this. Solide."

"Maybe it's the presentation. Plus I can't take this salesman."

"Il n'est pas discret."

The bed is displayed on a black-carpeted summit. The salesman lingers behind as we climb the steps to test the bed. He makes a joke as we sit together on the edge of the bed.

"Bad timing. Very bad timing. I'm getting out of here."

"Lucy, you're acting like a bashful child."

"I don't like his sense of humor."

We find peace at last in a furniture store initially launched in a country barn north of Lyon. It was inspired by Levitz, the salesman said, winking at me. Américain.

I succumb to an old habit and figure the cost in dollars. Levitz, my eye.

"This costs a fortune."

"Let me worry about that. Est-ce que tu es contente?"

"Yep."

"You take care of the tissu?"

"Fabric. Leave it to me."

• • •

The bed arrives several days later. The headboard rises in a wide, stately arc. It's comfortable and wide. Thick oak panels slide out on either side of the bed, eliminating the need for night tables. The bedspread is a soft brushed cotton and bands of irridescent color engage the light from the window. It steals the show and the whole room becomes impoverished. I wonder why we've never repaired the chest of drawers after all this time. Two drawers are warped from the humidity in the house and I can see the contents from where I'm lying on the bed. The poster from Carnaval is very wrong. I move toward Marc.

"Ça va pas."

"What's wrong?"

The bed, it seems, has thrown everything into relief. He pulls at the top of my sweatpants with one finger.

"My nightwear never bothered you before."

"It bothers me now."

"I don't believe in lingerie. You know that."

It's very quiet and I feel a reproach coming on.

"Alright, so what are you trying to tell me? That kind of shopping is embarrassing. In fact it's unthinkable. I don't go into those places. You didn't marry a cancan girl. O hé. Are you there?"

I think of that apartment years ago. The boutique with its spinning pedestals and shiny, exposed buttocks.

"Are we talking black lace here? Peekaboo underwear? You want a sex kitten, I gather."

"I'm not asking you to dress like a pute. Lucy, I'd settle for a nice nightgown. I'm talking about real pajamas."

"Let's return this stupid bed. This is all too complicated. Do you suppose Simone de Beauvoir and Sartre had this kind of discussion?"

"I don't know and I don't care. All I'm saying is that I feel I'm sleeping with a weight lifter."

"I find this a very middle-aged conversation. I'm going to sleep now."

"Ça tombe bien. So am I."

• • •

So it is that I enter a brave new world. We stop at the third floor of Nouvelles Galeries in Nice. Perhaps nightgowns aren't so derelict after all.

"What a bunch of fuss for something no one is ever going to see."

"Except for your husband."

"Right. Sorry."

"Regarde comme c'est joli."

He holds out something pretty, long and horribly expensive.

"That represents two weeks' worth of groceries, plus a night out, counting babysitter, film and dinner afterwards. You realize that? It is pretty, though. The last sleepwear I owned was a pair of babydoll pajamas I wore in seventh grade."

"And since? Before me?"

"There was no before you. I'm a child bride, remember? How long have you been harboring this boudoir fantasy?"

"Since last night."

We stand in back of another couple at the cash register. The woman is slightly larger than the man. He's holding a shopping bag from a sleek Italian boutique and a plastic sack from Prisunic. His wife hands the sullen cashier a red garter belt.

"Let me ask you one more thing."

He begins to laugh.

"I'm glad you're having such a swell time. Marc? Are we having a satisfactory sex life?"

It's our turn. We move toward the cashier together.

"Very. It's about to get more satisfactory."

"What's the matter? What are you staring at me for?"

"Nothing. I'm thinking about your hair."

"Stop there. Do you realize the concession I've made today?"

"You are artless, Lucy. You just don't know how to play."

"Mistresses play. Wives don't. At least American wives don't."

"American wives should. That's very dangerous thinking."

"Is that a veiled threat?"

"A what?"

"Chantage."

"Not at all. You've been gone seventeen years, Lucy. Why do you still insist on being so representative? And what is so holy about a ponytail?"

"I knew it."

"What."

"That I'd end up hearing about this one way or another. Was it the delegation of Italian hairstylists? The riveting afternoon with Madame Gonzalès and her hat collection? Brother. Actually, I'm not so intractable as you think. I just don't understand this stuff."

"You pretend not to. You're a snob. Simone de Beauvoir and Sartre! You still deserve lunch, though. Something fast, I've got to get back."

Checks continue to flutter in from mountain stations, bearing the name of a travel agency or a small country branch of the Crédit Agricole. Marc's prints seem to sit well in lobbies and the cool offices of some PDG, those ubiquitous directeurs generaux. The bed is shortly paid for as Arthur's optimistic missives float in, airy and light as paper airplanes. We replace the poster with a stark, linear artist's proof. It challenges every assumption I had about black. There are grades of it, degrees of it. The proof seems to reestablish black as a color and, studying it at night, I'm tricked into reading reds and hard, glassy greens into it. I finger the nightgown and imagine it leaving a light film on my fingers, like the dust on a moth's wing. Why a honeymoon now, in the midst of married life? Night dominates day and we follow cues without speaking. I don't think through this and wouldn't want to. The sharp, singular inventory of new pleasures is, for a while, enough.

Sometimes we read the same book and it becomes a kind of speed-read toward the first comic punchline or the exposure of a tragic dimension, when the subject is sober. There is furious page-turning and a lot of backbiting. When it comes to books and authors, we are profoundly nationalistic. Tonight I have the upper hand, as there is no translating Woody Allen. *Destins*

Tordus—what possible link can this title have to the original *Side Effects*? I argue the Laffont edition has not obtained a veritable Kugelmass.

The phone rings and Sam runs in to report that it is an unintelligible woman.

"You know something, Lucy? They've run off all the birds."

"Commerce and wildlife don't mix. You're in a shopping center?"

"I'm at home."

"Who's run off all the birds?"

"Why, the children. Now that children inhabit our trees the birds have all flown away. I can't even tempt my hummers back to the feeder. But these are small complaints. I'm ashamed of myself for bringing it up, though I do miss waking up to bird songs. Evidently your father's tree project is changing lives."

"That drastic?"

"For the better. Do you realize school counselors phone him with thanks? Newspaper people have been out here for the third time. The neighbors all withdrew their complaints because of the support he's getting. Tree house projects like this one are being planned on four other properties that we know of. All private parties. Two of them are old oil families. The way they tell it, they're sick to death of charity suppers and the Philharmonic. They miss the commotion of children."

"So what's your complaint exactly?"

"Do you hear that tapping?"

"Trouble on the line?"

"The trouble is at the kitchen door. Hang on."

She is gone for several minutes and sighs when she picks up the phone.

"What these youngsters don't need. Band-Aids and butter. Iodine. You'd think I was a state health clinic. There has been a lice outbreak here and half the children have shaved heads. Spooky, really, when I look out the window and see all these little bald children."

"It must be complicated. I think I see what you mean."

"I miss my male cardinal is what it boils down to. But a

bright redbird is a small price to pay for progress, I suppose. Your father is meaning to legislate trees."

"Mandatory tree houses? Mom, how can you legislate trees?"

"I wish I knew. This is all foreign language to me, but it has something to do with the impact of trees on the state of Oklahoma. Your father seems to think that with our shrinking forest and dwindling oaks we can never be serious contenders for industry. Get my gist?"

"Not exactly."

"I'm just trying to paraphrase what your father says. All this lobbying for trees gets to me. I don't see why companies should give a damn about forestry. Any business besides lumber, that is. If you want my opinion, your father's enthusiasms—well. I would personally like to see a firmer grip on reality. I mean, you could throw up an industrial park on the moon, if you ask me. Sidewalks and employee parking. A pleasant cafeteria. Frankly, if the day comes that a company enters a state because of its healthy timber, I think we're in serious trouble. But your father is finding supporters, Lucy. Not supporters, exactly, since he isn't running for office. But like-minded people write him letters. Phone him with advice. I have certainly gotten sidetracked today. I'm calling you because of the dog."

The collie, a fourteen-year-old fossil, could barely move the last time I was back. The utility room had been completely outfitted to suit the dog. She slept in a kind of outsized Easter basket and was being spoon-fed top-of-the-line ground beef and pulverized vitamins. My father and I have urged her to have the animal put away for years. She claims that their spirits are so much in unison it is like riding a tandem bicycle. If one falls off, the other is likely to go as well.

"I have killed the dog."

"You mean you had a vet put her to sleep."

"Let's not sidestep. I gave the vet the okay. Who's responsible, the general or the soldier?"

"That's going a little far, Mom."

"I held her in my arms when he gave her the shot. There

was a quiver and then she was gone. I thought you might like to know."

Robbed of the Be (Happy) Attitudes, my mother seems oddly exposed, like the embarrassing time I caught her stepping out of a steaming bath. I had never seen her unclothed and I backed away with an apology.

I crawl back into bed. Even after years of conversations just like this one, she can still knock me out.

"What's wrong, Lucy?"

"The dog's dead."

"You childhood dog?"

"My mother's childhood dog."

"Comment va Agnès? Quoi de neuf?"

"That's the problem. Nothing, but nothing, is new. Youth is being rehabilated around the globe and there's not a redbird in sight."

"Elle est drôle, ta mère."

But Sam is asleep, his hands folded over the broken spine of a cowboy book. Maybe he is riding the lonesome range in his dreams.

"Je ne suis pas bien."

"Ne bouge pas. Tu veux boire?"

He goes off barefooted in search of something carbonated. Was it news of the dog's death and its effect on my mother? The thought of my childhood backyard filled not with flashy redbirds but bands of bald children? Absorbing my mother's erratic messages has landed me a bellyache. My stomach is rolling as if I'm careening down mountain roads in a closed car. All this dyspeptic trouble despite my belief that things are standing more eternally still than ever.

15

My mother is right about one thing. At some point these trips home have become exotic and remote enough from my experience to merit a stolen soil sample. How did she put it? Flora and fauna. I seem to be in it for the strangeness, the news clippings and auto decals I haul back to France bear this out. I scour supermarkets for new clues to local mentality, scribble bits of conversations overheard in Church's Fried Chicken in a yellow notebook. I am a foreigner alright, but to what country am I now foreign? It was in this spirit of anthropology that I went to a charismatic church service one Sunday when I was home. One Sunday and then the following Sunday, leaving Schuller to my mother. Television is a warm medium. People's Congregation, by contrast, is red-hot.

I had taken Sam out to a catfish pond belonging to a farmer friend, promising a miracle as Sam grew increasingly fussy. The heat slapped our faces in waves as we sat with the poles between our legs. The fish weren't taking our bait. The miracle was not a tug on the line but a flotilla of red balloons. One broke rank. It drifted toward us across the pond and lodged fifty feet away in the branches of a cranberry tree. Sam was allowed to pop it only after I had read the message stretched across the side of the balloon and copied the address.

GET WITH GOD
PEOPLE'S CONGREGATION
7900 STATLER DRIVE

WE WILL RECEIVE YOU!

There was a point at which I nearly backed down. The building was located on the southern outskirts of the city, farther out than Oral's City of Faith, past all the neat theme residential developments that purported to have you living in England or Scotland when you had never really left Tulsa. City blocks gave way to country blocks and still I drove, following the red markers simply stating *PEOPLE'S*. And then with nothing in sight but old one-room jailhouses and truck farm stands, a traffic jam developed. There was a fabulous courtesy at work that held up despite the snail's pace. I nearly turned back at the entrance, though, when I spotted the militia. There were at least a dozen policemen supervising the entrance alone. They were not just directing traffic. They spot-checked trunks of cars and didn't smile. I was let past after a brief glance at my backseat. I rolled down my window. At ten o'clock the heat was already blistering.

"What's all this about, sir?"

"This is about harassment, Sister. This is about threats. First time out?"

"Yes, sir."

"In for a treat, I expect. Have yourself a good one now."

In the parking lot, I started to lock my car. A man in a black suit approached, shaking his finger at me. He handed me a sheaf of papers and implored me not to lock my car.

"Hi, my name's Rob. Oh, please don't do that. You're never obliged to do that at People's."

He walked briskly past me and continued doling out papers to other people. I noticed as I walked inside that most of the cars still had the keys in their ignitions.

The inside of the church was like an amphitheater. There was no stained glass and no pulpit, only a music stand with a microphone attached. The only religious symbol was a mural in back of the music stand, depicting Christ on the way to his cruxifixion, struggling uphill with His cross. There was an orchestra pit and a carpeted platform. If the mural had not been there the building would have been perfectly suited to any secular forum. Even the depiction of Christ was discreet. I had seen more violent interpretations of Christ in the children's art that surfaces everywhere in France around Easter. Then the members of the People's Congregation orchestra filed into the auditorium in single file. They were dressed in cheery sport coats and bright shirtwaist dresses. Members of the orchestra clapped and waved, then started an opening number that had a little of the lively tempo I recognized from "Let's Make A Deal."

The music went on for a very long time. There were several soloists, men and women. Some of them introduced their own music, for they were composers as well. There was still no preacher and the only signs of program guidance were internal. The music became softer and finally stilled. The woman sitting next to me took this as a cue to remove her chewing gum and introduce herself to me.

"Honey, my name's Ginny. You don't hesitate to ask for help if you need it. Hear?"

I had been spotted. What were the elements of camouflage, I wondered? Ginny was probably my mother's age. She wore braces on her teeth and a purple orchid pinned too low on her jacket.

"Thank you, Ginny. I'm Lucy."

"Have you received the gifts of the Holy Spirit?"

"I don't believe I have."

"Could be your lucky day, Lucy."

A man standing in the fourth row seemed to be the preacher. He had to push past several people. I didn't see why he hadn't chosen an aisle seat. He had ruddy cheeks and wore yellow-tinted aviator glasses. He wore a white suit and shoes with thick crepe soles that made no sound as he walked. He stopped several times on the way to shake hands or bend low to hear the whispery greeting of a child in a wheelchair. He seemed to be in no hurry to move from music to message. As soon as he took his place in front of the microphone, two men appeared on stage beside him with their hands behind their backs and their legs spread wide apart, like halfbacks being introduced before the opening kickoff. The preacher leaned over the microphone and took a wide-eyed look around.

"Can you folks hear me? Say halleluia if you can."

Halleluias rang out along with more hand-clapping and hooting.

"Did the Lord say it would be easy?"

There was a chorus of No, Brother Bud!

"But did the Lord tell you He would give you courage for the long march? And comfort through the long, cold night? And did the Lord promise ETERNAL LIFE through His only son, Jesus Christ?"

There was some foot-stamping then and more shouting—Praise the Lord! Halleluia! In Jesus' name, Amen! This continued for two or three minutes and then the congregation began to sit down. The sitting down took place with a great rustle that began with the first row.

"I have some news to share with you today. Some news about two members of People's who have decided to answer the call to move on. Brother Lloyd, I'm going to pass you the microphone. Tell us about your plans for the future, Brother Lloyd."

Thus began a round of constabulary information, who was going where with the Lord's message. What congregations were prospering and what promise gleamed in other parts of the world. There was enormous congratulating. Ginny's braces glinted as she smiled over the final, conclusive news that the Lord was on the march. And that the length of His stride was longer than ever. The two church members left the podium to sit with their families in the auditorium.

"There's a rumor going around. There's an ugly, unfortunate rumor going around that Christ is for weenies."

There is a round of appreciative laughter. Ginny reaches over, pinching me gently on the arm, and winks. Across the aisle from me a man tips his head back and closes his eyes.

"Listen to this, you all. I was standing in the aisle at Savon Drugs three days ago and I overheard the following conversation at the candy counter. Two little fellas not more than ten years old were discussing Christians. Right by the gum balls and hard candy at Savon you can also buy key chains and car stickers with gospel messages, and these two little guys were making up their minds about whether to buy sour balls or suckers with their money. One of them, the littlest, says to the other, 'But if we put our money together we could have one of them Jesus thangs.' The other one didn't miss a beat. He said, 'You dummy. Christ is for weenies.' Now the two of them didn't advance the discussion any further. But I, as pastor of this congregation, certainly did."

Brother Bud stepped back from the podium as people whistled through their teeth. The applause rose. He generated a little more enthusiasm in his smiling silence and drew closer to the microphone.

"I could refute it, couldn't I? I could say, 'Listen to what I heard. Two youngsters without a grain of sense.' But I'm not going to do that, because I know where that little boy is coming from. What he is referring to is a brand of faith soggier than the milk toast our mothers used to make us eat when we were sick.

"Spiritual weenies are counterproductive, my friends."

"Praise Jesus."

"Spiritual weenies are deadweights."

"Praise the Lord."

"Spiritual weenies are friction to the movement Jesus Christ generates among his body of worshippers."

"Amen."

"Yes, the Lord wants kindness. The Lord want honor among Christian men and women. But does the Lord want weakness in his followers? Should a Christian lie down in the road so the car that's aiming to run him down won't have to ruin a wheel jumping the curb? You laugh but I've seen that lying-down enough times to make my heart sick with worry and dread."

"The Bible calls us soldiers. But soldiers who won't fight are spineless. As a follower of Christ you must be ready to take up the sword in whatever sense the sword is offered you. Now, taking up the sword might mean you're going to have to tell a stranger about the good news. And taking up the sword might mean you have to lead a doubting spouse to the Lord. You might have to change the way you think and the way you live. It might mean you have to start a revolution in the place you find yourself as a Christian. Halleluia! There's no room in God's plan for weenies. God's work takes backbone. God's work takes courage. If we could turn around our public image maybe those boys and others like them could sweeten their mouths with the word of the Lord instead of five-cent candy balls. Halleluia!"

The flashy part of the sermon was over. He got down to work, directing the congregation to Corinthians. There were no further Halleluias or Praise the Lords. Brother Bud, contrary to what I had expected, was no dummy. Once he had their attention he turned scholarly. I couldn't see the reason for threats. Aside from a cheery sameness, I couldn't see what was objectionable about the People's Congregation.

The direction changed all of a sudden. There was still no obvious signal for the shifted course and this was what chafed. The mechanism was out of sight. They began speaking in tongues. Who cued them? How did they know when to stop or start? I was too afraid to look around. I closed my eyes and bowed my head as Ginny began to moan and cry. I only opened my eyes once during the whole thing, when I seemed to be losing my balance. Various men appeared in the aisles. They lifted fallen men and women and dried their tears. On the platform with Brother Bud a woman lay flat on the ground. I closed my eyes again and concentrated on the unity of the sounds, not on Ginny's gibberish or the sobbing of the man across the aisle. The combination of utterances surpassed speech. The congregation achieved a kind of music. Somewhere in the middle of the crescendo, Brother Bud applied the brakes. He whispered into the microphone:

"And when the day of Pentecost had come, they were all together in one place. And suddenly there came from heaven a noise like a violent, rushing wind, and it filled the whole house where they were sitting. And there appeared to them tongues of fire distributing themselves, and they rested on each one of them. And they were all filled with the Holy Spirit and began to speak with other tongues, as the Spirit was giving them utterance."

The sounds wound down slowly until there were only a few anarchic soloists. They were stubbed out like cigarettes by the same men who had appeared in the aisles. A few, still beside themselves, were led from the room. It was over. Brother Bud asked for prophecies and several hands went up.

"Praise the Lord. Brother Bud, I saw my dead sister Iona. She was dressed in a white robe and was surrounded by glorious angels."

"Brother Bud, I have seen the devil's awful face and can now say that we have nothing to fear. The devil is weak before our strength."

"Yes! I have seen cities destroyed today. I have seen cities burn and burn. Cities that have incited the Lord's wrath."

Brother Bud paid no attention to the woman lying on the floor beside him. Her ankles were crossed demurely. He made no effort to help her, and one of the men in the audience finally mounted the platform and brought her to. She cried a little as she marched off the stage. He was casual, though appropriately deferent about the miracle that had occurred during the service.

"Come on ahead, Abbie Dees. Don't be shy. How does it feel to walk? In the name of our Lord Jesus Christ, just how does it feel to walk? God! The GLORY OF OUR LORD!"

The little girl in the wheelchair rose unsteadily. Her mother's face was rough and red, as if she had been clawing herself rather than crying. The woman sucked her upper lip frantically as Abbie Dees made her unsure way to the stage. She wore a fussy, ruffled dress that stood out full on the ribs of a petticoat. Her legs were bent and thin. They were perfect in their deformity and seemed cast in a material other than flesh and bone. There were no bruises or marks of any kind. I stood up quickly to leave, dodging Ginny's grasp. I didn't want to see anymore. I kept thinking as I moved down the aisle that someone would leap out to stop me, but nobody did.

I was glad for the infernal heat inside my car, the kind of discomfort that was tangible. I sat until I was soaked through with sweat—it was rolling off my head by the time I finally started the car. Sounds then, human speech. I thought first of the Tower of Babel. A confounding of tongues, a confusion of speech for those audacious enough to build a tower to heaven. Then I considered People's Congregation, where the same cacophony of sounds became a gift of tongues to glorify and exalt God. I sweat on and on. Whether it was offered as blight or bliss, it seemed to me that we were crucially hobbled to our own obscure patch of sounds. Language, this aspect of it, was a divine grant doled out in private parcels, unknowable to even the nearest neighbor. The policeman who had assured me I was in for a treat was now crunching an apple. There was nothing to do but wave and roar out of the parking lot.

I returned the next Sunday, but had to leave before the rapture of tongues broke out, terrified that the next person the men in the aisles would have to revive might be me. All my Margaret Meadism was gone. I sat around too much after that, watching television with Sam and loading up on empty calories. I went to movies so I would have something to report on when I got back to France.

No hunter worth his salt would fire at an animal already crippled by another man's bullet. My brother reentered the state of Oklahoma the only way he could: half dead, as a weak survivor of eleven knife wounds. His derring-do got him over the state line and into Oral's hospital, where, according to the physician, "the power of prayer and the power of modern science combine to save lives." He even got his picture taken with the ex-governor of Mississippi. Catch Eckle couldn't shoot him now. Catch couldn't even hate him without losing face. In the ex-governor's own words:

"The citizens of Hattiesburg have asked me to extend their humble thanks to you, Cody Lerner, for saving one of our city's finest young women. Rainy Thomas is a woman who has it all.

Beauty and wisdom and the open heart that makes her vulnerable to people like Homer Sims. Cody, in risking your own life for one of our city's daughters, we would like to offer you the key to our city. I have written to Oral Roberts, expressing my wish to personally foot the bill for whatever treatment it takes to get a man like you on his feet. Cody Lerner, your intervention in the attempted assault on Rainy Thomas has given our city the green light on courage."

The photograph I have was taken in the hospital in Hattiesburg. The ex-governor and Rainy Thomas were standing by an open window. Sunlight poured into the room. What was most striking about the picture was not the gravity of the ex-governor as he read from the scroll nor my brother lying slack-jawed in the hospital bed. The most evocative sight of all was the crystal-clear outline of Rainy's wonderful legs under her sheer skirt. Rainy elicited tractor queens past, leagues of cheerleaders and baton-twirling Becky clones. She was blond, provocative and still alive, thanks to my brother. Cody's face was turned toward the open window but he wasn't looking at Rainy's legs. His eyes were on something outside the window.

My dream had been accurate. I scanned the picture with a magnifying glass, but Cody's face showed no damage from the knife. But damage had been done to my brother in some other significant way. Finding that damage was as tedious as bending over Sam's workbook. Eight pictures of the same man. Find the aberrant ninth with some small thing askew. I hadn't the energy to sort any of this out, and put the newspaper clipping in a drawer full of rubber bands and paper clips. Every ounce of patience was going into a series of phone calls and urgent telegrams emitted from a woman less intelligible than ever.

"Mom, you're not making any sense. According to this article—"

"I'm making perfect sense. I'm pointing out the holes in the story. And the great disparity between the Cody presented here and the Cody we know so well."

"What's so hard to accept? A woman cries out for help and my brother, recognizing a damsel in distress, rushes to her side. He gets a little banged up and as compensation the people of Hattiesburg turn him into a local hero and pay for his hospital bills. He's lots of things, but he's not a coward."

"Never claimed he was. I just want you to know these journalists have done a sorry job. They've given us a story outline, but they haven't delved into it. The result? We have no story at all. We have questions. By the way, Rainy didn't cry out for help. The tone of the article implies she did. But nowhere does it read that the woman cried out anything."

"What's your beef, Mom? Eleven stab wounds wasn't enough? Maybe you'd prefer a baker's dozen."

"Here you go. You move right in with all the familiar old grudges, the old preconceptions about my feelings for your brother. All I'm saying is I would appreciate knowing what really happened. Was it pure coincidence that your brother was hanging out at a diner in front of that pretty woman's apartment house? Is it typical of your brother to suffer insomnia on just the night Rainy Thomas is abducted? Cody could sleep through an Apache raid! And what was he doing in Mississippi in the first place? These questions are only answered in a superficial way and we're just not satisfied."

"We?"

"Which is why Becky plans to go right on down there."

"To the hospital?'"

"She's been there. Now she's going to rent herself a modest place and she'll return only when she's got hold of a fact or two."

"It's nice Cody gets such a warm welcome home."

"You think of your brother as having taken some kind of sabbatical! That he shirked the first real moral responsibility he ever had seems to have escaped your notice."

"Have you been down to see him?"

She didn't answer me immediately. I imagined her fidgeting with the red plastic timer or lighting still another cigarette.

"Still there?"

"You might be interested to know that I receive anonymous phone calls. Women I have never laid eyes on tell me my son is languishing, my son's color is poor. If he doesn't finish his green beans at noon, I know it by evening."

"So you haven't been down."

"Can't."

"You can but you won't."

"Oh, have it your way, Lucy. You always have."

Talk is cheap? We split our phone bills in half during Becky's Mississippi sojourn, launching endless scenarios that float or founder as the evidence rolls in. My mother's impassioned refusal to board any aircraft heading south draws outraged attention. The ladies of Hattiesburg, increasingly unbridled, finally go for the jugular vein. The president of the Junior League accuses my mother of being an enemy of Christ. She suffers their indignance with uncharacteristic control, neither dodging nor denying the charges.

"Mom, change your phone number! They're going to do you in."

"I wouldn't give those wagging tongues the pleasure. The less I say, the wilder their accusations get. You forget what a tough old bird I am, Lucy. It would take more than this petty campaign to roll over Agnes Lerner. Those women can't evict me!"

"Who's talking about eviction?"

"Psychological eviction, Lucy. Look at the big picture."

Possibly. Whether squatter or rightful tenant, my mother never really strayed from her own premises. When she buckled, as she was finally to do, it was with every conviction regarding her son quite intact.

16

In May of 1986 La Belle Eléna received still another visitor. This visitor was not a weary indigent stepping off an oversized toy train. Nor did our guest hail from earlier, bawdier times when Eléna herself presided. Our guest was dressed to kill. Four Vuitton suitcases for a one-week stay indicated that she meant business.

"Becky! Here we are."

"It's either jet lag or that new haircut of yours. I hardly recognize you. You look great, kid."

"I'll get a porter for these things. Marc couldn't make it. He's got to stake out the Palais de Justice this afternoon. Big Mafia guy is finally being tried in Nice."

"Mafia, really? Sam, you are getting so handsome. I could eat you up with a spoon. Give Aunt Beck a kiss, sugar."

Our car is full of shrieks and excited cries on the way home. I watch Sam's expression in the rearview mirror. He is amused and a little frightened by his aunt's gut reaction to most everything.

"I'm dreaming. A little old man with a beret carrying home a baguette. The sea! What makes it all those colors? How many shades of blue in all? I bought an automatic focus especially for the film festival. I hope you don't mind. I'll try not to embarrass you too much."

Cody's disappearance seems to have agreed with my sister-in-law. If Marc were to cut out for nearly three years would I look like that? She has done something to the color of her hair, lightly tipped the ends with gold. I once had my braid dunked in an inkpot. Somehow the results were not the same. La Belle Eléna?

"Oh, my. Oh, my, my, my. Big old place, isn't it? Cold in the winter, I guess."

"You bet."

"What strange birds these are. Pumpkin, are you man enough to carry Aunt Beck's overnight case? I thought so!"

Later in the afternoon, after she had examined every inch of the house and garden and sipped her Earl Grey tea, Becky wilted. I watched tiredness slip over her face all at once. The change was sudden and extraordinary. She looked, all at once, like a thirty-eight-year-old woman who had been through the mill.

"I guess you want to know why I'm here, Lucy. There's never been a better time to slip away now that things are back on track at home. And with the Cannes Film Festival on—"

"Then the two of you are doing alright?"

"The two of us have never been better. Now I'm not going to whitewash the situation and tell you things have been simple. And I won't eat my words, either. I told you all kinds of things about Cody and called him every name in the book. But something finally brought your brother to his knees. And we're making a go of it. The four of us. Libby has just about stopped smoking and Eleanor's letting her hair grow back in. It looks awful and spiky right now, but in a few months we'll be able to do something classic with it. Like before."

"What brought him around?"

"You'll have to figure that one out yourself. I just feel like somebody owes you more than these bits and pieces you get on the phone. Your mother gets so emotional and Cody won't recap any of this mess. That leaves me. The heat's off, Lucy. Who knows? You might even get to like me."

She went upstairs for a hot bath and a nap. During the week Becky stayed with us, La Belle Eléna was filled with sweet, unaccustomed odors. The mixture of mineral bath salts and a cloying, intense perfume seeped out of her room and down the stairs.

Becky embellished the story in unhurried episodes as we walked the Croisette in Cannes. In a bar called the Pam Pam, where we ordered sweet rhum drinks. On rocky beaches as we struggled to find comfortable positions. I had been given all the facts, but I was starved for extrapolation. The telephone, the sorry telegram can never convey innuendo.

"Beautiful alright, but this beach takes getting used to. Now, would you look at that? She has to be sixty years old—now why would she want to walk around topless? Have I missed the point?"

"You'll get used to it. Roll this up and put it under your neck. There, like that. Better?"

"A little. See, Daddy's instincts were always correct. I mean the detective business. The only thing is, he didn't hire the right one. She was right under his nose."

"You're talking about when you went down to Hattiesburg."

"Exactly. The good thing about the South is that people love to talk. If you stick around long enough and, Lord, smile, people always get to talking. Lucky for Rainy I'm an ethical person. With the dirt I've got on that girl, I could wipe her out so bad she'd never get back on her feet."

"You want some more tanning lotion?"

"Guess I'd better, hadn't I?"

The citizens of Hattiesburg never really forgave pageant officials when they didn't give Rainy the title in 1977. If ever a Miss Mississippi lived and breathed, if ever there was an ultimate Miss Mississippi, it had to have been Rainy Thomas. When she was named runner-up, the city's outcry was in its violent welcome home after the beauty contest. People's faith in Rainy changed over the next few years, but it never disappeared. Job after high-paying job came her way. For each she was underqualified, but this never disturbed Rainy. She finally found her calling as a professional fund-raiser. People went right on licking stamps and sending in checks and money orders whenever Rainy's big pretty face flashed up on the TV screen. They didn't think as much about the blind, the poor or the abandoned as much as they thought about Rainy in 1977 and how she had to come on back home without the crown. Rainy busted up her third solid marriage right in the middle of a United Way campaign. Remarks were made about how she might think about getting married herself and settling down. A lot of people heard these remarks at dinner parties.

"A woman named Edna Herald was one of her number-one supporters. She did a lot to maintain Rainy's rep. She deflected all the gossip she could."

The incident with Homer Sims didn't really surprise anyone. It was Rainy's exposure on television and in public places. Her willingness to spend eight hours a day in a shopping center if it furthered her cause. With her elongated facial features, Rainy made many people think of a true thoroughbred. And you didn't have to urge a thoroughbred to finish the race. The animal would run itself silly, break a leg or run until its lungs burst, getting over the finish line. It was just that single-mindedness that made Rainy a victim of aggression. She had most likely forgotten it was 2:30 in the morning when she left the ex-governor's place. Rainy had her own garage-door opener to the ex-governor's. She slipped her little Fiat in beside his black Bentley each evening toward 8:00 and would leave whenever their meetings about the hungry ended. On the morning in question that happened to be 2:30 A.M.

I snorted and Becky turned to look at me. She had been speaking with her eyes closed. Her lips were pasty and white with protective cream.

"Come on. Meetings about the hungry?"

"I'm serious. She said she and Dickerson were working on a plan to end hunger. Once and for all."

"Quel culot."

"If you mean the girl's got guts, you're damn right. You've got to respect someone like that. Now hush and listen. It gets even better."

It made sense. Not that a girl like Rainy would lock her car doors even at that dead hour. Not a girl with her heart in her hands. Not a girl always banking on the very best in people. She stopped for the red light, even as she saw Homer Sims on the street, his back up against the wall. What surprised her was it only took him two steps to get to the side of the car. Two steps and he looked like he was standing so far off. He hit Rainy once along the side of the head and then said, Why it's Rainy Thomas, isn't it? He made Rainy drive to her apartment as he held his hand between her legs. In his hand he held a sheathed knife.

"Good God!"

"Know what he is supposed to have said? 'I will cut you up in parts to mail to your blind and your poor if you make a sound. My name is Homer See Sims and tonight I want you to take care of me.' I would have died on the spot. Not Rainy, though. She managed to keep driving."

It is reported that my brother, suffering sleeplessness, was buying a pack of cigarettes from a machine in an all-night diner across the street from Rainy's apartment. The time was 2:51. He smoked two cigarettes from the pack, waiting, it is said, for tiredness.

"This part really bugs me. Cody told a reporter he had been encountering 'personal problems' for some time. And that night was difficult for him."

"That's kind of flat, isn't it? And incomplete. It drives my mother wild."

"Me, too. I'd much rather he'd just said it outright. 'I was just waiting to see if Johnny Dickerson had thought to save me some of his leftovers. I wanted a little piece, too.'"

"Becky!"

"Oklahoma crude. You've been gone a long time, Lucy. That's how jealous ladies talk these days."

Cody thought it curious that the couple across the street remained inside their car for such a long time. He saw the woman get out of the car with difficulty and then he saw her stumble. When the man hit her, he decided to act. Cody approached the two of them, and Homer, addressing no one or perhaps an invisible jury standing on the edge of her apartment building, began to speak. It was his lament.

"He was totally off his rocker. Completely. Cody told me his eyes rolled all the way back into his head once. He started yelling at Cody. 'Someone is always fucking with me. It always starts like this. Private bidnis gets to be somebody else's bidnis, and then it's THE WHOLE TOWN'S BIDNIS. Your time's up, faggot!'"

He unsheathed the knife he had held between Rainy's legs on the way home. The knife entered my brother's body eleven times. With the first blow, the staff of the diner, assembled on the sidewalk with rolling pins and paring knives, heard Cody cry, "Run, Rainy," which she did on her fine, long legs.

"The only reason Cody's even alive is because of the two cops that came around the corner in a patrol car. By the time they got Sims restrained, the man was literally out of his mind. He had completely forgotten Rainy. She managed to get back with four squad cars, no less. He slobbered like a baby and didn't even recognize her. So much for the '77 runner-up to Miss Mississippi."

Becky stopped talking and lay still. We had drunk beer with our sandwiches for lunch and I thought she was asleep. I felt cold and covered myself with an extra towel. The sounds on the beach seemed to draw farther away from me. Someone finally shut off the ghetto blaster. I realized I had dropped off myself when Becky spoke again.

"Yoohoo. You there with the skin cancer. I think even my fingernails are sunburned. There's some more. Listen up."

When journalists later reconstructed the evening's events in a special broadcast produced by a news team from Jackson, much was made of the weapon itself. It was discovered that one of Homer's numerous uncles was an antique dealer in a small port city. He dealt mostly in antique clothing, but disparate curiosities did turn up in his shop. There were hand-painted boats and ivory pipes. Plenty of old firearms and a whole top drawer devoted to iron handcuffs. But Homer had stolen his uncle's pride and joy. Hearing about the knife from a friend, Homer's uncle had driven clear up the coast under hurricane conditions once the owner decided to sell. It was an old dagger a blacksmith had once fashioned after an engraving he had seen of a misericorde, the medieval dagger used to give the deathblow to a seriously wounded knight. The broadcaster, in discussing the knife's history, made a considerable error in pronunciation. His gaffe produced a slew of outraged letters from offended historians across the state. Still, the knife contained a genealogy of its own and freed the crime of all ordinariness. It wasn't difficult for imaginative citizens of Hattiesburg to cast my brother in the role of a fallen knight. His room didn't remain barren for long. Women brought baked goods, and florists, hearing the arrangement was to be sent to that Cody Lerner, refused to accept payment. That Cody had called out the intended victim's proper name with the first blow of the knife drew little attention. It made sense, people said for the second time. With her history of exposure and all.

"Leave it to Cody. A run-of-the-mill scoundrel is one thing. But Cody edged himself into the first-class cabin with this one. I'm just about talked dry. You want to at least treat me to a soft drink? What's that mix of beer and lemonade they drink here?"

"Panaché. You're on."

On another day we took ringside seats at the Pam Pam. We were surrounded by celebrity seekers, people like ourselves, who were determined to remain blasé even in the face of Roman Polanski, who had just waltzed by.

"Things have certainly come full circle."

"What do you mean?"

"Well, when I first came to France light-years ago, his wife had just been murdered. Sharon Tate, remember?"

"Who could forget? Daddy bought Mama a pistol after that happened. Pretty little thing with a mother-of-pearl handle. And he taught her to use it, too. Took her out to the river Sunday afternoons until she could shoot anything moving.

What's he doing here? Wasn't he in jail or something?"

"He's just finished a big pirate film. A swashbuckler. I think he's given the ship to the city."

The drinks at the Pam Pam are bottomless. I lost interest midway through mine, but Becky finished hers and waved at the waiter.

"Gee, these are smooth. Ask him for another, Lucy. Now, back to your mother. Agnes, the ironhearted."

My mother did not rush to Cody's bedside. She waited for her rage to cool in Oklahoma, announcing, *I am staying put.* She was still as the eye of a storm.

"Nothing could rout her, Lucy. Not a one of their accusations got to her, none of their pleas. I was the first to crack."

She went to Mississippi alone on a Delta night flight.

"The girls were off with their boyfriends, so we had the house to ourselves. Forty minutes before I got on that plane, I was making love to Chico. Just to make sure."

"Sure of what?"

"Sure I wouldn't give in to Cody's allure. I wanted that son of a gun to pay. I read a murder mystery on the flight though ordinarily I do enjoy Barbara Cartland for air travel."

The first thing she did in Hattiesburg was to have the nurses shoo off all the visitors. She marched into the room, her heart pumping with anger and took a good look at all the things attached to her estranged husband's body.

"I'd planned on telling him he was one piece of shit. A bum. To really throw him out of gear I xeroxed a bunch of old bills. I figured we might open with a few past dues. Daddy treated Libby to her first real fur when she got the lead in the school play. I wasn't going to let on the coat was paid for. I sure wanted to give him hell."

But that's not what Becky did. Instead she whispered, Cody Lerner, you're some damn fool. Just look at what you walked out on. She undressed under the cold, flat hospital lights and walked over to Cody's bedside. Then, she began vigorously scrubbing up at the washbasin, something she'd neglected to do before leaving the house. She rubbed liquid soap into a thick foam on the inside of one leg and stared at her own image over the sink.

"I mean, when you hear about a man walking out on his wife, you automatically assume she's a real dog, right? I'm telling you all this by way of explanation, Lucy. My pride was seriously wounded. I asked him how long he'd been screwing Rainy Thomas."

Becky's opening interrogation lasted one hour. This discretion may have had something to do with the extraordinary equipment surrounding my brother and the nurses that entered without knocking to check his blood pressure or slip a tablet under his tongue. She wanted to know where he had been in winters and in springs and with whom. She wanted to know why he had left, but only if he could give a succinct answer.

"In emotionally sensitive areas people can only absorb limited amounts of data. When a man's gone three years you want a summation. I discovered the nitty-gritty step by step and all on my own. I did tell him about Eleanor, though. About how I fought to get her weight back up."

The only reproach Becky offered was Eleanor's bout with anorexia.

"The capper, as I told him, was when I forced her onto the scale in the bathroom and the needle held at ninety-five pounds. She had on her sweatshirt and tennis shoes, Lucy. After months of this health and exercise kick, I finally realized she was wasting away. And hiding it from me in those big, shapeless clothes. She was in constant motion. Family meals? Forget it. Eleanor would just wave her appointments notebook in front of my nose and run out the door. Her hidden agenda was starvation. We got through it alone, without specialists. Certainly without a father. I had to finally rock her in my arms like she was a little baby before she could face a plate of real food. Now what kind of specialist is going to tell you that? Cody really suffered when I told him all that. Which was just what I had in mind."

Then Becky's attention was drawn to Cody's own ordeal.

"I started thinking hard about what he'd been through. And I wondered if it were hard to stab somebody. I mean to push a knife all the way through skin and muscle must take a bunch of strength. I wondered how come all the wounds were around his back and abdomen. Seems like Homer would have thought about Cody's heart . . . anyway."

Becky left the hospital the next day. She looked at Cody's face, relaxed after an early-morning injection. She could, if asked, recite Cody's general whereabouts during his absence with some precision. But as to where my brother had actually been, she had no idea.

"I would not describe what I was feeling at the time as love. No, I don't think love was present in Hattiesburg. It came later, though. Maybe that's the most surprising part of this whole story. Whew! That woman looks like a million dollars, doesn't she?"

She kissed Cody's forehead and said they would talk again, when he reached the City of Faith. When Cody was well enough to move, he was flown to Oral's hospital at the ex-governor's expense. He settled down to full recovery in a room filled with yellow flowers Rainy ordered replenished each week. Daisies, pansies in pots, dozens of roses. This chaos of yellow was, as Rainy indicated on her cards, to give the impression of sunlight.

"It was enough to make you puke. 'May the sun beam down on you today, Cody.' That kind of crap. I unloaded everything on the janitor's wife."

Prayers were routinely said for my brother. They were not specially issued appeals or hasty supplications to fill in where medical science could not. Cody was on the mend. His chart said so. God was invoked as methodically as the physical therapist who appeared each morning after breakfast. It was in this atmosphere of occluded light and yellow flowers, in the daily prayer ritual applied as carefully as a poultice, that Becky felt the lifting away.

"Lucy, each day I was lighter. I felt myself lighter. I let go of something else, some old anger. I'm sure this was forgiveness."

Because of this new lightness, the freeing of her spirit from its long detention, Becky maintains that it was not actually Cody who was healed at the City of Faith, but her.

"Hate is a master. Anger is a shroud. Cody was gone for a long, long time. But he'd come back. Which was what I kept telling your mother."

Becky became a cafeteria habitué. She fell in love with the entire ORU student body. Members of the body befriended her at lunchtime. Several of them sacrificed study breaks to sit with her as she went through her painful conversion.

"Letting go of fury is hard work. I couldn't have done it by myself. Those kids were just wonderful to me."

My mother was successfully browbeaten by her daughter-in-law. She made her first visit to my brother not on the strength of a mother's blind love for her son. Rather, she was whipped into submission by the same pretty zealot who had, through an intricate series of luncheons and phone calls, won her heart so many years ago.

"We were watching the Donahue show. Your mother came crashing in with a brown grocery sack."

The sack was filled with orange yarn. She pounced on a folding chair and began to knit. She was at work on a series of projects for the disadvantaged. She planned to provide protection for two dozen disadvantaged heads come winter. Did she see the outline of her son on the bed? The impressive line-up of jars and bottles? She purled furiously.

"I'm not even sure she saw me, Lucy. She scared the daylights out of me. Bent over her knitting like that and then she just says, 'You might say hello to your mother. We could start there.'"

Cody may have been acting on some buried instinct. He didn't talk. He lifted himself out of bed with difficulty and went straight to her knees, pushing away orange wool and knitting needles. She helped him to his feet (or did he help her?) and in a confusion of tears and whys and sorries they began to treat the particular condition they had, that feverish condition of estranged mother and son.

"Cody told her he had been sick in his mind. That he had left us for the worst of reasons and stayed gone for the worst of reasons. She asked him why he'd bothered coming back and Cody made a big mistake. He laughed. And said he was back due to being stabbed. I think that laugh of his, which was Cody's old self bubbling up, got her goat. She said what a neat trick that was. To get stabbed and not die."

Then came Cody's second critical slip.

"He said God never rejected anyone forever."

She let him have it. Wrath lent her backhanded slap greater strength. Wrath and her wedding ring. The setting, dragged across Cody's cheek, made a nasty cut just under his cheekbone. Cody's face had survived Homer Sim's madness, but not Agnes Lerner's fury. She seemed unconcerned by the blood.

"Her parting shot was beautiful, Lucy. You come from such wonderful stock. 'So help me, you little bastard, if you dare speak of holy things after all this time. You're *my* son and I know what's in you and what's been left out. So don't try to lay any spiritual palaver on me. Turning born-again now would be too convenient.' You could have knocked me over with a feather, Lucy. She was breathing fire."

That evening Cody's blood pressure rose precipitously. His physical activity was immediately curtailed.

"Oh, that explains it."

"Explains what?"

"My mother's telegram. OVER A BARREL IN TULSA. FILL U IN LATER. I looked at that for days, trying to figure it out."

"All of us were stumped. And it wasn't like you'd think once he got out of the City of Faith. He didn't come rushing back to us. He took an apartment down on Riverside Drive."

"Pretty quiet neighborhood, isn't it?"

"More like an old folk's home."

Cody didn't speak of holy things. He launched a program of self-mortification as soon as he was released from the City of Faith. He resettled in a musty garage apartment. The neighborhood was filled with the clicking of canes and the low moan of wheelchairs. His landlady made only one request aside from absolute tidiness. Would he mind walking the dog for her? An overfed block of a dog, it had to be carried out the back door most mornings to pee. He cut her lawn without being asked, uprooted the poisonous mushrooms that favored the moist, shady corners of her property and only listened to the radio with headphones. She responded by calling him Dear. She reinstated her Thursday hair appointments, which she had long let lapse. Forgetting to adjust her hearing aid, she shouted the latest news into the telephone about her young man with the troubled past.

"I believe I am getting goosed on these drinks. Aren't you hungry yet?"

"I could stand an order of socca."

"What on earth is that?"

"Specialty down here. Wonderful stuff made from garbanzo beans, though it doesn't taste like it. No socca at the Pam Pam, however. I'll ask for nuts or something. Go on."

"I don't know if you're ready for this. But Cody went to work for Mr. Harry."

"No! I remember him. the pederast, the art collector. The menswear merchant and socialite. But I don't see Cody there at all. His store was always full of vicuna jackets and precious silk ties."

"Not so much expensive stuff since the oil market went. Still, you're right. It's not the spot for a guy like Cody. He didn't last long. I still hadn't let the girls know their father was back in town."

It was a bright, harsh day. The pharmacies had sold out their stocks of sinus remedies and hay fever pills by noon. The very young and old were urged to stay inside.

"They were sprawled on the floor watching MTV. I went in and cut off the television. All I said was 'Girls, he's back.' They didn't say a word. They got up off the floor and headed upstairs. I wasn't crazy about their costume change. Eleanor has this thrift shop stuff she puts on to make a point. Libby goes in for the child prostitute look. But I kept my mouth shut for once and prayed they'd let us in Nelson's. Lunch was dreadful."

Eleanor and Libby dragged chicken-fried steaks back and forth across their plates. They spurned food and drink and made polite conversation. Cody produced neat, trim lies that didn't trigger questions.

"He said strange cities only made people sad and lonely. It made them hungry for familiar things to touch and feel. Then he changed the soundtrack. Poor thing. Tried all of a sudden to be fatherly. He'd done a little homework, I guess. He had all these statistics on crack. Bless him. Eleanor just stared at him with a blank look on her face. Probably wishing her one wish."

"Which is?"

"To become a man. Isn't it clear to you? It started a long time ago with that paper route. Stuffing all her lovely hair inside that ball cap. Then trying to starve her way out of a woman's body later and practically shaving her head. This is pure theory, mind you. As for Libby, if you could've seen her that day! You have no idea how seductive a kid that age can be. And with her own father."

"Pretty disconcerting, isn't it?"

"I promised I wouldn't whitewash. I'd rather walk the plank than live through any of this crap again."

I thought of Cody, sitting in Nelson's Cafeteria on a steamy day, maybe looking at the exit sign that glows red at the back of the restaurant. Catch has captured what is essential about fatherhood. A loud, booming voice and weekends at the lake. Smells you can count on, like the leather in a shoe department and cigarette smoke mixed with the sharp scent of mouthwash. Rules and firm ideas about everything under the sun that add up to father love. Cody might have outfoxed Libby when she was small. But never scrutinous Eleanor, changing early into someone else with her ball cap and paper route, gliding past things like real fathers.

"Oh, my God. Look at the time. Marc has probably called the police by now."

The sun is setting. I point to the Ile de Llérins, just visible from Cannes, and tell Becky about poor Paganini, whose early musical genius was mistaken for the devil's own work. The French refused to bury him, and the boat carrying his body crashed on the island on its return to Italy. I find, as I recite tourist fact after tourist fact, that I have been decoding the menu, the milieu, and that it doesn't hurt a bit. We park the car for a minute on the Croisette and share a last cigarette. Polanski's pirate ship commands the harbor. Someone is waving a black flag furiously from the crow's nest. A high-masted, anachronistic beauty, the boat seems more the property of Sam's treacherous island than of the sybaritic city of Cannes.

17

Cody's return was not incandescent. It threw off about as much light as a match struck in a dark, windy field. There was no disclosure or redeeming conclusion. He bore Mr. Harry's trifling complaints and his landlady's increasing demands. He didn't reclaim his wife and daughters but observed a cringing distance, like a stray animal dropping in and out of view.

"He'd turn up from time to time, with a present for the girls. Or an idea for some outing. But he seemed to lack conviction. I guess Daddy sensed that. He moved in to push events to their natural conclusion, you might say. Daddy can be so persuasive when he wants to be."

Catch Eckle took out a store charge at Mr. Harry's. He wanted to undergo a significant wardrobe change, as he explained to Mr. Harry. He haunted the store, asking for Cody.

"Oh, he'd ask Cody dozens of questions. Like where a man's pants ought to break. What he thought about a particular color of salmon against his skin tone. It was flattering. Mr. Harry thought he had a real find in Cody, if he could generate that much business and customer appreciation."

Catch charged twenty thousand dollars in three weeks. He was casual about the amount, paying seven thousand in cash one day as a show of good faith. He lavished Cody with praise in front of Mr. Harry. Said he'd never known a harder worker or a salesman with finer taste. His purchases became hysterical. When Cody didn't have his jacket size, he bought one or two sizes larger and Cody cut it down. He bought two and three of some items and wrote down the date they were expecting a new shipment.

"Daddy looked like a fool. Almost sixty and dressed like a college boy. I thought he might be getting senile until he took it all back."

"All the clothes he bought?"

"Every single item. Cashmere coats, underwear. You can imagine the scene . . ."

Mr. Harry gathered up all the merchandise Catch piled on the store counter in an ecstasy of good manners and fine upbringing. Some of the articles had clearly been worn. He picked them up with the tips of his fingers and dropped them into a pile. Cody was fired that night.

As Becky and I talked a cat stalked a sparrow on the terrace. It was a young yellow cat the whole quarter was fond of. She was amply fed by two or three families, whose children coaxed her onto their turf with bowls of milk and plates of tuna fish. I got up to shoo the cat off.

"Let them be, Lucy. Don't interfere with nature."

The bird shot away and the cat, unconcerned, began digging a hole near a patch of mint. I did get up, ignoring Becky's protests.

"A garden is not a litter box. Scram!"

"They had it out later at Cody's apartment. I should say Daddy had it out with him. Cody didn't fight back at all. Good thing I was there. Cody might have taken his second beating. Daddy was that mad."

Catch dragged an armchair to the widow in Cody's room. He stretched his legs out in front of him and shut his eyes. The sun was setting and the room caught the last bit of red light. The part of the room where Becky sat was already eclipsed.

"Daddy opened with a line about the implication of a sunset. He said he couldn't understand what it was that made people so fond of them, when all they did was signal the loss of another day. He went on for a little while about that. I'll confess, Lucy. I wondered if my father had lost his marbles. He picked up this and that. One of the landlady's souvenir ashtrays from Vegas. Then he rubbed his eyes and lit a cigarette."

Becky cleared her throat and drew her hand through her hair. It was a pretty gesture, one that I had memorized by the end of a week's time. There was much that, grudgingly, I had come to find graceful in Becky. And appropriate.

"He told Cody that while he was following him he'd noticed the craziest thing. That he couldn't manage to keep clean. Spills, car grease. Dirt. Often he found himself changing clothes in the middle of the day. When he said it looked like Cody's filth was contagious, I jumped up real fast and poured us all some Gatorade."

Becky's voice dropped lower. Fear? Shame? I asked her to speak up.

"I said Daddy wanted a medical certificate to make sure he didn't have AIDS or venereal disease. Told him the staff at the City of Faith were a bunch of clowns and that he was sending Cody to a man he knew in Dallas. Then he announced he was taking him back into business as full partner."

"Catch's court of law."

"You bet. He had Cody pull his shirt off."

"How come?"

"So he could admire Homer's handiwork."

Cody went down to Dallas and didn't return until, in Catch's own words, he was pronounced cleaner than a bulldog after a tick bath. His first decisive act as a full partner was to fire the man who supervised the Fright Rider, a roller coaster Catch had put in at the 51st Street location. The man drank straight through his lunch hour and let pregnant women and children under ten get on the Fright Rider any afternoon. His first decisive act as father was to reinstate meals. He found Eleanor nonchalantly eating a frozen dinner at four o'clock.

"He told her dinner would be at six from then on. I sat back and mixed myself a Bourbon and Seven. And put my feet up, Lucy. You know how good that feels? I just sat there and took it all in for the first time in three years."

There were scattered protests. The unnamed descendants of Lovey and Dovey were released in the kitchen. Cody's lamb stew, two days in the making, was tossed out after yellow feathers and worse were found floating on the surface. Libby openly defied curfew, returning home at three o'clock in the morning in an ambulance.

"No, she wasn't hurt. She dates an ambulance driver. When Cody found her birth control pills it really hit the fan. Don't look at me that way, Lucy. I haven't been able to stave off just everything, you know. Single parenting is no picnic."

The final protest supposedly came from Chico. Catch himself swung by and drove Cody to work when it was discovered that each of his tires had been viciously slashed in the night. Cody's presence slowly became matter-of-fact. The personnel at each of the big three locations learned it would be Cody and not Catch who stepped out of the company-owned Seville. Eleanor and Libby combed Cody's drawers for warm socks and flannel shirts without fear of reprisal. This brand of scavenging they both recognized as their birthright.

"Since then things have just gotten better and better. We're a family again, thanks to Daddy's help."

"Help or coercion?"

"Firm help. And guidance, which is what your brother has always needed.

"So, Mr. Laugier. The coast is clear."

I stare at Becky, who's changed position again. She's sitting with one leg drawn to her chest, the other stretched out lazily in front of her.

"For whom?"

"For you. You can bring Marc home and settle this once and for all. We look like a family again is what I'm saying."

I think of the message on the red People's balloon again: *We will receive you.* Becky seems the most unlikely bearer of the grail.

"Just what are we settling?"

"The way you live. Which is neither here nor there."

"I live here *and* there."

"Same thing, Lucy. When are you going to wise up?"

I tell Sam over dinner that Aunt Becky's plane leaves tomorrow for America and that he will have to say good-bye tonight at bedtime. He pulls a long face and begins crushing green peas with the back of his spoon.

"Cut it out, Sam. Eat."

"Je n'ai plus faim, Maman."

"Alors, va te laver."

"Hurry up, Sam. Aunt Becky's got a little present for her nephew."

"Chic! Elle a un cadeau pour toi."

The pipes hum and we take our time over coffee. Sam's bathtime seems inexorably long and Becky looks at her watch.

"That little bugger. He's going to use up all my hot water. I'll go take care of bedtime and you finish the kitchen."

Sam stages an eloquent farewell gesture and is discovered playing dead in the shower stall. Marc and I race up the stairs together, hearing Becky's screams. I try to calm her as Marc hauls Sam's long, white body out of the shower stall.

"Marc, be careful!"

"J'en ai marre!"

Sam is wrapped roughly in a towel. He is true to the role throughout and lies slumped over his father's shoulder like a sack of livestock feed. I hear Marc's voice rise up out of control behind the closed door. Sam resists for several seconds and then gives way to violent sobs.

"Jesus, Lucy."

"Yeah."

My wising up goes forward despite the inelegant surroundings. I straddle a chipped bidet in the steamy bathroom. Becky, for her part, is seated on the lid of the toilet. Marc brings in three glasses and a bottle of whiskey after Sam quiets down. It's ten o'clock before it occurs to us to leave that bathroom for more appropriate surroundings.

When Becky left I turned La Belle Eléna inside out. Madame

Leconte launched a career late in life. She became a sought-after femme de ménage, while her husband plunged deeper into gardening and La Vie Tranquille. She returned home at noon in a white Mercedes taxi like a tired queen. Still, she found the energy to help me two hours a day and for a while I knew precisely where everything was. As I scoured and scrubbed, I thought about all Becky had told me. I was glad not to have seen my brother in extremis. Nor would I have been anxious to see him, convalescing in the City of Faith. Despite Becky's reportage, the evidence on my brother was still inconclusive—a shyster, an incorrigible womanizer, a fallen knight. If my brother had a small gift it was in generating conflicting reports and multiple versions. No one could stop making Cody up.

Cody's homecoming didn't trip off other returns. For a while I toyed with the idea that Eléna would return for a brief guest appearance. The knock on the door was not her, suggesting it was time to once again light the barbecue or cut up fresh fruit for a sangria. It was a neat, clean pair of Habib's boys, asking if they could spray. They each had a yellow tank of insecticide strapped to their backs and they set upon my roses, dark with suspicious stains.

The only coincidence of the period was a minute reconciliation. It bore significance only to the two parties concerned. Fittingly, the laying down of arms occurred in a dirty private clinic near a commercial shopping center advertising indoor waterfalls and fifty boutiques. My mother-in-law and I agreed on the nurses' sloth and the grime on the windowsill. We aired the room and discovered the exhaust from the cars and buses smelled worse than the combined odor of boiled sheets and blood. We watched Marc and took turns leading Sam to the public park a few blocks away from the clinic. From ten days of badgering staff for a fresh towel or a water glass free of fingerprints, an inadvertent concession seemed to have been made. We were not friends and would never address each other as Maman or Chérie. Sunday dinners would not be reinstated. We could, however, unite when the comfort of someone mutually loved was at stake. Marc walked out of the clinic on the arm of two civil women, both of whom were cheered by the sudden appearance of a nightingale on the limb of an almond tree. Marc had discovered, after enduring increasing discomfort in his left eye, that a maverick vein threatened his vision. It was rerouted on the operating table and he was obliged to wear an eye patch for several days. The patch was carried to school one Monday morning in an old jewelry box lined with red velvet. During La Petite Heure de Raconter, Sam described in detail what it was like to have a pirate for a father. A pirate who had seen for himself an island on the way to Corsica peopled by a sword-bearing, contentious tribe. When Madame Sarl called me in for a consultation I left Chan's suit hanging in the closet, choosing a more conventional uniform of jeans and hightop sneakers.

My father called in the middle of a furious summer storm. I was watching the desecration from the window when he phoned. A clump of cosmos was swiftly being flattened. I could see the widow watching from her window, too. Two yellow sheets clung forlornly to her clothesline. The wet wind howled.

"What's up, Dad?"

"Plenty. Most of it good."

"And the tree project?"

"Blooming. We're up to ten staff members and a Greenvision office is opening in Oklahoma City next year. But that's nothing compared to your brother's activities. He would have called, but he's going at a dead run. Approvals, papers to sign. He's got at least five companies bidding on every contract."

"A fourth location? Not more miniature golf."

"He and Catch are moving out of golf into something else. They're still in leisure, but a different kind. They're breaking ground on the new project next month and I know your brother would like to see you there. It's not something you people ought to miss."

"Why all the secrecy?"

"No secrecy. Something you'll just have to see for yourself. What do you say?"

"Love to."

My father's voice was choppy. I thought of the tin can experiment Cody and I set up as kids. We tried all kinds of empty cans, punctured and connected with string. Somehow our voices could never travel across that white line. Hello? Hello? We shouted ourselves silly.

"You'll have to speak up, Lucy. We're not going to take no for an answer this time."

"You don't have to. I said I'd love to. I'd love to come home."

"I know this interferes with Sam's school schedule—"

"At his age?"

"And, of course, your husband's work might make that kind of trip a little—"

"He has three weeks vacation coming to him. No problem."

"Well, you surprise me, Lucy. I thought I'd meet the usual resistance. I feel a bit disarmed."

"Put Mom on while you recover."

"Can't. She's at her Dale Carnegie course. Part of a new philosophy she has. She says the whole thing boils down to influence."

"Noun or verb?"

"Why both, I imagine."

I visited Marc in the darkroom that evening with the news. I watched an image slowly form in the tray of solution. The picture was of a man and his shadow. Marc had hung out of an office window to take the picture. The result was a bird's-eye view full of flat, dark planes and sharp angles. If you turned the picture the shadow appeared to be walking the man.

"Will you come home with me next month?"

He breathed a sigh of relief.

"Enfin."

He was referring to the successful print, but I telephoned Hélène Manotte for the tickets that evening. We spoke for a while about recent airport tragedies and the increased security measures in Nice. She asked about Sam.

"Deux billets, comme d'habitude?"

"Trois."

She burst out laughing. I'm not sure whether this was mirth

or relief. But there was champagne waiting for us at the airport the day we left. The head of customs is a man given to easy laughter. He wanted to propose a toast to the three of us in his stuffy office. But no one could think of anything appropriate, so we just drank and shook hands instead.

18

The state official requisitioned a tent at the last minute because of soaring temperatures. It is pitched in a deep hollow of land outside Ada, Oklahoma. Two miles north of this hollow lies a series of rocky caverns where accomplished robbers and hold-up men once stashed their loot. The caves are no secret. Scout troops scramble up the rocky slope to the caves on overnight junkets. They build fires and roast marshmallows in the damp, black holes. They tell stories of atrocities in the flickering light until they are restrained by the Scout leader, who fears recurrent nightmares and parental complaints. When the Scouts don't frequent the caves, amorous Ada teens do. All this will grind to a halt in the year 1990, the projected completion date for The Gateway. The caves have been bought by Eckcorp as part of a five-hundred-acre parcel. The concept of caves is under study by a public relations firm in Dallas. Five men and one woman are at a stalemate. The woman holds out on what may well be a moot point, maintaining that caves have a definite Old Testament feeling.

The tent, open on two sides, produces a kind of hot wind tunnel. Scorching air whips through in gusts. Ella stands between Marc and I. She has drawn her hair up into a chignon and perspiration produces an aureole of dark tendrils. She is wearing a cotton sailor blouse and a seersucker skirt. She produces several French nursery rhymes for Sam and her accent is surprisingly good. She tells me she takes the bus into Tulsa nearly every weekend. In several weeks, she may be only an outpatient.

"Did you get my letters, Lucy?"

"All of them."

"I guess they told you, though."

"Told me what?"

"That I'm about as batty as they come. The doctor says I've entered a holding pattern, though. Like a jet."

I draw her close and admire her hair ribbon, which she has set at a very saucy angle. I have brought back copies of *Marie Claire, Elle.* Two issues of *Paris Match.* We've spent lots of time dissecting the grand elements of fashion. She has applied too many different kinds of perfume and this is difficult with the heat. My aunt, seated several rows away, turns toward me meaningfully and mouths *Watch Ella.* Marc rocks back and forth on his heels as Catch talks. He has chosen as his focal point the birth of the Gateway concept. His description equals the pain and grit of true labor. The state official has removed his jacket. The searing wind blows against my back and I do the same.

"Sleep was remote at the time. I was a burned-out case. A spiritually burned-out case. There's no other way to put it. The miniature golf was prospering, alright. The figures were healthier than ever, but as every empty winner knows, the figures ceased to have meaning for me. I was searching for something. But what?"

Anita takes a pitcher of cold water to the platform where Catch is speaking. She hands him a small white towel along with the glass of water and returns to her folding chair.

"Thank you, sweetheart. My wife, Anita Eckle."

"The first ray of light, you might say, came to me as I examined Sunday. The traditional Christian Sunday. Rise, not too early. After the ten o'clock service it's lunch or brunch and then that endless Sunday afternoon. I might add, endless *secular* afternoon.

Typically, the kids shoot off with their friends, Dad putters in the garage and Mom gets back to her housekeeping chores. And if there's a family outing (take it from one who knows) it's miniature golf or bowling. There's nothing wrong with this. But the thread is broken. The spiritual thread is broken."

Marc lifts Sam in his arms for a better view. He's listless from the heat and ready to fall asleep. I wipe his face with a Wash 'N' Dry.

"You understand, Marc?"

"Of course. But when is your brother going to talk?"

"In a second."

Ella is humming what seems to be a passage from *Bolero*.

"Sssh. Ella, keep it down."

She stops and lowers her head, inspecting a corner of her sailor blouse.

Cody and Becky sit together in the first row, flanked by the girls. Libby is fascinated by the lanky cameraman. She watches every move he makes, while Eleanor remains aloof, her eyes on her grandfather.

"I began evaluating what I had under my thumb. Could all this energy, this possibility be rechanneled? Could we give our leisure activities some additional dimension? I watched my windmills turning, my Fright Rider rattling down the rails, and thought hard. I needed a catalyst. I'll just read the registered letter Eckcorp received last week from Mr. Johnny Dickerson, the ex-governor of the state of Mississippi:

> *Dear Sirs:*
>
> *I have kept abreast of the controversy surrounding The Gateway and feel that now is the appropriate time to offer my congratulations and pledge of support for your venture. It is a project that requires stamina and courage. I and others who have the good fortune to know Cody Lerner feel it is also the work of a visionary.*
>
> *Yours sincerely,*
> *John Dickerson*

"Now I want to turn the microphone over to my son-in-law. He is a young man with abundant ideas and ample hope. I say ample hope, because without it, we wouldn't have had the courage to present these ideas. We would have buckled under the polite catcalls of all the men and women who claimed it wasn't possible. Cody, will you come on up here, son?"

Visionary. This is a version of Cody worth coming home for. My brother mumbles his thanks and begins to speak. My mother whispers something to my father and shifts in her seat.

"The Gateway will not be a healing center. The Gateway does not claim to be a center for religious studies. The Gateway is a recreation park with an emphasis on the born-again experience. It is in this sense a theme park. The theme won't be ecology or fantasy or wildlife. The theme is God. His work and His word, the life of His son, Jesus Christ, will be depicted in a leisure park setting. Questions have been raised about propriety. Many people have become outraged over our alleged bad taste and our intention to pervert sacred elements. This is the controversy my father-in-law and John Dickerson referred to. I'm not going to enter a debate on aesthetics, but I would like to say a few words about the work that lies ahead."

He drinks from Catch's cup. Ella catches Marc's sleeve and pulls him toward her.

"I do hope Lucy told you that's not Cody."

"Ah bon? Who is it then, Ella?"

"I can document this."

"Sssh, Ella. Lower your voice!"

"I don't suppose you ever saw that movie where everyone turned into peapods."

"Peapods?"

"Not that, exactly. But these plants produced people doubles, you see. I mean the people looked, acted and talked the same. But the fact is, they weren't."

Marc nuzzles Sam and bends lower, listening intently. He's delighted to learn my brother is a peapod.

"I mean you had to have known my cousin before. This person has virtually nothing to do with Cody. What I'm wondering is exactly how many of the people gathered here are the same. Smilers, every last one of them. Born-again peapods. And just how many more does he plan to attract with this project of his?"

"Stop it, you two! And Ella, for heaven's sake, whisper. You're distracting Cody. Now be fair."

"The diffusion of God's word, traditionally, takes place in the church, the home. The workplace. I say traditionally. What about those many thousands of Americans who have not been spiritually solicited? They'll be loading up vans and campers in the summer of 1990. These people may be searching for a new concept in leisure. In its attention to the fact that these people will be seeking activities for their children in a changed and refreshing landscape, Eckcorp offers a very real Christian service. Effective diffusion of the word takes place in the world as it is, not the world as it should be."

Eleanor rolls forward a map of the Ada site and hands a pointer to her father. She strides back to her seat, unsmiling. A little roundness has returned to her cheeks. She pushes back with impatience the dark, soft wedge of hair that falls into her eyes. This break is unfortunate. Ella starts up again. My aunt turns to me, decisively this time, and I shrug. She whispers something to my uncle.

"Do you-all have Holy Rollers in France?"

Marc looks at her doubtfully, not understanding. She continues, not waiting for an answer.

"I personally can't stand it. I mean I used to hand out literature myself in public parks. Five steps and you were saved. *Fortunately* I took a course in Comparative Religion and I found out every one of them was based on the same principles. Now I see God in everything. Snakes. Rocks. You name it. Listen, do you smoke?"

"Thanks to our topography here in Ada, motorists will be able to see our statue of Jesus from a distance of up to twenty-five miles. Once summoned to The Gateway, this traveler will discover a simple, rustic setting. We will provide hotel and motel service here in the northeast triangle. Facilities will be simple and comfortable. We will also have thirty-five acres of cabin facilities in the highly wooded areas on the southern tip of our property. The Gateway will have no lake, no speedboats or waterskiing. There will, however, be a considerable waterway for swimming. All lodging will be linked by the artificial river now under construction. The velocity of water flow will be entirely automated, as sections of the river will be given over to biblical reenactments. Other sections will be open to swimming and sunbathing on sandy beaches. Tree-lined footpaths will follow portions of the river."

Ella smells deeply the cigarette Marc hands her, with her eyes closed.

"Oh, this reminds me so much of Paris."

"Ella, you've never been to Paris."

"Well, you certainly haven't changed. Except for your haircut. Same old nay-sayer."

"That might be. But you can't smoke in here. You'll burn the place down."

"Think so? What's he going on about now? His big old Jesus statue again? I'll just take this outside."

She leans over and kisses me softly on the cheek.

"Lucy?"

"Go on now. It's almost finished."

"Lucy? I love you best of all, even though I give you a hard time. You know that?"

"Hang on until lunch. It won't be long. Shoo, fly."

She wanders off to smoke and I relax. I hear a car door slam. Cody says something about the Red Sea.

". . . by dramatic means. The questions ahead all concern one thing. How to skillfully translate our text, the Bible, into our chosen motif. Family fun. To tackle these questions, we have hired the Adler Agency, a Dallas group. They are a widely respected firm whose clients are among some of the largest theme parks in the Southwest."

"Pas terrible."

Marc whispers his analysis of Cody's delivery—lackluster. Cody handles questions from one or two reporters. Marc wistfully fingers his camera and I realize I've let him down. My family is respectably dressed and well-mannered, homogeneous today as milk. And Cody the outlaw has turned himself in, body and soul. He is asked for his opinion on Christian rock concerts, the projected impact of The Gateway on the state economy. Someone asks if it's true the eyes in the Jesus statue light up at night. One reporter, showing off, makes a quip about Tulsa, the buckle of the Bible Belt.

"What kind of feedback have you had from the Tulsa ministry?"

"All very positive. We plan to offer around-the-clock ministry in our hotel-motel chain. The presence of a corps of trained clergy is vital to our program. Anyone who wants to accept Jesus Christ as his personal savior can do so, no matter what time of day or night."

The Eckcorp publicist stands up and announces her plan to tour the site with reporters. They will begin the tour with a visit to the caves. She is pretty, with the dark, strong features of a full-blooded Indian. She's wearing a business suit and her hair hangs free to her waist. The state official rises and interrupts her. They talk quickly and she hands him the microphone. He has to raise his voice, despite the loudspeaker, for a commotion begins at the back of the tent. The alarm there threatens to spread faster than the fire.

"Folks! Whoa, now. Hold on back there! We're gonna take this row by row. Just like when we were in primary school. Carl, you'll want to help the gentleman with the crutches. Row by row, folks! We've got all the time in the world. God's in here with us. Let's nobody panic!"

Catch rushes to the podium and grabs the microphone.

"Every person who's come up through the Oklahoma public school system will remember the dad-burned fire drill. And remember wondering *why?* Today is why, folks! No pushing. No shoving. That's the way. Ladies and gentlemen, our assembly is over. We're going to file out of here like Americans. Not a push, not a shove. The elderly first, row by row, if you please. This way, folks, and keep calm."

I feel an animal's terror. A slow, sleepy rootedness. I look at

Sam, curled into a small nut of fright against his father's shoulder. Orange flames crawl up the side of the tent. Fanned by the wind, they rise to form a cage of fire. Around me people are stomping and anxious. A man in a gray suit frees up each row, like a church usher. Marc puts Sam in my arms. He's crying and rigid, an awful burden. I don't feel I have any strength left in my arms. My clothes stick to my skin and it's harder to breathe.

"Marc, I can't hold him. You'll have to . . ."

But he's left us. Poised on a chair, then bounding off and bending to one knee. The Pentax shutter sounds like an automatic round. Watching him and feeling fury steal over me brings me to. Our row feeds out into the aisle. We're noiseless, cowlike and dumb. Who is this clown in the gray suit anyway? And is that really my husband, snapping photographs instead of leading his wife and child to safety?

"Salaud!"

"This is a chance in a lifetime. My God, this is fabulous. Just one more photo."

"Leave it to the television crew!"

"Maman! Aiieee. J'ai peur!"

"Oh, le monsieur va nous aider. Tiens, voilà! C'est notre tour."

Outside the terror siphons off into foolishness. Nervous jokes are made about bonfires and Smoky the Bear as the first siren is heard. A woman bursts into tears and walks off from the crowd, sobbing. Watching the woman and wondering how I might help her, I see Ella sitting in a patch of weeds, her legs spread slightly apart. She's smiling, her eyes on the fire and smoke. She holds a can of gasoline in her lap as innocently as if it were a lunch pail.

My aunt succumbs. The heat, the sight of her daughter in a squad car exacts its toll. Her hat tumbles off her head first, signaling a fall. She collapses slowly, in sections, with a little cry of alarm. We catch her before her head strikes the ground.

"Somebody get water quick!"

"Here, little lady, have some of this. I always carry a little something in my glove compartment."

An onlooker pours something down her throat and she comes to, coughing and gasping. She bats at him at first, then drinks fiercely from his silver flask. She's helped off the ground and led to a shady spot. Cold cloths are applied to her neck and cheeks. My uncle sits in the squad car answering questions and Dad has his arms around my aunt's waist.

"Come on, lean on me. Rest here until your strength comes back."

"Well, a squad car. They might have put her in an ambulance, Wade. Look at her. Right out there where everybody can see her. They've got her trapped in there like she's a criminal. Why don't they shut off the damn light? Those big shots, trapping a poor, sick girl and treating her like she committed murder."

"More like arson. Lucky for us she's so inept. Sadie, think for a minute of what your daughter had in mind for all of us. I'm afraid our Ella's gone pretty far afield today."

"Our Ella. You sanctimonious ass, Wade. She's my Ella and she's sitting in a police car at the moment. But I guess you wouldn't know how that feels, now—would you? You're in your glory today. Two fine, grown children, one of whom is going to clean up nicely with his religious park. The other drags home her fancy, French-talking husband and son. You've got yourself a nice, neat set of family jewels. And me? All I've got is that pretty little lunatic nobody can save. And now they're fixing to take her away for good."

I stare guardedly at my cousin, starved for last looks. Her mind and its workings, more thick and matted than a wild animal's nest, have long been closed off from me. What's new now is the sense of something deadly and intentional in her that we've all failed to see. We have tried to integrate Ella by reducing her to a farce, an engaging, offbeat anecdote. She retaliates by trying to burn us alive.

Sam is at the wheel of the fire engine. Police and firemen abound and Sam's in heaven. Marc is shooting close-ups of his son in an Ada fireman's hat.

"Happy beyond measure?"

"Exactement."

"I find your behavior disgusting. You took a life-and-death situation and turned it into a picture for a photo album."

"A family photo album. Doesn't that redeem me? Voilà! Comme ça, Sam."

"You've become an unthinking, unfeeling camera lens."

"I didn't photograph your cousin."

"But you wanted to. Well, the show's over. Catch has moved and it has been seconded that we go to Howard Johnson's to recover."

"Who is Howard Johnson?"

"You're about to find out."

But we haven't seriously affected the hollow of land outside Ada. The patch of land, barren and dusty so long, has known Indian councils and civic pig roasts, years and years of prison rodeos. Plant life here has been sent packing. The fire, fueled by a canvas tent and little else, was already languishing by the time the fire department arrived. There is smoke now and milling people, some of whom are discussing food and where to get it. Others are shepherded into the publicist's Jeep for an abbreviated tour of the Gateway site. The effect is post-theater. An empty stage and dimming lights. All the relative insignificance of a single afternoon's performance.

The family convoy heads toward the Howard Johnson's on the old interstate. It's air-conditioned; and free, presweetened iced tea is being offered all day long. The temperature is holding steady at 112 degrees.

"Malheur. This is Howard Johnson?"

"Right. Motel and restaurant. Nothing else out this far. You're in for an all-American eating experience. Wait until you tuck into Jell-O."

Marc handles it with aplomb. Iceburg lettuce drowning in thousand island. He blithely butters a thin slice of white bread and pounds the bottom of the ketchup bottle along with the rest of us. He deflects all discussion of Ella by drawing attention to the behavior of Americans in an emergency situation.

"Really, I was impressed today. The order and the discipline! The French would stampede. We can't bear to stand in line in the supermarket. How would we have functioned in a situation like we saw today? Mr. Eckle, perhaps you said it best. 'We're going to file out of here like Americans.'"

I wonder if he is bluffing. But an expression common to ideological converts everywhere steals over his face and I think not. Have I created a Frankenstein?

"And the police and fire department were there in minutes! I'll tell you something. Lucy and I were at the beach in Antibes and what we saw will show what I mean. An ambulance driver pulled his vehicle up to the sea wall and turned his radio up full blast. Then he went windsurfing! Of course a call came in and by the time he got to shore, arranged his windsurfer and dressed, I'm sure the person was dead."

My mother shakes her head in disbelief. My aunt and uncle's absence are forgotten as Marc generates more discussion. Cody watches quietly, smiling to himself as Catch grows more and more discursive. He grabs Marc's forearm as he explains the principle of the smorgasbord.

"Doesn't exist over there? Shame. I guess that has to do with the American notion of plenty. Now you take my wife Anita. Honey, you don't mind if I use you as an example? Assume we invite you to dinner. Now, it may be pretty standard fare. Simple. You get me? But my wife won't be satisfied until she hears the magic words. 'I couldn't eat another bite.' Or, 'Anita, I am just stuffed.' So believe it when you read that banner outside that reads *All You Can Eat for 11.95*. In America, you can go back for seconds and thirds—matter of fact, I'm gonna get just another bite of that roast beef."

"Catch, you want to get me another slice of that cornbread, too, while you're up?"

"Cornbread? With the Miami trip coming up? I wouldn't, Anita. Agnes, how's about seconds on that fruit salad?"

"Aunt Lucy, what's Sam saying?"

Sam, seated far away from Marc and I, is dazzled by cousins and attention and the Ho Jo Children's Special, a medley of bland food stabbed with paper umbrellas. He is also enjoying the impunity of not being understood.

"Tu es bête comme tes chaussettes.

"Ferme ta boîte à Camembert. Tu l'auras pour ton dessert."

"He's just being silly. A lot of nonsense, really. Sam, assez!"

The girls dote on him. They show him how to make rings and bracelets out of dandelions they've picked and stuffed in their pockets. Eleanor cuts an unyielding slice of turkey and when he turns a water glass over, she rescues it from the edge of the table. She draws some of her old baseball cards from a canvas tote and with mime and animation, and a small dose of foreign language requirement, gives Sam a rundown on each of the players. Catch moves to the end of the table to perform for Sam.

"The hand, please remember, is faster than the eye."

Coins flash and disappear. Sam squeals with pleasure, plunges both hands into Catch's pockets. While Sam is preoccupied, my mother shyly offers Marc the first of many Lucy anecdotes. He smiles and nods, pretending comprehension. Later tonight, lying in the twin double at the Best Western, he will probably ask me what this story means.

"She must have been, oh what, Wade? Five? This poor girl made the mistake of second-guessing Lucy. She brought out a Roy Rogers for Cody and a Shirley Temple for Lucy. Now, Marc, these are fizzy pink drinks for children. And the drinks are exactly the same except for the name. Well, Lucy was livid! Wouldn't rest until the waitress brought her a fresh drink, for she wanted a Roy Rogers, too. Now, my question is this. Did she want to be like her big brother Cody or was she actually expressing a desire for a man on a horse?"

My mother sighs and settles her chin into the cupped palm of her hand.

"What a lot of catching up we have to do. Oh, and Lucy tells me you're having a show in Paris soon! We'll want to hear all about that."

I go back to get the food Catch has forgotten. Making my way through the crowded dining room I am surprised to notice we are undeniably a clan. A kind of dreamy attentiveness is obvious. It is this self-absorption, rather than shared physical features, that makes our table little different than any other where a family gathers for the first or fiftieth time.

"It's funny how things dovetail."

"Which things, Lucy?"

"Well, ideas. I mean you and Catch doing The Gateway in Ada, Oklahoma. Meanwhile plans are underway for a Disneyland in Paris. There's this international hunger for amusement parks or something."

"I wouldn't exactly put this on the same level as Disneyland."

"I'm not. As far as I know there aren't any visionaries championing Disneyland. Just plain old promoters."

"Johnny Dickerson's full of hot air."

"Mmmm."

My mother's knee is pressing mine under the table and her finger slowly taps one cheek. I back down.

"Do we get free passes?"

"You betcha, Sis."

"You look wonderful, Cody. I haven't told you just how terrific you do look."

Pursuing Cody is, of course, futile, as Catch and others have learned. His beauty and shattering smile are as much his fence today as they ever were. Any discovery will always be pure serendipity.

"Could've spiced up your speech, Cody. It wanted hyperbole."

"High what?"

"Hyperbole. Oh, extravagant statements. Bold figures of speech. Like Catch and Dickerson use."

Cody looks over at Dad, who has wandered away from us to a window, and smirks.

"Know what, Lucy? I'm thirty-eight and I can't climb a flight of stairs these days without turning blue in the face. I'm fresh out of hyperbole."

Purses and hats are gathered up. We may escape without a concluding statement. Catch, spent and rumpled, seems content to just pack it up and go home. It's Sam who demands the last word in a song I promise to translate verbatim. He sings with his short legs spread apart, as if braced against a fall. He clenches his fists for every high, inaccessible note. The song is innocent. It's about the escapades of a fellow named Pirouette who lives in a house made of carton. The mailman breaks his nose on the way up the paper steps, otherwise the song is mild and free of tragedy. We are attentive and, even though it is sweltering standing in the parking lot, we remain assembled and ungrumbling right through to the end.

About the Author

Linda Ashour is an American writer who has lived in France. She was born in Oklahoma and is a graduate of Denison University. *Speaking in Tongues* is her first novel.